Praise for
THE NORTHERN LIGHTS

"Enchanting....*The Northern Lights* is a startlingly fresh work, an innocent and humorous story about the fundamental strangeness of life."
— Barry Lopez,
author of *Arctic Dreams*

"This is Howard Norman's first novel...an entirely unforeseeable book and an entirely indispensable one."
— *Los Angeles Times*

"Howard Norman has evoked the lonely reaches of northern Canada to tell of the Cree and French community there.... An endearing little gem."
— *San Francisco Chronicle*

"Does cultural imperialism know no limits? Here's an American author who presumes to write about...our very own north country...and, what is worse, does a wonderful job of it....Unforgettable."
— *Toronto Sunday Star*

"Funny, inconsolable, tender, risk-taking...a book like the first tracks on a field of new snow."
— Ursula K. Le Guin

"This gentle, stylistically inventive novel is fresh as wintergreen...enchanting, replete with gentle whimsy and hauntingly evocative prose. IT IS A SIGNIFICANT ACHIEVEMENT."
— *Detroit News*

"*The Northern Lights* is a fresh work that is rich in its characterization, crisp in its thought, deft in its use of place, and original in its imagery....IT SUCCEEDS BRILLIANTLY."
— *Worcester Evening Gazette*

·THE·
NORTHERN
LIGHTS

Howard Norman

WASHINGTON SQUARE PRESS
PUBLISHED BY POCKET BOOKS
New York   London   Toronto   Sydney   Tokyo   Singapore

This novel is a work of fiction. Names, characters, places and incidents are either the product of the author's imagination or are used fictitiously. Any resemblance to actual events or locales or persons, living or dead, is entirely coincidental.

A Washington Square Press Publication of
POCKET BOOKS, a division of Simon & Schuster, Inc.,
1230 Avenue of the Americas, New York, N.Y. 10020

Published by arrangement with Summit Books,
a division of Simon & Schuster, Inc.
Library of Congress Catalog Card Number: 86-30044

ISBN: 0-671-65877-8

First Washington Square Press trade paperback printing April, 1988

10 9 8 7 6 5 4 3

WASHINGTON SQUARE PRESS and WSP colophon are registered trademarks of Simon & Schuster, Inc.

Printed in the U.S.A.

For
Jane Hannah

CONTENTS

"WILL YOU PAINT A BEAUTIFUL PICTURE OF ME FLOATING IN THE WATER?—NOT IN ANY PAIN YOU UNDERSTAND—BUT FLOATING EASILY AND PEACE-FULLY IN MY ETERNAL REST."

"WHAT?"

"AHA! THAT STARTLED YOU. GO ON, ADMIT IT. THAT STARTLED YOU, DIDN'T IT?"

—NATSUME SOSEKI
THE THREE-CORNERED WORLD

CHAPTER ONE

Unicycle

My father brought home a radio. "It's got a sender and a receiver," he said. "Now you can talk to people other than yourselves." He fit the earphones over my head. And the first news
I heard was that my friend Pelly Bay had drowned. Pelly had
fallen through the ice while riding his unicycle. That was April
1959.

Our house in northern Manitoba made up the entire village
of Paduola Lake. We were on the map only because of my
father's work as a cartographer, and we were about as isolated
as any family we knew about. There was my mother, Mina, my
younger cousin, Charlotte, and my father, Anatole, whom my
mother called Anthony. Our house was situated at the end of a

rocky peninsula. On the front door Anthony had painted in bold, white letters our last name, Krainik, and under it 58° lat., 101° long. Made of logs and large, oddly shaped stones, a moat of cement around each, our house had five rooms and a pantry. It was built in 1931 for a wealthy sportsman from Winnipeg who intended it as a fishing lodge. Rumor held that he lived in it one summer month, had bad luck fishing and hunting, and never came back. He finally sold the house to the government.

When you walked in the front door you entered the kitchen, which had a sink with a pump-handled spigot; the well was out back across a short stretch of yard from the outhouse. The outhouse had its own woodstove. The kitchen also had a stove, with pots, pans, and ladles hung from pegs above it. We ate at a table with four lyre-backed chairs that had been sent up from Toronto one by one. The kitchen window had a hand-sewn red curtain. The living room, whose broad window faced south over the lake, had a stone fireplace, two overstuffed chairs—one beige, one dark brown, each with a matching straw-stuffed hassock—a foot-pedal sewing machine, and a small table for magazines. Mina kept a framed photograph of her parents on it. Two bedrooms, side by side, faced west, each through a single window. Both bedrooms had a porcelain wash basin and a pitcher on a bureau beside the bed. One basin was ivory-colored and pear-shaped, the other round with a pastel scene of French country life. The third bedroom, which Charlotte occupied, was directly off the kitchen. It had a small brass bed while the other beds were of simple wooden construction. Its wash basin was white with a picture of a barrel tumbling over Niagara Falls.

Pelly lived with his aunt Hettie and Uncle Samuel in Quill, a small village ninety or so miles over scores of pothole lakes to the northeast. I had already spent three summers in a row with them. But Pelly did not have the unicycle until the fourth summer, 1958. That June, when I arrived by mail plane, he stood waiting proudly beside the unicycle, wearing the rough blue corduroy jacket he seldom took off.

The pilot's name was Moses Dog Toussaint. He was part Cree Indian, part French Canadian, more on the Cree side, with closely cropped black hair, a round face, and a gap-toothed smile. I had not flown with him before. In the roughest turbulance he hummed in a monotone as if to steady the plane. "We, should . . . mmmm . . . hmmmmm . . . mmmmm . . . get there, soon." He also spoke with pauses between syllables as unpredictable as the choppiness of the air.

Moses managed a smooth landing on Piwese Lake, near Quill. He taxied a ways, then shut down the engine, the plane bobbing on its floats. Moses reached back and took the anchor from the supply box. Securing its rope to a hook under his door, he climbed down onto a float, then swung the anchor into the lake. Crouching on the float, he smoked a cigarette. Soon a Cree man, Samson Autao, arrived in an old wooden rowboat and took us to shore. "Coffee, I get, now," Moses said. "See you, later, sometime, eh?" Moses and Samson walked toward the Hudson's Bay Company store.

Pelly rode up, circled me a few times, and said, "Whattaya think?" The unicycle was silver, the spokes of its wheel caught the light. Pelly tried a fancy spin and fell off. He stood up, laughing, and brushed himself off. He righted the unicycle, which stood just over waist high. "Well, Noah," he said, "you lose your tongue since the last time I saw you?"

"What is that?"

"Called a *unicycle*."

"How'd it get here?"

"Sam and me brought it up from Montreal."

We walked the unicycle to the Hudson's Bay store. The proprietor, a wiry, fastidious man named Einert Sohms, came out on the porch. "Some contraption, eh?" he said. Before I could answer he was on his way back inside. "Got to make sure Moses Toussaint don't drink every last drop I've got."

"Boy, Sohms's got his hair slicked back even thicker than usual," I said.

"Hettie gave him some otter grease for a present. He didn't know how to say no. Put some on right away. Four or five Indians watching. No smiles, no frowns, just that in-between look. I held the mirror. Whew! Now I can smell Sohms from across the lake."

The store had Quill's only porch, which ran across the entire length of the building. The main part of the store was a large room with a counter. Behind the counter was a mail-and-key hive. Sohms had managed to save it from the fire that tore through the hotel in Flin Flon, where he had been a desk clerk. I could see him shipping the hive from place to place until he took the job in Quill. There were far too many slots for the number of people who received mail, so he used the hive to store jars of nails, inks, medicines, spices, buttons, anything that would fit. The store had four aisles of tall shelves stocked with canned goods, tools, Stanfield underwear, wicks, snowshoes, dog harnesses, boots, knives. I never saw the day it stocked radios, though. Along the rim of each aisle rested a sliding ladder fixed on runners.

Quill was originally a Cree village, but by the time Pelly lived there its inhabitants were French Canadian, Norwegian, and Finnish as well. Referring to its mixture of people, Sam called Quill a spice-box place. Life ran with the least friction between the Cree and Norwegians, who had had families in Quill for two generations. But things were congenial among everyone. Neighbors kept an eye on one another. No one went too hungry.

The different nationalities met in English, which usually worked well enough, though at times a conversation ended mid-sentence, at a standstill between thought and speech. A language of gestures figured importantly in getting any communal task done. Odd things brought people close. Once, a French Canadian named Isabel Montminy collapsed on a February morning. After resting she bounded back with disquieting energy. She sewed five quilts in nine days, each revealing a haphazard pattern. Her fingers were scabbed with pinholes. She toured the quilts around, offering them as gifts. People accepted the quilts and right away knew Isabel was in trouble. As many families as could afford to pitched in money. Sohms arranged for a plane, and Isabel was sent to Winnipeg, where she made connections to Virginia to visit her sister, whom she had not seen in ten years. When she returned in spring, she visited each family to whom she had given a quilt. "May I have the quilt back?" she said. "That wasn't really me who made it."

Before the first snows each autumn, Quill lost a lot of its people. Most Cree dispersed in family groups to winter hunting camps until spring. Day labor, in towns and cities, drew many others away. They would take up hotel residences in Flin Flon, Winnipeg, sometimes as far away as Regina in Saskatchewan. Their children were always the new ones in school. New Year's Eve, wherever they were, they would wait their turn at the Hudson's Bay Company transmitter and try to reach Quill, to say Happy New Year to Sohms and ask after Hettie and Sam, the Malraux, the Amundson, the Koivisto families, who always stayed through winter. This was Sohms's big night. His usually sparse quarters were now festive. Chairs and tables were set out, each with a tablecloth. The rafters and windows were festooned with different-colored crepe paper. Sohms dressed up in a bright suit with a maple-leaf lapel pin and bowtie. His thick, dark brown hair would be painstakingly designed, as evidenced by the pleats on top of his head, the uniform sidelong waves, and manicured sideburns.

I attended only one of Sohms's New Year's parties. It was the winter before Pelly drowned, and Pelly was there with me. Typically he sat all night in a corner, singing along, making sketches of everyone in his notebook, mercilessly teasing Sohms. "What's that hair scent you got on, Einert?" he said. "It could kill a rock." Liquored cider was heating in a saucepan on the woodstove. The enormous phonograph, hooked up to a cell battery, was playing loudly. Sohms favored the Big Bands, especially Paul Whiteman and Tommy Dorsey.

He had been sampling each new pan full of cider since we had arrived, at about nine o'clock. By ten he was drunk, regaling everyone in the room with boisterous monologues. Stories of his childhood in Halifax, of the great explosion of the ship carrying nitroglycerin one foggy night in the harbor there. Once he even bellowed laughter. This amazed us, it was so unlike his usual self-contained manner. "I didn't get my nap today," he shouted before swigging from a flask. "That's okay—I'll take it while I'm asleep tonight!" His slurred logic was appreciated only by himself. But no one cared one way or the other. The drinking was steady and in good fun. Sohms could be put to bed if he fell over, dragged back inside if he wandered coatless outdoors to piss or to make a braying noise and gallop full force into the side of the porch like he had the New Year's Eve before.

Sohms kept the door to the storeroom closed. Through it the radio's static sounded like a scratchy record with the needle stuck in its last groove. It was the radio over which Sohms communicated with mail pilots and cities. Drunk, Sohms did not hear when a voice crackled through. He was alerted, however, by the sudden hush of our voices and shift of attention toward the door. Abruptly stiffening his spine, he stood up and performed a sharp military turn. Then he saluted the door and intoned, "Voice from a distant metropolis, I am at your command!" He hurried in to the radio, closing the door firmly behind him. He wanted all such conversations to be private. Then, as the night's host, greetings were relayed through him. When he finally appeared, he said, "That was Mrs. Zwicker. Calling from Winnipeg. She—" He stopped and stared at the phonograph. A barely perceptible coil of smoke came out of its bottom. Walking toward it, he removed the record that had just ended, placed it in its cardboard sheath, and set it on a shelf. He then surveyed the quiet room. "Don't anyone move," he said.

Sohms picked up the phonograph, the smoke now gathering around him like a hood. He walked through the store, kicked open the front door, crossed the porch, and in a gray-wool-stockinged feet walked down the two steps into the snow. Sobbing, he sank to his knees and held the phonograph out in front of him before setting it down in the snow. The rest of us crowded the doorway. Fixing his sight on Pelly, he said, "Pelly, a shovel, if you'd be so kind."

In a corner of the store were the long-handled tools: shovels, riving hammers, axes, barking spades, and brooms. Pelly picked an iron-blade shovel. He then walked back out to Sohms, facing the phonograph, which sparked and hissed. In three shovelfuls Sohms buried it, cell battery and all. He then secured the shovel handle down, like a grave marker. Pelly helped Sohms back inside the store, where two metal tubs of hot water in which they could thaw out their feet were prepared.

The rest of the night was musicless, except for the occasional Finnish dirge offered by Aki Koivisto, a large, bearded, long-faced man. Koivisto's own drunkenness was illustrated by melancholy apologies to his wife, Hedda, for having gone whoring in Montreal. "Oh, Aki," Hedda said consolingly, rubbing his head and quaking shoulders as he sprawled on her lap, "that was nearly twenty years ago."

Koivisto seemed disturbed by this. "Oh, God," he groaned, embarrassed equally by nostalgia and remorse. "It seems like just last month!" Hedda rose angrily, delivering Aki to the floor. As he rolled over he looked at Pelly and Sohms, both soaking their feet in the steaming tubs. "Einert, my good man," he said. "It was brave of you to smother your beloved phonograph to save the store. To save us all from certain death by fire. You're a brave, brave man, Einert. Poor, poor old phonograph, going to be as rusty as . . . as . . . as a phonograph left out in the snow, is what it'll be as rusty as. That, and nothing else. It is what it is."

In his sketchbook Pelly had chronicled the party. He drew Sohms pouring cider into the saucepan. Quickly flipping the page, he drew Aki flat out asleep on the floor. It was a view from Aki's boots, all the way to his big hands held in delicate repose, inches apart, just behind his head. As he meticulously sketched a bootlace that had strayed from the top eyelet, Pelly brought his face close to the page. He always drew with great detail. You could almost tell from his drawing that Aki was snoring. He then captured Rupert and Marjorie Malraux dancing, arms locked around each other, eyes closed. Rupert was well over six feet, and Marjorie barely five feet tall; Pelly caught how Rupert bowed over while dancing to spare Marjorie having to press her face against the rough wool of his suit. Even after all of Sohms's guests had fallen asleep, heads down on the tables, and Sohms was asleep on his cot, Pelly sketched away. I turned off the radio. Then he drew a picture of me turning off the radio. Then a self-portrait: Pelly sitting in a corner, sketching.

Pelly Bay.

It has since haunted me, how his name referred to water. He was named after the arctic port where his grandfather was born. A whaling song located it exactly: *Oh, I'm an icy berged and splintered ship, tossed round in ghosty spray/Through Repulse north past Igloolik, I'm pray bound for Pelly Bay.* Pelly never got to visit the place. We were both fourteen when it sounded to me as if he had drowned inside the radio.

He was thin but not gawky, tall for his age. His step was leaning, buoyant, decisive even when moving between rooms. His face was angular, his nose bent slightly to the right. Sam joked that it cast a shadow on his ear. He usually wore a slightly harassed expression, even when speaking calmly. He had sad brown eyes and sloe-black hair that reddened in the sun. He was usually quiet, reticent, though when something he had been thinking about welled up inside him, it flew out in an impassioned flourish of talk.

This brings my third summer in Quill to mind. Again in early June Pelly was there to meet my plane. Without even so much as a hello, he started in about his battle with Tommy Okipet, a muscular, storm-faced Cree who was at the time about sixteen. The problem was Sarah, Tommy's younger sister. She was twelve and lived with her sister, Tommy, two sets of cousins, aunts, and uncles, both of her own parents, and three surviving grandparents in an arrangement of shacks and cabins just at the outskirts of the village. Sarah was a lithe, thin girl, a bit high-strung, dark-skinned with black hair down to her waist. She kept to herself, which is no doubt one reason Pelly felt a kinship. Her elder sister and mother were corpulent, and perhaps Sarah would eventually be, too, though the fact that she liked to run everywhere made that hard to believe. Her nickname was *Vootisin*—"Breeze." She made excellent round quill baskets, having apprenticed herself to her father's mother, the best basket maker in Quill. She would take the foam rubber inside of a pillow (several foam pillows stayed unsold in the store for years; people preferred feather pillows) and go searching for a porcupine. When she found one she would throw the foam rubber at it from close range, coming away with a whole pincushion of quills. She would prepare the dyes in saucepans, soak the quills for days, sew them in geometric patterns or animal faces to birchbark frames with gut thread and a bone needle. Midsummer she would trek with Tommy or a cousin to a highway to the south. There they would set up a makeshift table and sell the baskets to tourists. They would stay in a three-dollar-a-night motel and bring back stories of drunk logging-truck drivers, whores, loud families in matching outfits, who traveled in silver airstream trailers, stayed in campgrounds, and bought frozen fish, which they cooked near trout streams.

Anyway, Pelly was severely agitated. "I've been sweet on her a long time, you know," he said. "This ain't no surprise to you. Met her behind the store a few times. Didn't touch her, not ever. Stood a ways apart, talking is all. But I'd been thinking about kissing her. Then I came out and said it: 'I'm thinking about kissing you.' I told her that. She just shook her head no. I gave her some drawings. Of herself. Portraits, like I do of everyone. I started drawing her day and night. So Tommy, he gets wind of this. He's had it in for me for a long time. You tell me why, I don't know. So now he's steaming pissed off and he walks right up to me, no one else around, and he socks me down with his fist. Jesus F. Christ—what? In the face. I'm down. He takes out this new hunting knife. From the store. Then he kicks me. Then he sits on me. So now he's sitting on me, and he pulls out from under his shirt all the drawings I gave to Sarah. He got them away from her. So now he stuffs one into my mouth, I'm choking. Then he tears the rest up like confetti. Asshole fuck, he says to me, fuck-prick, he says, things like that. He gets up. Walks away. So I follow him. Pretty stupid when I think about it now. Down to the river. Come up behind and leap on him. On his back. He's swinging me around. Back down on the ground. He's on top. Socking my face again. Now, get this. He takes off one of my shoes. Throws it right into the river. Just throws the shoe in. After that he goes away. We glare at each other. I don't go behind the store anymore. So, how have you been? Your father been around lately?"

It was known around Quill that Pelly hardly slept, at most two or three hours a night. In summer he would sit in a cane-bottomed chair on the porch. It was uncanny how he could sit there all night, even if there was a suffer of blackflies. Some nights he would set out a table, place an oil lantern on it, and paint by its light. In winter he would paint in his room. Using Sam's old brushes, he would make portraits of the various mail pilots and people in Quill. Each portrait was on an eight-by-ten piece of manila paper. He did a pencil sketch first, then painted. But sometimes the pencil outlines remained visible. When he painted a resident of Quill, he or she was always shown leaning against a door. The one exception was Sarah Okipet. He painted her running, leaning against any number of doors, sitting on the porch, looking adoringly at him, working on her baskets, even clobbering Tommy on the head with a jagged rock while holding Pelly's hand. Perhaps his most intricate compositions, though, were of mail pilots. These were impressive likenesses. A number of pilots brought photographs of other pilots, friends, immediate families, and asked Pelly to use them as models, even offering modest fees. But never more than five dollars. He kept to simple backgrounds. Mostly doors, as I mentioned, or a cobblestone chimney, which was curious since no such chimney existed in Quill. I think he saw a cobblestone chimney in a book once. Some winter nights he would go out on snowshoes tacking up portraits on doors and trees. People would find them the next morning. Almost every household owned a portrait signed *Bay*. But the walls of his room were bare, except for the months he had pictures of Sarah up over his bed.

Sam called him a cabin-fever orphan, because Pelly's folks had fallen apart inside the long winters. Jake and Margaret Bay were their names. For four and a half years they had lived in Churchill, the port town on Hudson Bay about three hours by plane from Quill. They lived on the ground floor of a two-story hotel along the Churchill River. Jake Bay had worked as a railroad brakeman until he fractured a thumb in a switch accident. After that he sold tickets and managed the station's luggage room. Margaret had worked for a correspondence school, tutoring students who lived in remote Canadian villages. Her specialty was European history. "Truth be told," Sam said, "I liked her more than my brother. She felt an injustice was done to her, though, having to live in Churchill. She claimed the place was forgotten. No—that it never was civilized. Even though every spring all sorts showed up there. Eskimos, Russians, Finns, let's see, who else? Well, a few Poles, French, Indians, of course. Sometimes the place favors a rough breed, I'll grant her that. Grain-boat sailors and the like. Still, you could have a family life there, and a good one. Plenty do."

As his folks' drinking and quarreling worsened, Pelly had begun to spend more and more time in Quill. For a few years he traveled back and forth, not knowing month to month where he would be. As Sam put it, he had a strong constitution, which helped keep him hopeful. One day, however, he asked to live with Sam and Hettie. "Imagine," Sam said, "he had to *ask* to leave home. He was pretty heart torn to see how quickly they agreed to it." I never learned what happened to Jake and Margaret Bay, how they ended up. "I imagine they went ways separate as a snapped wishbone," Sam said.

When we met, Pelly had not seen Jake and Margaret in over two years, and he never mentioned them to me. When I asked about them once, he said, "It doesn't matter," and the belligerent, then downcast look he gave me stilled the conversation.

Pelly's aunt Hettie was a stout, lively Cree woman who had married Sam when she was eighteen and he was twenty-four. Mixed Indian-white marriages had taken place in the region for centuries. In Quill they were neither advocated nor discouraged, but more or less tolerated with varying degrees of hope or doubt.

Hettie had been born in Quill around 1900. She had light brown skin, thick eyebrows, and black hair usually woven up in a tight braid coiled atop her head. Sometimes her hair flowed loosely or was braided along its sides. She always wore housedresses, sometimes with more than one apron. Hettie's walk was almost as much side to side as forward, as if she were heavier than she actually was. She was resolute in most ways, even-tempered, attended to daily chores according to a strict agenda, and expected Pelly and me to do the same. Yet she could be bawdy as well. "Noah, I'm going to flirt right at you," she would say. "You need practice at it." And she would grab me by the belt, push me against a wall, and grind up against me, laughing heartily, then go about her chores, all the while glancing at me as I warily watched her move around the room. Each week when she placed fresh spruce boughs for fragrance along the floorboards, she would call, "Nooo-ahh?" When she had caught my attention she would pinch her own considerable behind, waggle, and say, "Noah, I know what, you're thinking. You should cry in shame, Noah. I'm going to tell it, to your mother." But I wasn't thinking anything, except that Hettie was acting crazy again, enjoying herself by embarrassing me.

Hettie spoke English with more proficiency than most of the Cree in Quill. On occasion Sohms hired her to translate for him. The Cree would come around to buy rope, steel fishing hooks, kettles, cigarettes, and to have pelts appraised. Hettie worked haltingly between Cree and English, but she seemed to understand everything Sohms said. Whenever Sohms attempted humor, Hettie saved him from failure. Instead of translating, she would take on a serious expression and tell him, "That's not funny in Cree."

Pelly's uncle Samuel carved decoys for a living in the shed behind his house. Along with Aki Koivisto, who fashioned fine sleds and toboggans, and Rupert Malraux, who made whirligigs, Sam was among the finest woodworkers in Quill. He made all the northern waterfowl but specialized in ducks. In Sohms's store he displayed one harlequin and a mallard but sent the others south by plane. In cities they were bought by hunters, who would bring them back north. Such were their erratic migrations.

A tall man with light brown unruly hair, Sam had a stiff,

hesitant smile; his eyes, taut at their edges with wrinkles, revealed his humor. He had large hands and wide, bony shoulders. When he put on a shirt, it looked as if it were still on its closet hanger, except that Hettie hung his shirts on nails along their bedroom walls.

Sam owned a collapsing green pickup truck with a wooden tailgate. He had bought it one summer in Flin Flon and had driven it up along the old, rutted logging roads, one of which ended in Quill. He kept it parked to one side of Sohms's store. He would let anyone drive it, even if they hardly knew how or learned while doing it. Mostly the truck was used to haul wood. In my entire time in Quill perhaps two tanks of gas were used up. Each spring a ground squirrel's nest had to be got out of the muffler.

"How about let's sit in the truck." Pelly said.

We climbed into the musty cab. The black Naugahyde seat had been torn and mended in several places with electrician's tape. The dashboard had a layer of dust on it. Dried mouse pellets were on the seat and floor mats. The ashtray was open, crammed with butts. The unicycle was in back, as if we were about to drive somewhere. The key was in the ignition. The dust made me cough. "Great place to talk," I said.

"Yeah," Pelly said, "real private." This made us both laugh, for out the window we could see a logging road sequestered by thick spruce, beyond which lay ten thousand square miles of wilderness.

Pelly turned, glanced at the unicycle, then said, "I first saw a picture of it back in March.

"This one night I was awake painting. As usual. Still very dark outside. I'd been working real good. Was trying to finish a painting of Wilfred Gaboriault. You know, the pilot? So I'm sitting there painting. Hettie and Sam are asleep, and I was working right along. Then I hear something. Like a fly in my ear at first. So I go to the window. I see this plane going down.

24

Jesus F. Christ, I think. Smoke's coming out and a little fire. It's all spinning down. Right smack into the trees. I get on my coat. Get on snowshoes. Set out for the accident. All the time I'm thinking I've got to keep a clear head here.

"Right away I find parts of the plane on the ground. Most of it's up in the trees, though. Engine was hissing up there. Then I see Wilfred. He's half fallen out of the plane. His mouth's open and blood's trickling down his chin. Didn't even call up to him. He wasn't moving at all.

"Packages and letters were scattered all over the snow. Blowing around. Couple of canvas sacks, too. They were open. Letters spilling out, swirling around.

"I was going to go right back. Wake up Sam and Hettie. Tell 'em what happened. Bring 'em out to the plane.

"Instead, I don't know why, I started gathering up the letters. Putting them in stacks, neatly like I was folding shirts in a drawer or something. Then I tie closed the sacks. So there's these stacks of letters, and I had 'em weighted down with pieces of the plane. One stack I had weighted down with one of Wilfred's shoes. Now and then I look up at Wilfred. The whole time the radio's squawking away. Wilfred's got this look on his face like he's trying to figure it out, what the radio's saying.

"Don't tell this to anybody, okay? The thing was: I felt like climbing up and sitting with Wilfred. Just for a while. I even tried, but kept falling back down. Couldn't get a grip.

"So I'm finishing with the mail. I got all the packages in one pile. And I find this catalog. One of those warehouse catalogs with the order blanks. It was full of everything—all kinds of radios, and I'm out there, Wilfred's up in the tree, and I'm paging through like I was just in the kitchen or something. I don't know *what* I was doing. So I stuck the catalog under my coat and went back.

"I wake up Sam and Hettie. Walked right in. Snowshoes and all, and I'm shouting things panicky. 'Get up, get up . . . ' I don't remember what. 'Wilfred Gaboriault's in a tree!' Hettie and Sam, they jumped right up. Got dressed and right away go knock on doors. Me, too. I'm over at Aki's house knocking. I'm over at the Amundsons.

"Pretty soon lanterns are coming through the dark. Lanterns going toward the porch. Lanterns on in the store. Could see Einert holding one up near his face, looking out his window.

"Now there's most everyone. We start out and get to the plane, and these Cree men climb up. Jason Two and Abraham Bass. They climb Wilfred back down.

"Then this crazy argument breaks out, Noah. Well, a quarrel, at least. Wilfred's half-froze, see. And Jason Two was pushing Wilfred's hands together. Wilfred's arms were broken stiff, and Jason wanted his hands clasped together. But Aki says, 'Who cares? Let's just get him back.' Then Hettie says, 'No! Hands should be up next to him. That's only right.' And all the while Jason Two's holding Wilfred's hands together, then he binds them up with a bootlace. 'Goddamn it,' Aki says, 'poor Wilfred ain't under arrest!' But Jason Two just turns away. And Hettie's pinching tiny red icicles off Wilfred's beard.

"Then Wilfred's laid out on a toboggan, and Sam and Aki pull him back. Sohms says to put him on the porch. He goes in and brings out a blanket. Aki wraps Wilfred up in that. Sohms gets a tarpaulin. Aki wraps that around Wilfred, too.

"Some of us go inside the store. Sohms right away goes into the radio room. He's very jittery. Doesn't even shut the door. He starts right in trying to reach Winnipeg, emergency station. Can hear him shouting, 'Come in! Come in!' No luck. He's in there for maybe an hour. Finally comes out. Just shrugs. Sits down with some coffee. Won't take a drink that both Aki and Sam offer. He's concentrating on Winnipeg. Goes back to the radio. Sounds pretty frantic now. 'Come in! Come in!'

"By now it's light out. Winds have calmed down. We hear the plane's radio. Still squawking, the sound carrying in. This starts to spook Einert. Makes him cover his ears. 'I wish to God they'd stop trying to reach Wilfred,' he says.

"Aki says, 'I doubt they will, Einert, until you get through and say what's happened up here.'

"Now there's me, Aki, both Kathryn and Olaf Amundson, Rupert, Hettie, and her cousin Edna Blackduck, all in the store. Hettie and Edna are sitting in chairs. Everyone else is talking about Wilfred or Sohms, but Hettie and Edna, they're talking about everyone else. I brought them over cups of tea. Edna, you know how she's younger than Hettie but looks older? Well, when she got woke up like that in the middle of the night, she really looked old. She spit some tea on the floor. It tasted all right. She was just disgusted at how people were behaving around a dead person. She said Wilfred shouldn't be talked about for a long time. Hettie was nodding but said we were doing the best we knew how.

"Finally, it's late morning and Sohms gets through. Asks for a plane to come and get Wilfred, for someone to tell Wilfred's wife. Einert comes out and says, 'They say the weather's too rough to send a goddamn plane up. Predict it'll be ten days, maybe more.' Rupert says, 'What'll we do?' Aki says, 'Deliver Wilfred to the train.' Sam says, 'Sounds about right.'

"So they start planning. You know how the train runs between Winnipeg and Churchill? Well, Aki says it'd take three full days by sleds, at least, and hoped the train had an ice car. They decide to travel to the Etawney Lake, North Knife region, where the train goes through. Then Aki asks Sohms to radio Winnipeg, so they can radio the train of their plans.

"They start packing up three sleds. It's Aki, Jasper Autao, Jack Ominik, and Olaf who're going. Olaf gets his huskies. Sohms gets some tents. They get food and whiskey. Caribou shoulders, smoked fish. Let's see, what else? Oh, yeah—pemmican. Other supplies. They tie Wilfred to one sled. He's still wrapped up tight.

"I admit to feeling pretty sick by this time. The whole thing's starting to hit me. Finding Wilfred and all that, his mouth bleeding. I'm in the store watching things through the window. Einert's in there, too, trying to concentrate on some ledgers. He's got his pen out, but he's not writing. He's just real shook. Me too, and I'm trying to think of something to do. So I take out the catalog. Still had my coat on! I take out the catalog and start paging through it. I get to the bicycle section. Bicycles. Tricycles. Then I see the unicycle.

"I look over at Einert. I knew that Aki and the rest, they'd be gone soon. So I walk over and show Einert the picture and say, 'Einert, what do you think of this?'

"Well, here's a surprise, Einert catches right on. 'Why don't I write out a check,' he says, 'You can pay me back later.' 'I'd appreciate that,' I say. So he does just that. Writes me out a Bay Company check.

"So then I fill out the ordering form, tuck the check in an envelope, write out the address of the warehouse in Montreal, and lick a stamp. Einert gave me the stamp. I go out and find Aki and ask him if he'd deliver the envelope to a train conductor or porter, I didn't know, anybody on the train who'd send it for me. Otherwise, who knew how long it'd take if I waited for a mail plane? Aki says sure thing. He puts the letter in his coat pocket.

"Now they're about to leave. Dogs are fighting, getting the reins all knotted up, so Aki kicks the lead and drags him by the scruff, up to the front. He gets the reins untangled and checks to make sure everything's on tight. Checks to see if Wilfred's packed in tight.

"Then they head out, and the snow's starting, and by the time they got past Piwese Lake we couldn't hardly see them.

"Bad weather goes on, and two weeks later they get home. Jasper Autao and Jack Ominik, I mean, and Olaf. Olaf says that Aki decided to go to Winnipeg with Wilfred, go to the funeral and give condolences and all. When Aki got back he said he sent my letter.

"About a month goes by. No planes. No unicycle. Einert says, 'Whattaya expect? *Emergency* supplies sometimes take forever! A body's been taken to a train from here, and you're worried about a contraption?'

"Now Hettie, she knows Sam and me are going to Montreal, and she really wants to go. She wants to see the city at least once. But both her folks are sick, so she can't go. Just me and Sam go. We took a plane to Flin Flon, the train from there. Stayed in a hotel. Had a porch ten times the size of Einert's. Huge fireplace in the lobby. Wide seats on the porch, covered up till summer with tarpaulin. I went and took a tarp off one. It had a metal frame, and when I sat in it it rocked, almost like a rocking chair. We stayed in a room with a bed and a pull-out couch. Sam said he was going to build Hettie one of those chairs. We walked around a lot. Went to visit some of Sam's old friends. This man named Harry Salter, who owned a sporting goods store, where he sold a lot of Sam's decoys. A kind of bent-over man named Arthur Calder, who Sam said used to visit Quill quite a bit but doesn't anymore because of his health. He did cough a lot. He had a motorcycle but said he hardly ever drove it, except to the grocery store, which was only a block away. He got on it, started it up, and drove to the store and back, right while we were watching. We even visited a museum gift shop. Sam had a few decoys there. A duck and a grebe. I stood in the shop awhile, hoping somebody would buy one just so I could see that, but no one did.

"One morning in the hotel I tell Sam about ordering the unicycle. 'Where's the mail-order warehouse?' he says. Right here in Montreal, I say. 'Well, maybe it's on its way up to Quill, wouldn't that be something?' Sam says. 'But let's go take a look.'

"We took two busses, then walked a ways and found the place. Man there hands us a long box over the counter. The unicycle's in it. He says, 'Another week or so, it would've been on its way. Haven't sold one in so long, we were considering taking them out of the catalog.' 'Glad you didn't,' I say. A tire pump came with it, and a spoke tightener.

"Something else. Wait here, I'll get it."

Pelly all but leapt out of the front seat of the truck, ran to the house, and promptly returned with a thin pamphlet: "Go ahead," he said, placing the pamphlet on my lap. "Take your time. I've got it memorized."

In the pamphlet was a photograph of a circus bear on a unicycle, the world's tallest unicycle (shown in the living room of a mansion, its tuxedoed rider bent over so as not to bump his head on the ceiling), Parisian marathon racers wearing striped outfits, a man in a suit weaving through a London traffic jam, a boy trolling fishing line from the wooden bridge he's pedaling across, a young woman herding sheep down a slope on a unicycle whose spokes are fretted with carnival ribbon, a unicycle-riding monkey holding out a tin cup to onlookers as an organ-grinder with a long, droopy mustache turns the organ's crank.

"Soon as Sam and me got back home to Quill," Pelly said, "he helped me put the unicycle together. I wheeled it directly over to show Einert. He sat on it, balanced against the porch railing, but didn't try and ride it. 'Just checking the merchandise,' he said.

"I started to practice right away," Pelly said. "Out on the landing strip."

There was an old tar landing strip about a hundred yards from Quill. It had moss growing in cracks and hadn't been used in years. Each morning before breakfast, the wetlands steaming in the early light, we wheeled the unicycle out there. Pelly went through a few basic exercises, inventing as he went along. I watched. After a week I learned to judge, advise, encourage, and cajole, but only about things Pelly himself had taught me to look for. First, Pelly would try to pedal in a straight line. "A little wobbly," I would offer. He would try again. "Not so wobbly that time," I would say.

Next, he would practice abrupt stops, trying not to fall. "You leaned too hard into the turn," I might say, advancing the obvious as expertise.

After breakfast (usually oatmeal, sometimes eggs and fried potatoes, which we prepared ourselves) we went right back to the strip. There I would take out my list of stunts. "Let's start out with a simple turn, then a couple of spin-arounds," I would say. "Follow this with riding the whole length down, and zig-zagging back, then work your way through the figure eights." Pelly improved so quickly that I found myself working harder and harder to think up interesting routines. But I felt useful and he felt coached, and the unicycle drew us close. When he rested, we discussed traveling from town to town, where he could perform.

"We'll need a tent," he said.

"Sure, in case it rains."

"I'll paint posters. You can hand 'em out."

"Go down to Winnipeg, maybe."

"Drive around in the truck. Names on the side. Girls."

"Let's practice some more."

Afternoons we gathered wood for Sam's decoys and went on hunting forays, each with a twenty-two-caliber rifle. Usually we shot ptarmigan, rabbits, sometimes squirrels. Then we would fish for lake trout, pickerel, whitefish, either out in a canoe or off the rocks along Piwese Lake or any of a dozen other nearby lakes. Sam usually went hunting by himself, and since most families were in the same situation, meat was shared—moose, caribou, duck, geese. No tabs were kept, but few debts went unheeded. Occasionally we bought canned soups from the store.

Hettie prepared whatever Sam, Pelly, and I managed to bring

home. Almost every night we had stew. Hettie, I was told, was the first Cree woman in the village to use spices. As a wedding gift, Sam had given her packets of thyme, basil, and pepper. Kathryn Amundson shared recipes with her. Ptarmigan stew, for instance, was one recipe that Hettie, a fine cook in her own right, learned from Kathryn. This was something of a joke. "Norwegians themselves," Sam said, "pretty near faint from pepper."

Hettie would skin and draw the ptarmigan, wash and cut it into pieces. She put the pieces in a heavy pot, along with onions, pepper flakes, barley, salt, and water. She brought it all to a boil, then let it simmer. The smell, wild and pungent, mixed with the fragrance of spruce boughs to fill the house. A little while before the stew was ready, she made a paste of flour and water, added it in, and stirred it every so often to keep it from getting lumpy. Then she made dumplings of bear fat and water and dropped large spoonfuls on top of the stew. About this time Hettie's old father, Job Gathers, would arrive and ask, "You using, spices, in supper?" Job and Hettie's mother, Mary Walks, both disliked spices, and although they were invited every night to eat with us, they would refuse if spices were in the meal. They would simply wait until later in the evening to visit.

Sam would come in from his shed and the four of us would sit down at the long wooden table that took up much of the kitchen. Head bowed, in a deadpan voice, Sam would offer a rhymed prayer that he made on the spot: "Thanks to the forest for the things with feet, thanks to the hungry boys here for leaving me and Hettie something to eat. Amen."

After we cleared the dishes, Pelly carried in the unicycle. He leaned it against the kitchen wall, then meticulously oiled the pedals and spokes, using a squeeze can with a long spout from the Hudson's Bay store. Then he brought the unicycle into our bedroom. That was the entire house: the kitchen and two bedrooms. He would prop the unicycle against the wall.

I would take down the shortwave radio from its shelf and set it on the table between our beds. It was a brown Grundig-Majestic, about two feet high, with a grainy tan screen over the speaker. Each corner had a white plastic treble clef surrounded by dancing notes. On either side of the push buttons for selecting stations were the volume knob and the ferrite rod antennae control knob, each nearly the size of a doorknob. A third large knob was for fine-tuning through the wave bands. This required a delicate touch, an ear pressed close as a safecracker's as he notches through a combination, his livelihood entirely dependent on his concentration. We lay on our beds, listening in the dusk. At eight o'clock, *Great Men of Vision* came on. "Tonight," the announcer proclaimed, "a biography of someone who changed the face of the world." Inventors, scientists, dictators, explorers. I was duly impressed by the way individuals could make history, yet equally so by the announcer's ability to condense such accomplishments to half an hour. This was done through theatrical language and vital anecdotes related as if in the voices of the historical figures themselves. Never mind that Ponce de León sounded just like Louis Pasteur, Marco Polo like Albert Einstein, Marie Antoinette like Eleanor Roosevelt. The only thing that mattered was that spectacular events and important lives were brought all the way to Quill.

At nine o'clock, *Great Books* connected us to the libraries of the world. This program began with the reader, Fabian Bennet, announcing in a British accent, "Here, once again," then a background voice hushing him. Bennet would say, "So sorry," and lower his voice. "I find myself in the Provincial Library in Toronto," he would continue. "Tonight, what great good fortune to have happened upon a volume of . . . " You could hear him settle into a squeaky, leather chair, switch on a lamp, and open the book. Throughout the summers, we heard Tolstoy, Kipling, Swift, George Eliot, Louisa May Alcott. There were offerings of Dickens: *The Pickwick Papers, Sketches by Boz, David Copperfield*. A *Tale of Two Cities* was read one summer in its entirety. "So, without further delay, let us begin." We heard the page turn. "It was the best of times, it was the worst of times . . . "

In the morning Hettie asked, "How is Fabian?" It was true that after hearing him night after night, we could tell how he was beneath the professional voice—if he had a cold, if he was tired. Hettie had a compassionate concern, and not a little curiosity, over this man who entered our house nightly. Since his voice was all we had, we could of course only guess at his appearance.

"He's too skinny," Hettie once conjectured. "He stays talking radio at night, because his wife, she don't like doing it no more with him."

"Oh, come on, Hettie," Pelly said, "you don't even know if he's married!"

"It's what I think. You go to radio place. Then come back, tell me if I'm right. Go ask Fabian's wife, how it is to sleep with Fabian Bennet."

Other mornings she might say, "I been thinking about Fabian Bennet," then decipher this and that, his sorrows, his joys, all from his voice.

After the ten o'clock news, *Lights Out*, a fright show, came on. Hearing the first chilling notes of its theme song, Pelly would rise up like a corpse from its coffin, draw his quilt over his shoulders, and act as though he were playing the organ. Then from the radio came an exaggerated wolf howl, unlike anything heard in the north. "Must've tortured some poor dog senseless," was Sam's comment when he first heard this. Usually the episode involved a murder.

In the dark I would face the radio away from me. That way I

could see the tubes and think of their delicate tributaries of wirelit orange as the routes the characters took to reach us.

As I nodded off to sleep, I would be vaguely aware of Pelly getting up from his bed, dressing, gathering up his paintbrushes, moving toward the kitchen or the porch. Often when I woke the radio was still on, and I'd hear maritime weather reports, soccer games from South America, an orchestra from Amsterdam, wheat surveys from Saskatchewan, a soprano trilling up the scale in London, medical advice from Boston. Pelly may have turned the channel, or one frequency may have simply replaced another just as day replaced night. I would get dressed and walk outside. Pelly would be waiting next to the unicycle.

I had always left Quill by mid-September, but that year I stayed on through the month Nimituhumoowepesim, as the Cree called it, "deer-rub-their-horns-time." By early October, Pimuhumoowepisim, "migrating moon," the thousands of waterfowl departed. Grebes, loons, and ducks all seemed to disappear, often camouflaged by morning mists rising off the ponds and lakes, suddenly bereft of their voices. But dawn to dusk the precise, leaning orders of geese, with their hoarse, insistent chorusing, filled the air. Hettie had a song: "Good-bye, geese taking summer. Taking summer," which she repeated, sometimes mumbling, in varying cadences while cooking, attending to other chores around the house, or sitting at the table with her parents. Many of the songs she knew evoked birds, weather, and seasons, especially winter. "Others leave, you stay. Raven." That was another one. "One day you're walking on leaves, ptarmigan. The next on snow." Or: "Duck, you got caught! Sudden ice."

I stayed on through November, Akwutinoowepesim, "frost moon," and that month it snowed every single day, sometimes all day long. The families who had intended to leave Quill were gone by now. The skies lowered, dense and gray. On occasion there would be a reprieve, a bright blue day. By December the air was bitterly cold yet dry compared to the damp cold of November. Now it was Yekewutinoowepsim, "rimey moon." Quill was snowbound. The acoustics were strange. One day someone crunching home on snowshoes might be heard a mile away, and yet a mail plane might appear out of the clouds, bounce on its skids, and skim across the lake ice, all in total silence, as if there were a wall of glass between the lake and Quill. It was not unusual for the temperature on mid-December days to be five or six degrees at noon. The nights dropped well below zero. January and February mornings you would get a crack of icy static in the nostrils when first stepping outside and have to shade your eyes against the harsh glint of snow, if the sun had worked its way through. Certain days neighbors were seen only on their way to their woodsheds. Chimney smoke was our windsocks. Enormous drifts had built up against the houses, sculpted in various shapes. Even brief walks were taken on snowshoes.

Winter might be seven months long.

Daily agendas remained about the same, except that going out in deep snow to hunt or ice-fish required more preparation, thicker clothes, of course.

There were a dozen or so fishing shacks set up on nearby lakes, but not on Piwese Lake, since that was where the mail plane landed. Pelly, Sam, and I would spend afternoons in our cramped shack, the oil stove cranked up, the smell of whitefish, pickerel, trout, on a lucky day, thick in the air. In the first minutes out of the cold, huddled close, we would sit as still as possible, letting the chill in our bones subside. "Put your hands down around your peckers," Sam would say, demonstrating. "They'll warm up fast. Do I have to tell you that every time?" He would laugh. We remembered, but we liked to hear him say it. Then Sam would chisel out the hole, frozen over from the day before. Sometimes he would bring a flask and let us each have a swig of whiskey—just one, and right away. We had simple wooden poles, and for bait we used fried dough, fish guts, strips of bacon, sometimes combinations. Some afternoons winds might flute the shack, rattle it. Other afternoons were calm; the heat inside would make us drowsy. Sam would doze off sitting up on his wooden bench.

It was on the ice that Pelly revealed his true artistry. He had tried out different lakes and a long stretch of stream. Finally, he settled on an oval-shaped pond open to a snowfield at one end and horseshoed in by spruce at the other. He learned its surfaces and borders. He sprinted its circumference, arms spread wide, hands tilting like keels in the air. On abrupt stops, the unicycle sprayed ice.

He pedaled the alphabet in wide, sweeping letters in newly fallen snow. He hoped to write a message clear enough for Moses Dog Toussaint to read from the air. When he unicycled by moonlight he made an obstacle course of the shadows.

Often someone else would come out to watch with me. In early December, I stood for several night hours with Aki Koivisto, shuffling back and forth, chuffing visible breaths, clapping our hands against the cold like slow applause. "He's got that figure eight pretty good," Aki said.

"We're planning a big performance," I said. "The whole routine."

"That so? The kids will love it. Everyone will."

Pelly was Quill's only circus ever.

In the ensuing days I got lost in Pelly's acrobatics, they were so mesmerizing. He had all but perfected a full spin in the air, a zigzag, and the "fake peril." That is what we called it, the fake peril. It consisted of his tilting low to the ice, rolling a dizzy spell up in his eyes, and making the unicycle wobble. He then swerved dangerously twice or three times, flopped over a snowbank rim only to pop up, and then, like a movie run backward, climbed onto the unicycle again. After reversing these antics, he got off the unicycle in the middle of the pond, bowed

with a great flourish, and waited for my applause, which ricocheted off the trees.

A week before Christmas Moses Toussaint handed me a
letter:

Dear Noah,

    *When Moses told us that you would be staying on at Quill,
Auntie was happy that you were having a nice time. She would
not write you, for fear of taking you away from Quill, especially
if you do not wish to leave. But she wants you to come home
for Christmas. So do I.*

Love,
Charlotte

Suddenly I realized that no matter how steeped I was in life
in Quill, I had been negligent toward my family. I told Moses I
would be leaving with him. Then I found Pelly in his room,
drawing. "Got to go on the plane," I said. "Moses is waiting." I
handed him Charlotte's letter. He read it, nodding. Then he
went back to his drawing. I packed hurriedly.

"We had some extra months this year, though," he said.

"Yeah, and June's not that far off."

"What about I teach you to ride next summer?"

"Maybe, I don't know. Don't think I could do it. But I sure
wish I could stay for the show. It'll look great on the ice."

"I'll do it for you out on the landing strip."

"The whole routine, okay?"

"You bet. You're my coach. Got to show off for my coach,
don't I?"

"I better finish up here."

"Meet you in the store, okay? I don't like watching people
pack suitcases."

"Okay."

The unicycle was leaning against the railing. Samson Autao was dragging a toboggan full of supplies in from Moses's plane, which we could hear idling out on the lake. It was Sohms's habit to hire someone on the spur of the moment to fetch goods, carry mail to and from a plane. Often this required three or four trips. Meanwhile, the pilot usually sat by the woodstove drinking coffee, taking down supply orders. His next stop would be Paduola Lake. Then he would continue his rounds: Chartrand Lake, Grandmother Lake, Nesbitt Lake, Abrahm Lake, Handle Lake, Muskego Lake, Little Footprint Lake . . .

We walked to the house so that I could say good-bye to Hettie. This was always difficult. Her strategy of avoidance was different each time. This time, she faced the woodstove, staring into a stew pot but not stirring or adding ingredients. "*Maybe*, see you next summer?" she said flatly.

"Hettie," I said, hugging her from behind, "you know that's true." She just leaned closer to the stew, humming, ignoring me.

I walked to the shed, opened the door, and stepped inside. Wooden ducks lined the shelves. A preening harlequin. A dozen or so mallards. A whistle drake. A white-winged scoter with metal eyelets, Sam's favorite. Its head was a rectangle of rough leather, its body made of cork. A metal ballast was nailed to a wooden rudder on its underside. Few people made this type of decoy anymore. Sam would never sell it. On the sawdust floor were two Canadian geese, their necks bowed and stretched the way geese feed. A row of goose-headed canes, another kind of decoy which a hunter could set out over a mud flat, were stacked in a corner like a gentleman's walking sticks.

"Say hello to your mother and cousin for me, will you?" Sam said.

"And my father," I said. "Should I say hello to him?"

"Word has it I'll see him before you do. He's supposed to stop in Quill on his way to your place. Said he'd bring me a two-way

39

radio set. Going to bring one to you, too. Figured you and Pelly
might like to talk to each other over it."

Sam stood up from his bench. We shook hands, then he
cuffed the top of my head. He went back to work on his decoy.
"Good traveling," he said.

Pelly walked with me to the plane. "Maybe check that catalog
of yours for circus tents, okay?" I said.

"Soon as you leave."

"I'll work up some new ideas for the act."

I climbed into the plane and leaned back against a sack of
flour. Moses got in the pilot's seat, an unlit cigarette dangling
from his lips. "Got plenty, coffee, in me," he said. "You ready?"

He taxied over the lake, arced up, and leveled, snow sweeping from the wings. I looked down to see Pelly start to write a
large A into the grainy snow on his pond, moving swiftly but
with great deliberation on his unicycle.

"Pelly, he'll be at the end of alphabet, by the time we get to
Paduola," Moses said.

He veered the plane southward, pitching it slightly, and we
were out of the clouds. "Pelly says he gonna teach, me to read,"
Moses said. "I can't read words. Know how to read numbers,
the meters on dashboard, here. But can't read. Can talk over
the radio, okay. He's gonna make words in the snow, know
what I mean, eh? Gonna start, with my name. Big letters, my
name. Moses. Dog. Toussaint. Gonna surprise Mr. Einert
Sohms. Just gonna walk in and say, 'Gimmee that paper to sign.'
Receipt for the mail. No more thumb in ink. I'm gonna sign it.
Moses. Dog. Toussaint."

In a while we circled Paduola Lake. I could see chimney
smoke, the roof under it. I mumbled the latitude and longitude
coordinates. "What, did you say?" Moses asked.

"Nothing," I said.

When we landed, Charlotte ice-skated out to meet the plane.
"Hey, Noah!" she shouted. "Hey, how are you? Hey, Moses!
Take these letters, Moses, okay?"

Mina had given Charlotte a stack of letters wrapped in string.

"Charlotte, hey," Moses said. "Little while I am writing to you a letter. What to write you, eh? Anything you want?"

Charlotte shrugged. "I don't know," she said. "How about telling me what you see up in the sky?"

"See you skating out."

"You just *told* me that much!" Charlotte said, laughing. Moses laughed, too, but looked slightly confused. "Don't worry," Charlotte said. "If you write 'See you skating out,' I'll be glad."

"I will do that," Moses said, pleased. "Maybe a month or two, a letter, eh?"

"Okay, Moses. So long. Good-bye now."

Out on the ice Charlotte jumped up and down, pulling my suitcase, trying to skate toward our house all at the same time. "Tell me *everything*, Noah!" she said. "Everything from Quill. Then I'll tell you everything that's gone on here, with Auntie and me."

"I got absolutely nothing to say," I teased.

She yanked the suitcase away from me, snapped it open, and crouched over, facing me. "I'm going to empty this all over the lake," she said, taking small, choppy steps backward on her skates. "Shirts over there, socks over there. And I mean it, Noah!"

"Okay—" I tried to keep from laughing.

"Okay, start talking."

We started back toward the house.

"And don't leave out a thing!" Charlotte said.

At the beginning of April my father came home. He had been gone since the previous December. He just appeared in the doorway. It was a windy day, so we had not heard the plane. He nodded an almost formal hello, took off his boots and coat, and set a small crate on the kitchen table. He opened a drawer, found a screwdriver, then pried the crate open. He reached in and took out a radio.

There was always tension when he returned after his long absences, sometimes worse than others. The very worst, to me, was when he would silently inspect things. He would pick up a coffee cup, say, and act as though it were an object fallen from the moon—as if he had long been away from civilization and had to demonstrate it.

Now we could see he was excited. He sat down at the table and turned the radio toward him. Mina stood behind Charlotte in her bedroom doorway. She had one hand on Charlotte's shoulder, the other nervously stroked her hair.

"This is a two-way set," he said. "It's got a sender and a receiver. Now you can talk to people other than yourselves. I was just over in Quill. I saw Sam and Hettie. I saw Pelly. I saw his funny bicycle."

"Unicycle," I said.

"That's it. I saw him riding the *uni*cycle."

"You're back early this year," Mina said.

"Well, we got a lot of mapping done this winter, so they let us go."

"I see," Mina said.

"Anyway," my father said, "Sam's now got an identical two-way set. A little gift from me. Sam's become a regular communications expert, what with the shortwave, and now this. See, what I figure is: first, Sam catches an orchestra from the air. They're floating around all the time from cities. He can catch one just by turning a dial the right way."

"We know how it works," I said.

"Okay—okay. But now, listen carefully. Since Sam has a duplicate two-way"—he gingerly tapped ours—"all he has to do is put the transmitter from *his* radio next to his shortwave's *speaker*"—he was demonstrating all this with his hands—"and presto, a philharmonic!"

"One radio talking to another," Mina said. "We just listen in on their conversations, is that it?"

The anger in Mina's voice had to make my father realize that his circuitous radio strategy had backfired. He knew that she had long wanted to leave Paduola Lake. She had had quite enough of our isolated existence. She wanted Charlotte and me to have formal schooling. On every one of my father's visits, we heard them arguing. He would say, "Next year."

"Goddamn you to hell next year!" Mina shouted. "Well," she would say, lowering her voice, "of course, Anthony, I wouldn't want to rush you about this. Not something this important to me. Why not think about it another ten years or so."

If we had to continue living at Paduola Lake, at least the two-way would be an improvement. Our two classical albums, Rachmaninoff's *Variations on a Theme by Paganini* and Stravinsky's *Rite of Spring,* and their cell-battery player were worn derelict and scratchy. We had listened to the two albums so often that we had taken to placing the needle anywhere but their beginning, simply to allow for variety.

Finally, ignoring Mina, my father squared the two-way in front of him, fit the earphones over his head, and adjusted the dials. He spoke into the mouthpiece. "Sam? Sam, can you hear me? This is Paduola Lake calling. Sam, can you . . . do you have an orchestra there?"

A moment later Sam must have come on because my father interrupted. "Sam, one second. Hold on." Then he slid the earphones from his head and placed them over my ears.

But it was Hettie's voice that crackled through:

"Listen, Sam is all broken. He's sat down. He can't talk. Listen, some bad news, from here. I can hardly say it. An accident. On the pond. Pelly went through. Fell through. He gathered us, for watching his tricks. Everybody. Was there. On the unicycle he was. Sam and me we had chairs waiting for us special in the snow. We sit in them. We have blankets. On our laps. Especially at us Pelly is waving. He did tricks. Funny ones. Then he did going backward.

"That's when it happens. Out in the middle." Her voice cracked. "A few men they crawl, out there, but too late. It was too late, he's gone. Pelly is.

"We just don't get next now what to do."

Earphones still on, I stopped listening.

Seeing I was deeply shaken, my father switched off the two-way and lifted the earphones from my head. With a few hesitant laughs, he said, "Didn't think talking with Sam would upset you so much." He glanced around. Both Mina and Charlotte were staring at the radio. Then, toned down, a little unnerved, he said, "I mean, son, you look like you've seen a ghost."

CHAPTER TWO

Paduola Lake

"Life's give and take," Anthony had once declared. "The government hands you a job, but no telling where they'll make you live."

He was employed, at least for a while, in mapping the interior: northern Manitoba, that is, and eastern Saskatchewan. "The more exactly I map a place," he said, "the more overwhelming what's around it seems."

I knew him only in glimpses. He was not tall, though robust. High, broad cheekbones and black hair combed back from a smooth forehead are what I remember best about his appearance. Also his eyes, which were pale blue. His parents were Ukrainian. As with most subjects he was brief whenever he mentioned his family. He once showed me an old photograph in which his mother, an elegant, small woman wearing a pleated coat, scarf wrapped around her head, leaning on a cane, stood next to his father. His father, a rangy-looking fellow with wild white hair and a fierce squint, wore a dark shirt and held an overcoat over his shoulder even though snow was on the ground. The back of the photograph read "March 1930." They stood in front of a shingled cottage. "That's in the Ukraine," said my father. "They were at about the same latitude as we are here."

In rare, light-hearted moods he was given to deep laughter and, especially with Charlotte, outright affection. There was a large, faded map of the world on the wall of Charlotte's bedroom which Anthony had given her for her tenth birthday. Whenever he was home, he came in to say good night to her. I heard their conversation from my bed. Anthony stood at the map and tapped his fingers rapidly against it. "Where's it raining?" he asked into the dark.

Charlotte guessed. "London, England," she might say. No matter which city she named, she was always correct.

"Right," Anthony said. "Now, who is it raining on?"

"An old woman, but she doesn't have a raincoat on."

"Wrong. It's raining on a man and a woman, talking with each other. She's holding an umbrella."

"They're trying to figure out where to have supper."

"No, they're not. They're arguing about something."

"No, they get along fine. They just can't figure out where to eat."

"That's the reason they can't get along. They should just go to a place, sit down, and have a good supper. Instead, they're out in the rain, arguing."

"Yes, they should just get inside."

"Now, what are their names?"

Some nights he stood by the map until the people had professions, troubles, complicated lives. If Anthony's question or disagreement went unanswered, it usually meant that Charlotte had fallen asleep. Then he would quietly walk into the living room. I'd hear the chair springs.

His face grew more whittled with each visit. I say "visit" because we so rarely saw him. Mina never threw out a calendar. She saved all fifteen from our years at Paduola Lake. In the squares under such mottos as IN THE GRIP OF WINTER BE IN THE HUG OF STANFIELD UNDERWEAR, she summed up each day's thoughts and activities in a few sentences. I remember her sitting at the kitchen table, a candle lit, mulling sentences over before jotting them down. Later, when I examined the calendars, I found that my memory was correct—Anthony's usual pattern was to stay with us for a few weeks each June and December.

To me he was like an awkward guest. This was partly because of the strained civility with which my mother spoke to him, attended to his meals, saw that his clothes were laundered. As if our house were an inn. They slept apart. Anthony slept in the spare bedroom and, after Charlotte arrived, on a pallet on the living room floor. Even within our house he kept to himself.

Claiming exhaustion from his travels, he sat in a chair, feet propped up on the hassock. *The Dictionary of Musical Instruments*, with its hundreds of illustrations, was usually open on his lap. It was a book he seemed more to occupy than own. If ever he felt me watching him, which I often did half-hidden in a doorway, or from the kitchen table, he would look up nervously and say, "I'm in the O's . . . oboes, ox horns." He then showed me the relevant line drawings, searching my face to see if I was properly impressed. "Beauties, aren't they?" he inquired. Then he went back to studying the page.

I now know why he burrowed into that book for hours at a time. It was a connection to a world he had once been part of. As a young man in Toronto he had played French horn on the weekends with a small orchestra and had worked in a music store to pay for night classes in geography, toward earning a certificate in cartography. One night the horn was stolen from his room. But the thief had left the battered case. "After that," Mina told me, "he usually had the case with him, but he stopped playing for good. He simply would not buy a new horn. The theft made the decision for him. Once I said that it looked rather silly, him carrying an empty case around. It caused no end of trouble. It was best to say nothing."

One snowy morning I watched him trudge into the distance carrying the case, filled as usual with his clothes. Earlier, watching him pack, Mina, Charlotte, and I had struggled to keep ourselves from laughing. "Let's see," he said, taking careful inventory. "Socks, underwear, two shirts." He snapped shut the case.

That night I dreamed that Anthony was detained in order to perform a solo for the local owls. He set the black case down on the snow and pulled out his French horn from under the shirts. I knew it was a French horn because I had seen a drawing of one, but I'd never heard its sound. The dream had to invent that. Anthony stood up and began to play. The solo took days to complete. At the end of the dream Anthony returned to our house and flew into a tantrum. "How can I earn a living," he shouted, "with those goddamn owls holding me up?" He kicked aside cardboard tubes holding maps and flung tripod quadrants out the door. Then he collapsed in a chair, breath steaming forth from his mouth as if the room were just as cold as outside.

I startled awake. Charlotte was perched on the edge of my bed watching me. "You okay?" she said.

"Bad dream again. Terrible."

"Sounded like it. I brought you some tea."

"There were these owls."

"That one again. Uncle Anthony and the horn?"

"Yes, don't tell Mina."

We sat a while without talking, just sipping tea. Then, with a mischievous expression on her face, Charlotte brought out a shoebox from behind her back. Opening it slowly, she lifted out Mina's "secret" collection of postcards, each one an illustration of the Ark. "These'll cheer you up," she said.

Mina's interest in the Flood, which she had had since childhood, became a consuming passion during our years at Paduola Lake. She kept her postcard collection hidden among boxes in her closet. Whenever I was ill, or in bad spirits, or woke loudly from dreams, Charlotte smuggled the cards into my room. She sat on the bed and fanned them out, anxiously awaiting my choice. I picked one at a time—perhaps an irreverent one, two giraffes smoking cigars, two leopards roller-skating up the plank. Or the Asian naive with a parade of color-sail junks, each filled with animals, their destination a bamboo Ark looming in the storm-swept horizon. Then there was the fabled griffin, half lion, half eagle, in line with twin antelope, horses and swans. ("Why only one griffin?" I once asked Mina. "Because," she answered, "it's *already* two animals.")

Mina forecast her arrival with shouts and threats, the broom end waving in the doorway. "Who's the thief?" she would shriek, feigning a witch voice. She would hurry in, a look of exaggerated hurt and anger on her face, and demand an apology. But the next moment she was transfixed alongside us on the bed, explaining where she had obtained each card, whether in Vancouver, where she was born, or Calgary, Edmonton, or Winnipeg, where she had grown up. Of course we knew it all by heart. Still, each telling captured us all over again.

Then, with a sudden look of wistfulness on her face, she became Mrs. Noah. "That was a remarkable voyage. My husband treated me with great kindness. There were hardships, of course, but we never lost hope."

She actually said things like that. Charlotte and I just lis-

49

tened. "Well, then," she would say, snapping back to the present, "on to other things. Charlotte, go back to bed."

"I'm five feet three and one-half inches tall," Mina once said, her gray-green eyes brightening, "the tallest woman in my family. Of course, there was just Mother and I."

She had moved to Toronto at age twenty-five, when her parents finally returned to Vancouver after years of transiency. There she found work in a movie theater, The Northern Lights, and took a room a block away. Her salary was twenty-eight dollars a week, her rent eighteen dollars a month. Six evenings a week she waited on customers from behind the refreshment counter. It was also her job to arrange the cardboard displays in the lobby and out on the sidewalk. She especially liked putting up the cutouts. "Out-of-date ones," she told me, "I took home. I remember I had cutouts of Myrna Loy—well, you don't know what she looked like, of course, but she was beautiful. And Clark Gable, and many others. I kept them pressed to one another in my closet. Sometimes, when I had a guest to dinner, I'd say, 'Just put your wrap in the closet there.' As soon as the door opened the figures sprang out like from a jack-in-the-box!"

One night in 1941 Anthony walked into The Northern Lights. "He had on a greatcoat and a fedora hat," Mina recalled. "There was a double feature playing—*The Shanghai Gesture*, starring a wonderful actress named Gene Tierney, and Victor Mature, and *Seven Sinners*, with a mysterious woman named Marlene Dietrich, and John Wayne. I'd placed the cutouts of Victor Mature and Marlene Dietrich close together on the sidewalk. I suppose it implied a romance. But of course they were in different movies. I did what I pleased with the cutouts.

"*The Shanghai Gesture* played first. It was about a tycoon who is seduced by evil. His own daughter is used to lure him into an

Oriental gambling den. It was a silly story, but I sat through it four Sunday afternoons in a row; Sunday was my day off.

"Anthony, however, had wandered out well before the intermission between movies. He looked around the lobby. At the drinking fountain, the candy bars, the exit sign, as if they were all of equal interest. Finally, he walked up to the refreshment stand, but didn't order a thing. Instead he stared at me.

" 'Mature and Dietrich aren't in the same movie,' he said.

" 'You don't say,' I said back.

" 'I do say. It's deceiving the public.'

" 'You're the only one complaining.'

" 'I'm going outside and move them apart.'

" 'You do that, but don't plan on getting back in.'

"One might say we had struck up a conversation. Soon it was intermission and the lobby had filled with people.

" 'I've got to get back to work,' I said. 'Besides, you keep talking and you'll miss the second show.'

" 'I'd rather hear you tell me about it than sit through it, anyway.'

" 'Suit yourself.'

"When *Seven Sinners* began, I told him its plot. I guess I just became interested in him. He seemed so eccentric, but with purpose. He wasn't like anyone I'd met. Then he got around to inviting me to see his orchestra play. At first I refused him. He stood around the lobby a while, then left. He came to the theater every night for a week. He'd buy a ticket, but would never go in to see the movie. He'd stand there talking to me. That was our date. We'd be at the movies but would never watch it. If he had a night class, he'd be there to walk me home.

"Finally, I did go see his orchestra play. In a gymnasium at a high school on Jarvis Avenue. A dingy old place with echoes.

"Anyway, December of 1941 we were married. We wrote to each other's parents. Anthony's were in Finland at that time. Mine were in Vancouver. We told them the courtship had gone on much longer than it had. The wedding was in my apartment. There was Anthony and me, Mr. Rouche, the owner of the theater, who else? Oh, yes, Edward Wherity, a very fat violinist, and of course a justice of the peace.

"Just before the ceremony, Anthony insisted that we take the cutouts from the closet and place them all over the room. So we did that. Olivia de Havilland was in a slinky gown. Errol Flynn had on swashbuckler clothes. Dick Powell wore a striped suit and smoked a cigarette.

"The justice said a few words about the past and future, and then we were married. Anthony moved in. I kept my job at the theater. Mr. Rouche gave me a week off with pay, and we honeymooned in Niagara Falls. That's where the wash basin came from, the one with the barrel. The hotels there were designed to make you feel special, but since there were so many other newlyweds, we didn't.

"When we got back, Anthony worked at the music store and finished school. He also worked in the map room of the library. We stayed at those jobs just over two years. You were born in 1943. Then we moved downstairs, to a bigger apartment. We wrote to each other's parents again, telling them about you. Then Anthony got the job in the north. Couldn't pass it up, he said. Jobs were terribly hard to find. He was of age to be drafted, as the war was on, but the government sent him north instead. We wrote to the parents again. Neither of us had met the other's, still haven't. When we left for Paduola Lake, you were just a year old.

"Nearly eight years, Anthony coming and going, before your cousin arrived."

In June 1952, when Anthony came home, he announced, "Your cousin's coming to live here."

Charlotte's mother, Eloise—Mina's sister—and Henry, her

father, had both died in an accident in Halifax. They had worked in a salmon canning factory along the wharf, and one morning the roof collapsed and thirty-eight people were killed. Eloise was pinned under a conveyor. Many factory reforms resulted from the accident, but Charlotte was orphaned by it.

"How did you hear about all of this, Anthony?" Mina said. "And how did you make these arrangements? Not that we wouldn't love to have her." The latter Mina meant quite sincerely.

"Had to be in Halifax to get some technical equipment," Anthony said matter-of-factly. "Naturally I looked up Henry and Eloise. Their house was all locked up. Charlotte was in a foster home. The accident was all over the papers. That place she was in—terrible. Just awful. I couldn't leave her there."

Wilfred Gaboriault, the pilot whose plane Pelly eventually saw crash, was working the mail route at the time, and Anthony arranged for him to fly us to Flin Flon, northwest of Lake Winnipeg, to meet Charlotte's train.

At the depot we sat on a wooden bench for a few hours until the train pulled in. A porter helped Charlotte down the train's metal stairs. She was wearing a green coat and black shoes with white knee-high socks, and she had a cried-out look about her. Setting down her suitcase, she glanced around desperately for a familiar face. Charlotte had met neither Mina nor myself. "Uncle Anthony!" she called out when she saw my father. She waved, her hand held close to her face, and then sat down on the suitcase as if the gesture had exhausted her.

We walked over to her, and Mina kissed the top of Charlotte's head, hugged her tightly, and said, "Welcome home, darling. Now, let's take a look at you."

At the time Charlotte was seven, two years younger than me. She had black hair tied up in twin braids atop her head; its shade reminded me of birch knotholes. Nature had given her beguiling, slightly Oriental eyes that held her quickness. On her upper forehead was a small violet birthmark that, a few weeks after her arrival, she had tried to erase with turpentine. Her skin blistered and ached for days. When it healed, Mina sat Charlotte down and told her that the birthmark meant she had a rare, stubborn character, that it was a curious fate to have such a thing, but a gift as well.

"You're lying!" Charlotte sobbed.

"I'm not," Mina said. "Things like this can make you stronger. But you won't understand that for a long time."

Next to the train I gave Charlotte a small bouquet of daisies wrapped in waxed paper. "I like three other flowers more," she remarked in a tone that was my introduction to a very opinionated girl. "First, yellow roses. Next, day lilies. Third, violets, but there has to be a whole field of them or it's just no good."

Under her breath I heard Mina say, "You and I will get along just fine." Mina laughed nervously. Turning to me, she said, "Those have got to be the first flowers you've ever bought, isn't that so?"

"Yeah," I said. "And if she doesn't want 'em, I'll throw 'em under the train."

"Don't be a jackass," Anthony said, cuffing my shoulder. "She's just saying that about her favorites so you'll know for the next time."

Mina looked at Anthony incredulously. "Father offers son advice," she said. "Now, how about buying *me* some flowers, Anthony?"

"We've got to get a move on," Anthony said. "Noah, give your mother one of those daisies, will you?"

Mina took a daisy from me and quickly handed the bunch to Charlotte. "They're for you, honey," she said.

"Will you carry my suitcase?" Charlotte asked me.

Anthony had rented a Ford pickup truck. Crammed into the one seat, along with a basket of sandwiches bought at the depot, we jostled along crude gravel and dirt roads for two days. We stopped overnight in a field and slept in the back of the truck, in sleeping bags and under extra blankets, except for Anthony, who slept in the front seat. Our destination was the small town of Nelson House, where Anthony had arranged for us to meet Wilfred Gaboriault. Testifying to her exhaustion, Charlotte slept much of the way. In Nelson House we waited half a day for Wilfred to arrive and return us to Paduola Lake. As we boarded the plane Anthony said, "Got to return the truck." Then he turned back to the truck and climbed into the front seat. After honking the horn in a pattern of short bleeps like Morse code, he waved and drove off. His abrupt departure was a new thing for Charlotte. For the second time in two days, she waved. In the plane Mina told her, "You'll see—he comes and goes."

There could hardly have been time for Charlotte to catch her breath, considering the shock of losing her parents, the long train journey alone, waking one morning in Paduola Lake amid strangers when only a few mornings before she had woken in her own house in Halifax. Perhaps Eloise—the aunt I never met—had prepared a breakfast of cereal, toast, and orange juice that morning, after which Charlotte had walked to school with other children.

It is possible that the sheer magnitude of such changes re- quired of Charlotte a nearly oblivious adaptation, a complete giving-over to the present, because to look back for even an instant would simply have been too painful. Yet for a long time after her arrival, we heard her crying in her bed well into the night, and we felt helpless. And she would mope around the yard for hours, staring into the woods.

I knew the surrounding lakes and woods, had hunted and fished them, taken hundreds of day-long treks, and had my share of close calls. Close calls never had to do with animals, but with hazards of terrain—suckholes formed by the spring melt-off had unpredictable locations. There were certain rock formations where, if you were careless in climbing, you could jam a leg into a crevasse, snap an ankle. In winter the contours of snow could be deceptive. I once went careening down an otter slide that had been camouflaged by freshly fallen snow, had locked snowshoes and badly bruised a leg and broken my nose when I catapulted off an ice hummock at the bottom of the slide, landing hard facedown. On streams, ponds, and lakes the sturdiness of ice had to be constantly tested. A thaw in the middle of a pond might occur in January, and no one could ever explain it. It just happened.

It soon became clear that Charlotte would take to the woods at her own cautious pace, one brief, tentative walk every day. It was not the animals that troubled her, though she had only seen them in zoos or in books, but the whole estrangement from the city. We mostly *heard* the animals, at night, anyway. Porcupines mewed, called in high-pitched cackles or staccato coughs, and gnawed at our outhouse. The caribou snorted like pigs or emitted guttural bellows, forced gusts of breath through their nostrils when they foraged near our house, kicking away snow to find ground cover. Occasionally we heard the echoing shriek of a lynx or the industrious scraping of its claws on a branch. A wolf glimpsed at the edge of the yard. Even rarer, a bear rummaging in the compost heap, ransacking the fish-drying shack I had built.

That first winter Charlotte was with us, she was captivated by crows. Without fail she was awake before anyone, the moment she heard their first early-morning squalling. Charlotte met their insistent call with scraps of fat and crusts of bread, which she flung out the door.

Unlike other birds that came around—sparrows, jays—crows were walkers. You could sense their weight. Now and then one would break through a thin snow crust. Even though the bird easily regained the surface, the event sent a panicked cacophony up from the other crows, an outburst Charlotte found splendid. Knowing I watched from a window, she would stand on our step and start up her own repertoire of crowlike noises. The crows, even those grappling with the larger pieces of food, looked up, listened tilt-headed. It was as if by some projection of their vanity that Charlotte's head moved woodenly, like a ventriloquist's dummy.

Charlotte's comical, intense devotion to the crows led Mina to observe, "I believe that if I didn't give her others things to do, she may well spend her entire day watching them." Charlotte took in details, telling them to us at supper. "Today there was this owl out there. Big snowy owl. Just sat there blinking and looking at my crows. They didn't like that, not at all. They made such a fuss! They went right after the poor old owl and chased it into the woods."

It wasn't until Charlotte lived with us that I realized how seldom Mina used to laugh. But now a free-wheeling, even raucous laughter drifted in from the living room where Mina spent each morning teaching Charlotte how to knit. Balls of yarn were strewn all over the floor, and darning needles were lined up on a piece of black felt. It was as if they read each other's minds. I'd stand in the doorway, able to detect only that they both concentrated on their knitting. Suddenly, without even looking at one another, they would burst into laughter.

Charlotte quickly took to knitting, though her first knitted pair of mittens had dwarf thumbs, and one mitten was considerably larger than the other. Soon she began knitting likenesses of crows into mittens, scarves, and sweaters. "Don't you want to try something different?" Mina inquired.

"Not really," Charlotte said. "Well, maybe crows flying along the arms"—she held up a half-completed sweater—"instead of on the front."

This, too, all but collapsed them in laughter.

They cooked together, washed each other's hair, sat fishing from boulders at the peninsula's edge. Afternoons the three of

us worked through reading and writing lessons, using primers
sent in by plane. Although she had no formal training, Mina
was a disciplined teacher. She conscientiously studied the
primers, taking detailed notes. She was a stickler for grammar
and handwriting. When Charlotte and I compared handwriting, Charlotte would roll over on her back, gasping laughter,
her legs cycling in the air—my handwriting resembled barbed
wire. It was cramped, and the tallest consonants veered off at
odd angles. I did not work hard at my writing. Charlotte labored
over hers like a monk, stacking lined paper covered with finely
crafted letters in the kindling box near the stove.

In those first weeks Charlotte lived with us we bickered
constantly. We went out of our way to be cruel, to tease each
other mercilessly, flinging insults, even allowing ourselves temper tantrums in Mina's presence. The morning of the first hard
snow, Charlotte and I were out back of the house. She packed
a snowball and tossed it into the air. I ran to catch it, and then
purposely let it strike my shoulder. I squinted up my eyes and
without warning tackled her, smothering her under my weight.
Then, despite her protests, I crammed snow down her leggings,
under her coat, down her galoshes. Bloated with snow, her
arms were forced out stiffly as if tied to splints. I could not bear
the rage on her face, so I pulled her stocking cap to her chin.
In muffled screams, she cried, "I hate you!"

Mina appeared in the doorway. "Both of you—inside!" she
shouted, a tremulous note running through her voice.

Charlotte ran to her room. When she came into the kitchen,
she wore a cotton bathrobe a couple of sizes too big, and she
was still shivering. Mina placed a cup of tea in front of her.
Charlotte's face was set stubbornly, and she spoke only to Mina.
"I don't want to eat breakfast with him, I don't want to do
lessons with him, I don't want to look at him. I hate his guts."

Mina took a chance now. She saw that attitudes could have
hardened, and both Charlotte and I might have cordoned off

our lives from each other for quite a while. So she said, "*Decide*, both of you, to get along. Decide it for yourselves and me. We're out here alone. It's not like other lives. Not like life in Halifax —forgive me, I know that's difficult for you to hear, Charlotte. This is, shall we say, an unusual life. Whatever we have, perhaps whatever we will ever have, is all right here. That includes each other."

"*You* and *me*, Auntie," Charlotte snapped. She crossed her feet, pressing the one on top down hard, curling back her toes. She looked at the floor. "Not *him*."

"All *three* of us," Mina said. "Get it through your heads, both of you. This house—it's . . ." She paused. "It's like an ark, one that's drifted into a part of the world which, well, it has dangers. The only way to live through the dangers is to protect one another. To take care of each other. . . ."

Mina broke down crying. Charlotte and I both went to our rooms, distressed, ashamed. We each returned in a few moments. "You tell Charlotte you're sorry," Mina said.

I looked at my cousin but could not manage an apology. "I won't beat you up anymore," I said.

"He didn't apologize," Charlotte said.

So we were wary of each other. We did separate chores around the house. I brought in wood, ice-fished, cleaned those fish I caught, occasionally cooked a meal. I wandered in the woods, hunting with my twenty-two. I began to work alone on my school lessons. Yet Mina and I spent time together. Often I asked her about Anthony. Once past her initial discomfort with the subject, she answered in detail. Bitterness would creep into her voice. But she would always end by saying, "Of course, you'll have to make up your own mind about him."

Often we talked well into the night, long after Charlotte had gone off to bed. I remember her saying: "I really didn't expect life to be this way. Never *dreamed* it would be. But what *should* I have expected, then? Your father and I, we got into a bad habit. Whenever we learned a thing about each other, truly learned it, it became the very thing we could not bear to know. We became strangers. Can you understand this? Intimacies— just a way I'd like my coffee very hot, couldn't bear it cold— grew all the larger because of this. They grew larger and larger, almost monsters sometimes, living in our house, pushing us apart with huge hands of enormous strength. The larger the intimacies got, the more we ignored them. We went days without talking. Weeks! And of course, he was gone for such long periods of time. Until it came to pass that we no longer really recognized one another. When we were young, in Toronto, when we lived in the apartment with the cutouts still in the closet, I never dreamed of life being the way it's turned out."

On Sunday afternoons I dragged the bathtub from the pantry to the kitchen. Then I filled the caldron that hung in the fireplace with water and built up the fire beneath it. I heated water in two kettles and two large stew pots on the woodstove, coordinating things so that all the water was ready at about the same time. With a steady pace, like a one-man bucket brigade, I walked from caldron to tub, tub to caldron, scooping out water with a wooden bucket, finally a ladle, until the caldron was empty. Then I added water from the pots and kettles. I kept to my room while Charlotte bathed, and Mina sat at the kitchen table. Mina taught Charlotte Acadian folk songs and love ballads, whose tunes she quickly learned, although she had difficulty recalling a second verse to any of them. She would merely hum along, linking up whenever she remembered a phrase, even a word. Charlotte's voice was of a fragile, hesitant timbre, though she could rise to full-throated contributions when inspired by Mina's enthusiasm. Mina's soprano was lovingly practiced, if limited. Charlotte added complaints to their duet, "Too hot!" or "Too cold!" as Mina poured rinse water over her head, continuing to sing without breaking stride. "Stop yammering," Mina would finally say, "I'm not your nanny!"

Each Sunday Mina sang her favorite ballad without fail. Charlotte, resigned, would make her request as if suddenly recalling the song. "Auntie, sing about the selkie, will you, *please?*"

"All right, darling," Mina would say, "you've talked me into it."

"Selkie" was a maritime word for seal, and in Mina's mournful ballad, a seal-gunner is married to a selkie, who often changes form, from human to seal and vice-versa. So even though he takes pleasure in knowing that she basks in the sun and capers about in the sea, he is tormented by the possibility that he might not recognize her among the other seals when he goes hunting.

"Please don't become a seal," he pleads.

"Don't hunt in my waters," she stubbornly replies.

It is an exchange full of foreboding. One clear day the gunner shoots a seal that is, of course, his wife.

Mina knew a dozen versions, each more tragic than the next.

The ballad inevitably ended Charlotte's bath. It was as if the song, having traveled the spectrum from joy to loss, left little to be said. Silently Charlotte would stand, wrap a towel around her, step from the tub, and go to her room.

"Noah, Charlotte's done!" Mina would call. This prompted me to empty the tub for Mina's bath and refill it. Again I would lay on my bed, daydream, listen through the door, read a broken-backed copy of a Jules Verne novel, until Mina called, "Noah, your turn!"

I would repeat the entire process, heating water, filling the tub for myself this time. In those first weeks Charlotte saw my bath as an opportunity to advance our little war. While Mina kept to her room to offer me privacy, Charlotte, now dressed and wearing a towel around her head, invented reasons to be in the kitchen. She searched for this or that in a cupboard, clattering about, feigning frustration at not finding what she wanted. Or she would carry her notebooks and pens to the table and pretend to concentrate on her homework. Fuming, but not wanting to give her the satisfaction of my anger, I would sit hunched up, arms hugging knees, unwilling even to scrub my back with the new brush Mina had ordered from the Bay Company store in Quill.

One time Charlotte actually began to bake cookies. "Don't think too much about my being here, Noah," she said, flattening out pieces of dough with a spatula. "It's not that interesting to watch a scrawny goat bathe." And after placing the tin sheet in the oven, she left.

With the smell of baking cookies filling the kitchen, I sat in the cooling water. When Charlotte returned, she took out the tin, placed it on a ledge, and removed the cookies to a plate, which she set on the table, all in slow motion. "Want one?" she asked.

"No thank you," I said.

She walked from the kitchen attempting a ballad, whistling where she had forgotten the words.

In the end there was no one orchestration of a truce. In time Charlotte relaxed her incessant teasing, first by damning me with faint praise ("You're short, Noah, but not *too* short. Being short must be tough for a boy, though. You're brave"), and then, miraculously, she actually seemed to enjoy my company. A cautious deference to each other's presence had begun.

That Christmas Anthony was home, and we had a small tree on a cross-stand in the living room. Charlotte had knitted colored crow ornaments, which hung among the spruce needles. We had a big meal: a wild turkey, which Anthony had brought, canned corn, mashed potatoes, stewed tomatoes, rice. And we drank cider. Anthony was drinking more liquor than usual for him. First, he drank rum mixed in with the cider. Then he switched to whiskey, mixed with a little snowmelt. Finishing one glass, he walked to the front door, opened it, crouched on his knees, and carefully measured out a portion of snow, which he pinched into his glass like a chemist. Returning to the table, he added the whiskey. He kept silent through the meal, until I placed on the table the pumpkin pie that Mina and Charlotte had just baked. Then he spoke up. "What kind of Christmas is this, anyway? I remember real *Christmases*! With all sorts of *talking*—stories! Stories, that's the ticket. Let's have some stories!"

"Sleep it off," Mina interrupted. "We'll have stories in the morning."

Anthony squinted hard and stared at Mina, bringing her into focus. "No, not tomorrow," he said, "right now, when we're all here at the table. With all the bones on the plates. All the food, the . . . pie. With the pie." He stumbled through his sentences. "Mina," he continued solicitously, "Mina, my wife of . . . many years, you begin. Mina, a story!"

Charlotte and I looked at our plates.

"No, *you* begin, Anthony," Mina insisted. "Tell us something. From your *travels*. You know, from out in the *world*. The children have heard all of my stories far too often."

Anthony leaned back in his chair. He glanced around the table, then at the open gift boxes sprawled on the floor. Next to some of them lay the clothing Charlotte had knitted, all of it decorated with crows. He closed his eyes, inhaled deeply, then let out his breath in a long, moaning sigh. He took a deep swig of whiskey straight from the bottle. "I'll tell you something," he said. "Matter of fact, there's a crow involved. Over near Quill, east of there, actually. I was with a crew, and one of the men started coughing up blood. Blaach! Blaach!" He imitated coughing and retching noises. Mina pushed her pie away from her and laid her head on the table, facedown.

"Had a pain in his chest as well. Thought it was pneumonia.

So, we were out a ways from civilization, and didn't have an ounce of medicine among us. Tobias—that's his name. Toby, he was laid up.

"We'd heard of an Indian doctor not too far away. Decided to take Toby to see this doctor. Word had it—according to a Cree we'd been using all along as a guide—this doctor, his name was Sipawese, pronounced *See-pah-wes-ay*. According to our guide, Sipawese once took a crow out of a man's chest. A man had a crow right in his chest, and Sipawese actually got it out somehow. See, this Sipawese, he's a special kind of doctor. Knows how to sweat fevers out of you. Knows how to mend bones by talking in animal voices, and the like. That's what was rumored about him. He wasn't ordinary.

"Anyway, we travel with Toby, who's sick as a dog by now, and we finally get to Sipawese's place, godforsaken as it was. Right away this scrawny hound comes out snarling at us. I throw a rock. The dog slinks behind a cabin.

"Now old Sipawese himself comes out. He's wrinkled, old trousers tied up by a rope belt. Comes out to one side of his cabin.

" 'Dog says you aren't come here to kill me,' he says.

" 'No,' I say. I point to Toby's chest. 'This man has got some trouble in there. Heard you once took a crow out of somebody's chest. Thought maybe you could find out what's wrong here, too.'

"Well, old Sipawese just stares at me. 'Who told you that was half-wrong,' he says. 'I first put that crow—in.'

" 'In his chest?' I say.

"Sipawese, he just nods. I ask him did he take the crow out again.

" 'Yes,' he says. 'Want to see it?' he says.

" 'Yeah, sure,' I say.

" 'A dollar.'

" 'I don't have that much with me,' I say.

" 'How much, then, you have with you?'

"I reach into my pocket, take out a few coins. Hand them to Sipawese. He takes them, and right away throws them in through his cabin door. They hit the wall and fall on the floor. Then he walks inside his cabin. We follow him. I'll tell you, that was one sorrowful peculiar place of residence. There's one table. Right in the middle of the room. On the table—guess what? The crow. Stuffed with scraps of paper, spruce needles, dry reeds all sticking out. Feathers all faded.

"Sipawese says, 'Was a good crow, before it went in his chest.'

"I looked around. What else is in the cabin? I'll tell you. On the wall is this statue of Jesus Christ. But it's got a necklace on, and the necklace is made up of dried-up leathery paws. There's a bare cot. A few plates, bits of food. Plastic knives and forks. Couple of coats hanging on nails.

" 'How long will Toby have to stay?' I ask.

" 'Two days. Maybe three,' Sipawese says.

"Toby says, 'I'm not staying two minutes.'

" 'Hold on,' I say. 'Let me ask something else.' But Sipawese'd already gone out the door. When he's halfway between his cabin and a shed out back, I shout at him, 'Where are you going?'

"He doesn't turn around. He shouts, 'To my house.'

" 'What are we standing in, then?' I shout back.

"Now he turns around. '*Their* house!' he says. He's referring to Christ, and that torn-up crow.

" 'Who sleeps on the cot?' I say.

"He points at Toby. 'He will,' he says.

"Sipawese goes to his shed. Now the notable thing to know about this shed is that it has a door on each side. Four doors. Each one's got a window. Window of sheet plastic nailed to a wood frame.

"Sipawese goes in one of the doors.

"I walked up to the shed and there's his face, right behind a plastic window. All distorted-like.

"I walk to the right side of the shed. His face appears there, in that window.

"I'm walking slowly around the shed, and at each window there's his face to meet me.

"I turn and look at Toby. I say, 'I agree now, let's get to a town.'

"After that we took Toby to Kirstein Lake, got him by plane down to Flin Flon. Heard later he was all right, but for some scarring up on his lungs. In bed for a few weeks."

"Poor crow," Charlotte said thoughtfully.

"Thank you very much for that lovely Christmas story," Mina said, raising her head.

"You're entirely welcome," Anthony said. He struggled to his feet, walked to a chair in the living room, reached down, and took up the scarf, hat, and mittens that Charlotte had given him. He put them on, opened *The Dictionary of Musical Instruments,* and promptly fell asleep.

Anthony left the day after New Year's 1953 his usual way. First, he would announce the general time of his departure, something along the lines of, "I'll be going early afternoon." When in fact, he would always leave around dawn, having awakened everyone with his rustling about and his muttering. Mina packed sandwiches but never handed them to Anthony— she would leave them on the table. Charlotte was responsible for emptying out half of each rum and whiskey bottle, filling them again with water before Anthony chose one or two to take with him. I would make sure he left us a check or some cash so that we could pay for food and other items. Mina was deeply ashamed when she had to ask, via a pilot, for credit. Sometimes before helping to fold Anthony's shirts and pants, I would search the pockets for money. Then, carrying his French horn case and a gunny sack, Anthony was off. He would have made arrangements with a mail pilot to be picked up at Paduola Lake, though he would never inform us of such details ahead of time.

That summer, I met Pelly for the first time. Anthony had mentioned Pelly once or twice. He had met him along with Sam and Hettie while mapping in their region. Anthony and Sam had discovered a common affection for radio music, though at the time Anthony did not own a radio. Sam, like Einert Sohms, liked swing and jazz, while Anthony preferred classical. They had, as Anthony put it, friendly discussions over this.

One morning in early June Wilfred Gaboriault landed his plane on Paduola Lake, then paddled a pontoon to shore. Mina, Charlotte, and I met him. "Wilfred," Mina said with surprise, "you're out of schedule, aren't you?"

"Yes, ma'am," Wilfred said. He was a shy, tall man about forty, with a ruddy face and thick red beard. He was wearing his Canadian Air Force flight jacket. "I've stopped for one reason," he said.

"Well, come in for tea, at least," Mina said.

"Really can't," Wilfred said. 'We're about to get some weather. I have to get going. What I dropped by for, was to give you this."

He handed Mina an envelope, which she opened immediately. "It's from Samuel Bay," she said. "That's the man Anthony mentioned."

"He's a fine man," Wilfred said, "with a fine wife, fine nephew."

"That would be Pelly," Mina said.

"That's right," Wilfred said. "Look at this, will you?"

Wildred slid a rubber band off a scrolled piece of paper, which he unrolled and held by its corners. On it was a portrait of himself. "That Pelly, he's got talent, don't you think?"

"Yes, I do," Mina said.

Charlotte and I nodded in agreement.

"Auntie, what's the note say?" Charlotte said, tugging Mina's sleeve.

"Let's see here," Mina said. "It reads: 'Why not send your boy over for a visit? All of you visit if you like.' " She brightened. "I think it's a wonderful idea," she said. "Maybe you can attend school. That would be a fine thing to do."

"Missionary teacher's there most of the summer," Wilfred said.

"Besides, you can get to know Pelly," Mina said, "and then you'll be back in a few months. Of course, Charlotte should have playmates, too. But first we'll see how it goes with you. What do you think?"

"Let's all go," I said. "If things turn out wrong, I'm stuck."

"I fly in once a month," encouraged Wilfred. "Twice some months. You know that."

Clearly Mina did not want Charlotte to leave. I suppose she worried that she might be lonely to a harmful degree if she stayed on alone. How many times before Charlotte's arrival had she said, "Noah, I'd be mad as a hatter if it wasn't for you being here!" Still, there was something odd about her not leaping at the opportunity to visit Quill. Uninvited, she never would have, unless Anthony moved us there. But now she had an invitation in hand!

"Mina," Wilfred said, "there might be something to this invitation. Now, it's none of my business, but the truth is, you've been out here a long time. You've often mentioned going to town, even a city."

"I fully realize that," Mina said sharply.

Wilfred lowered his head. "I'll take you on over to Quill if you want to go, is all I meant."

"Thank you for that," Mina said. "You're a friend for offering."

"It's nothing at all," Wilfred said. "I just know they'd like your company over there, too."

"It's between me and Anthony—my staying here," Mina said. It was an uncharacteristically candid confession, especially to an aquaintance, though I think she meant it as a standoffish comment and nothing more.

But Wilfred took it to heart. "Then he's got both sides of the coin," he said. "He's got you wanting to stay here and be long gone, at the same time. You can't win, Mina."

I think Mina was worried that she had forgotten how to live among people, that she could never fully regain the knack of it. If Quill, with its eighty or so residents, involved such a hardwrought decision, what must the thought of a larger town, a city, have done to her?

"Just try it," Mina said to me.

There did not seem much time to think it over. Wilfred, Mina, and Charlotte were all looking at me.

"All right," I said, wondering how the decision would work for or against me.

"Fine," Wilfred said. "Good luck in weather, and I'll be back two mornings from today. The lake we'll land on is just a short ways from Quill. I'll radio ahead. There's a Hudson Bay store there. Run by a Mr. Einert Sohms. I'll tell him you're on your way. He'll tell everybody else. Somebody'll come out to meet you."

CHAPTER THREE

Preacher Tempted by Land-Otter Girls

"Don't blink or you'll miss it," Wilfred said. "I'll double back." He banked south, lowered our altitude, and circled Quill. "That building in the middle—with the porch. That's the store. Now, to your left, that house at the edge of the clearing? There's where you'll live."

Cabins and small houses that comprised the main of Quill were aligned roughly in the shape of a triangular kite whose southern corner had a meandering tail of four additional cabins, each perhaps an eighth-mile apart. Clusters of three, four, and five cabins were at the outskirts in the other directions. The landing strip was just to the east. The spruce forest grew right up to the edge of the village.

"Now Sam Bay, he's liable to insult me. But it's just us lampooning, eh? Don't mean a thing," Wilfred said. "That's him there." He pointed to a man in a rowboat. "Sit tight, now." Wilfred eased the plane down on Piwese Lake. "All's you have is that cardboard suitcase, right?"

"That's it," I said.

Wilfred did not anchor. "We don't drift much, not with the wind elsewhere," he said. Sam maneuvered the rowboat between the floats. "Thanks," I said to Wilfred. He handed Sam my suitcase. Sam, on the middle slat at the oars, placed the suitcase on the slat behind him. I climbed onto the front slat. "This here is Noah Krainik," Wilfred yelled. "Take good care of him, eh?"

"Nothing here could be as bad as flying with you, Wilfred," Sam shouted over the engine noise.

I looked at the two figures on shore.

" 'Cept maybe rowing with you," Wilfred shouted. "Noah, make sure you get to shore by dark, eh?"

Sam rowed straight to an inlet surrounded by boulders, deftly guided it up to a brief stretch of rocky beach, where Hettie and Pelly waited. Pelly helped pull the boat up. He took my suitcase and looked at me, saying nothing. On shore Sam said, "This is my wife, Hettie. My nephew, Pelly."

"_Towa'w,_" Hettie said.

"Means welcome," Pelly said. "There's room."

Wilfred's plane took off. I watched it disappear over the trees. Turning back, I looked at Hettie. "_Towa'w,_" I repeated.

"Nope," Pelly said, shaking his head. "You'd say _nunaskwon-owin_—thanks."

Pelly turned away and started walking, holding my suitcase.

I followed him, Sam and Hettie followed me. When we reached the front of their house, Hettie pointed to it. "_Tutoka-win,_" she said.

"Household," Pelly translated.

"Does she speak English?" I asked.

"I speak," Hettie said. "Fine, I speak it, good." With a quick sweep of her hand, she said, *"Wuyuwetimik."*

I looked at Pelly, already relying on him. "Out-of-doors," he said.

We walked into the house and stood in the kitchen. The entire house was made up of two bedrooms, a kitchen, and a pantry. The kitchen was similar to ours at Paduola Lake, only smaller. It had a pump-handle spigot in the sink, a large wooden table, a few cupboards. It had three windows, though: two curtains of yellow cloth, one burlap. Hettie said, *"Etokumik."*

"Kitchen?" I tried.

"Indoors," Pelly said.

"Genius, pure and simple," Sam said. "Now he'll know if he's indoors or out in two languages."

I sat down at the table. Hettie poured me a cup of tea. *"Nepesu,"* she said.

"Nunaskwonowin," I said haltingly.

Hettie shook her head. "Taste first," she said. "Then if, you like, it, speak."

I sipped the tea, which was terribly sweet. It must have had two or three spoonfuls of sugar in it. I grimaced but said, "It's good."

"Mewewin," Hettie said.

"A gift," Pelly said.

"I have enough trouble with English," I said, worried.

Hettie touched the kettle. "Tea *wuskik,*" she said.

"Tea kettle," I managed, *"Mewewin?"*

"No!" Hettie scowled. "Not a gift. It's mine."

"It's her favorite thing in the house," Pelly said.

Hettie sat down in a chair. She ran her hand over the top of the table, then acted as if she had picked up a splinter. "Ow!" she cried. "My thumb, it invited the splinter." She looked at me. "I speak it, fine," she said.

"Hettie will help you," Pelly said when he saw my puzzled expression.

It was true. From the first day Hettie spoke Cree around the house, translating the essence of what she said for my benefit. Pelly was a fluent-enough Cree speaker to have long conversations with Hettie. And though I stumbled feebly through my early attempts, Sam encouraged me. But he cautioned, "It's right you learn to speak it, but keep in mind a white man can't think in Cree."

I was immediately taken by Hettie's language, the sound of it. The way certain phrases went from long vowels to abrupt, almost slurred consonants, then quickly to a final vowel. Phrases that emanated from so deep a hollow in the throat that they seemed like whispers. The shifts in cadence and inflection, and the travels, within a single sentence, from scratchy monotones to lilting, buoyant strains.

"It helps to listen in on people talking," Pelly said. "Hang around the porch."

I took his advice and sat on the porch every morning and waited. Eventually Cree men and women, mostly elders, happened along. They leaned against the porch or sat on the steps, completely ignoring me, talking for hours. I was pleased to catch even the topics they discussed. The men smoked cigarettes; they shared one between them, each taking a quick draw, hardly inhaling. When the cigarette was passed around, no one spoke. The elder women preferred pipe smoking.

One morning, after about two weeks of eavesdropping, an elderly man, Abraham Sukimas, whose name meant "mosquito," tossed a stone at me. He was standing in a group. "How much do, you get?" he said, pointing to his head.

"How much?" I said.

"How much Cree?" he said. "Words—which?"

Surprised to be addressed at all, I answered proudly, "Some. Not much. Yesterday I knew you were talking about checkers."

"What—did you get?" Sukimas said.

I thought hard for a moment. "Checkers," I admitted. "I heard just the word 'checkers.'"

None of the group said a word. They looked away from me.

"Today," Sukimas said, now looking at me, "we are standing here, and talk—about you."

I stood up from the porch step and walked away, turning around to see what they were doing. Sukimas was imitating the way I walked. He swung his arms wildly, stopped, looked around with a bewildered expression as if unable to decide which direction to walk in. Then, much to everyone's delight, he sat down on the ground. He looked over at me. "Checkers," he shouted. "Checkers—hey!" He then added something in Cree. Sukimas had named me for the single word I had caught the previous morning.

Actually, it was through checkers that I began spending time with Hettie's father, Job Gathers.

"He's been looking for someone to play with him for a long time now," Pelly told me. "I used to, but how slow it goes drove me nuts."

Then one afternoon Job said, "You play checkers?"

I nodded yes.

Immediately he walked to his house, returning with an old checker set in its original cardboard box. Standing at our door, he asked Hettie to bring out a fold-up table, which she promptly did. She then brought out two chairs. Job opened the table and set the checkerboard on it. I lined up the pieces. "Sit," Job said.

Job had light brown skin with fine wrinkles like fishing net at the corners of his eyes. He was a small man who had lost part of an index finger in a forest crew mishap, back when he was advised he was too old to work with the crew. He usually had on worn corduroy trousers frayed at the pockets, dark flan-

74

nel shirts, a belt with a wide western buckle shaped like a steer's head and horns. His hair was neatly combed with a little grease. His old athletic socks, most often the ones with black ankle stripes, were rolled down enough to reveal a second pair made of gray wool, both pairs purchased at the Bay Company store. At certain times, if the light was just so, Job seemed ageless. That is, his youth, middle years, and old age were all harmoniously present in his face.

We played late in the afternoons. Like most Cree, Job played at a remarkably slow pace. We seldom spoke, just nodded or said "Hmm" if an especially intelligent move was made—although what was considered intelligent by Job was hard for me to figure. Sometimes he was so satisfied by a particular alignment of checker pieces, it was as if he had spotted a constellation he had not seen in the sky since childhood.

He would make a move. This was followed by an outburst of talk from the dozen or so spectators who had inevitably gathered, all Cree except for Pelly, who usually sat nearby making sketches. People wandered off for a piss. Children ran past, jarring the table. The elders, who patiently stood by, muttered comments, blew smoke toward the checkers, looked at me in sympathy when it was clear that I was perplexed by this game, ruled as it was by whim.

If I made a move too soon after Job's, it implied his had been hasty and was thought to be an insult. Perfect Cree etiquette would dictate that a game consist of two moves and last a lifetime.

I would make a move. Job would light a cigarette, take a few measured draws on it, extinguish it on a checker piece, then study the board.

Job always initiated the close of the game. After a considerable hiatus between moves, a kind of seismic activity took place: with sudden acceleration, twenty or so moves were performed —jumps, kings moved backward, zigzag sprints across the

board. Then Job put his hand over mine, stopping me. "Done,"
he would say. "Good-bye."

During a game in late June, Job said, "You, Pelly, want . . .
check on bear? In the morning."

I mentioned Job's invitation to Pelly. "I've gone with him
before," Pelly said. "The trap's usually about two hours in some
direction by canoe. Job usually goes with his cousin's boy, Billy
Mwoak—you know, that tall, skinny kid? But Billy's away,
working a fire crew. You want to go?"

"You ever see a bear in the trap?"

"Once I did. Job shot it."

"I never have seen that."

"You just might this time."

We told Job we wanted to accompany him. He seemed
pleased at our enthusiasm, yet dismayed as well. I think he
really wanted to go by himself or with Samson Autao or someone
else, and thought we would slow him down. Yet he felt an
obligation, since Hettie, we found out, had been asking Job to
take us out into his hunting territory at least once.

Just after dawn we got into Job's canoe. It was a chill, clear
morning, a few stray clouds on the eastern horizon lacing the
sun, loon calls echoing from Piwese Lake. A lone crow flapped
across the lake, then four or five beckoned in succession, or one
crow with many voices, it was difficult to know which. Job sat
back on his knees, pushed the canoe off with a paddle, then
maneuvered us through the inlet out onto the lake. Pelly took
up the paddle at the bow. I sat on the middle slat. "Down—
that way," Job said, nodding south. "Then—to a river, small.
Then—to a river, bigger. Trap's out there."

"That's about as much of the future as he's likely to mention," Pelly said. "Don't talk about what you're *going* to do when
you get back. Job says talking about the future insults the land.
Makes it seem like we think there's no dangers that could kill

us. Animals are always listening in, too. They won't give themselves up on a hunt, if they think we're taking it for granted that there'll be plenty to eat. It's best to think just about what's in front of you. That's what Job says."

Job paddled in even strokes. "No talk now," he said. Pelly and I looked out over the smooth, slate-gray water. Job started up a slow chant: *"Ne'mosom, omos'mimaw. Panokwun . . ."*

"What's it mean?" I whispered.

"Something like, 'Grandfather, my grandfather. He comes in sight,' " Pelly said.

"Grandfather?"

"The bear's his grandfather. Everybody's grandfather."

"No talk," Job reprimanded. He began to sing again, until the song's cadence, *"Ne'mosom omos'mimaw, Panokwun, Ne'mosom omos'mimaw, Panokwun,"* and his paddling locked together.

Across the lake we portaged in a small inlet. We got out, and Job pulled the canoe up between boulders. He walked into the woods to piss. While looking out over the lake, Pelly and I heard Job let out an ungodly groan. We ran over. Job was squatting next to a dead owl. He held it up, moving its stiff wings, testing for any life. He set the owl down, then began to rummage frantically around the woods. Muttering, he kicked away moss, tore up clumps of wet leaves, lifted up rocks. Then he sat down, panting.

"What's going on?" Pelly asked, standing next to Job.

"We—get back now, to home," Job said emphatically. "Right back. No bear trapping."

"What's all this about?" I said.

"Mamakwasew," Job said. He held out his hands horizontally, a few inches apart.

Pelly looked at me. "Dwarfs," he said. "Tiny people. Supposed to be a whole tribe of them. They have villages under rocks. Sometimes they live in tunnels."

"They killed the owl?" I said, some doubt in my voice.

"Maybe—yes," Job said, a look of consternation crossing his face as he stared into the woods. "Maybe now, they turn over our canoe. Maybe now, they laugh, so loud, till"—he covered his ears with his hands—"we are deaf. Maybe, they just fly the bear trap, somewhere else."

We walked over and sat next to the canoe. Job took out a cigarette and lit it with a match. He took three quick draws, then a longer one, then smothered it against his belt buckle, wiping the buckle with his hand. He put the remainder of the cigarette in the chest pocket of his coat, took off his coat, laying it on the ground. He then produced a leather pouch, loosened it, took from it a roll of masking tape, bit off a piece, and taped closed the pocket holding the cigarette. Reaching back into the pouch, he took out a sewing kit, threaded a needle, and sewed the piece of tape to the pocket material. Chuckling yet looking about warily, he shook his head in amazement. "*Mamakwasew,*" he said, "do anything—for a smoke."

We paddled back. On shore Job turned over the canoe and pegged down its mooring rope. Then we walked back to our house. Inside, we sat around the table.

"What?" Hettie said.

"We got across Piwese," Pelly said. "Job found a dead owl. Then we came right back."

Hettie looked aghast at her father. "Who killed, the owl? Something, terrible could happen, if an owl's—dead."

"*Mamakwasew,*" Job said.

Without hesitation Hettie asked, "They get a smoke?"

Job tore the tape from his coat pocket, took out the cigarette, and inspected it. "One's been smoking it—goddamn," Job said. He handed it to Hettie, who also examined it closely.

"Think it rode, back, with you?" Hettie asked.

Job just shrugged.

"*Mamakwasew's* coming here," Job said. "It's that—preacher's fault."

Job blamed the least mishap in Quill on the resident missionary teacher, Rev. J. A. Mackay. Job generally felt his presence brought bad luck, though he never explained his feelings; they were a gut-level response. He did not entirely disavow Christian teachings, either. He had gotten along well enough with previous clergy. This was an intensely personal conflict, between Job and Rev. Mackay. Job's attitude bordered on contempt, and he did not hesitate to speak of it. Rev. Mackay knew better than to knock on Job's door. Sam said, "Part of it has to do with one time when Mary Walks was sick. Mackay kept after Job to send her to a hospital in Winnipeg. *Real* doctors there, he claimed. Job said, 'Get lost.' Job said that Mary's bones were leaving, and that Jason Bass—local medicine doctor, been in Quill fifty years—would take care of it. Mackay spoke against sweat baths, chanting, Bass's medicines, and the like. Said it was all useless. Said he'd pray for Mary. Well, when Mary improved, Mackay tried to pay a call. Job spat, 'Her bones came back and you didn't have a thing to do with it.' There's a lot more to it, but that's it in a nutshell."

Rev. Mackay was in Quill under the auspices of the General Synod of the Church of England of Canada. At the north end of Quill was the one-room wooden schoolhouse, painted red with black shutters, where he lived and taught. It had three south-fronting windows, the direction Mackay faced in when lecturing or giving sermons. Against the wall behind his podium was a cot, wash basin, and wooden bureau with four drawers and metal handles. There were fifteen students' desks with palette-shaped tops and chairs attached.

He was about forty-five, slender, pale. "He reminds me of Abe Lincoln," Sam said, "except without the beard." He often pressed his lower back with his hand to keep from stooping. He had an oratorical voice befitting his calling, although his throat often dried and his sentences cracked.

He seemed an intelligent man who belonged nowhere near

Quill. He was clumsy in so many ways. When he tried to clean fish with Cree women, he nicked and scraped his hands and ruined edible parts of the fish. The women were angered and feared that the fish were insulted in death and would purposely taste rancid. Another time he vomited at the sight of a newly skinned beaver slowly turning over a fire, sputtering fat in tiny detonations into the ashes, its yellow teeth protruding.

He was a stubborn man, much like his predecessors, I was told, in his belief that Christianity would finally swallow centuries of Cree thinking. That is not to imply that the missionaries had been total failures. In Quill, as in hundreds of other Indian communities, a considerable number of Cree had been baptized. Most Cree owned Christian first names, though seldom addressed one another by them. Yet to an outsider they might refer to themselves as Christians. Their notion of what that meant, however, most certainly differed from what any missionary had in mind. The Cree took from Christian teachings only what they felt was strange, humorous, or useful. Sometimes they combined realms. For instance, certain biblical characters were said to dwell in the north. So you never knew in which Cree folktale Goliath might defeat a neighboring Indian tribe or Abraham might lead his nomadic congregation of caribou.

Mackay was tolerated, kept an eye on. His behavior was predictable enough to make it unthreatening. Even at his most dramatic, when he waved his arms and spouted moral indictments, the Cree merely thought him entertaining.

Mackay worked hard at the language. Before coming to Quill, he had been tutored by certain Cree vagrants his church had sponsored in Winnipeg. In exchange for being sobered up and fed, they gave him lessons. In Cree, his sentences faltered and he had to repeat himself with slight variations, but he usually got his points across. In lectures and sermons he sometimes combined languages, making for a kind of pidgin. Each evening

Mackay sat with a few elder Cree, whom he paid, taking down words in his notebook, consulting a Cree-English dictionary published by his church. The next morning in class he would try to assimilate his expanded vocabulary, supplementing his lectures with cardboard illustrations of biblical stories.

Mackay focused most intently on folktales, insisting on hearing traditional stories. It was known that several elders made up stories on the spot, to entertain themselves and to be hospitable to Mackay without maligning their oral tradition. Mackay was truly delighted to hear these stories, as they seemed to bring him closer to the workings of the village. "His own stories," Pelly observed, "*sound* Indian. But he always slips the characters a Christian way of thinking."

Sam had a different complaint. "Other preachers," he said, "had some quiet about them. They stuck to church business. If you got curious about something, you went to them. Otherwise, they left you alone. But this one, Mackay, I don't know. He's got his nose in everybody's business. Asks the kids what the parents are saying around the house. Seems he's frustrated that he can't be everywhere at once."

In mid-July an episode took place that Mackay eventually used against me, confirming Sam's assessment of him.

Late one morning, we were out gathering wood for Sam's decoys. "You know Kathryn?" Pelly said.

"Kathryn Amundson?"

"Yeah."

"You want to go see her?"

"I see her all the time."

"I meant *see* her."

"No," I said. Then: "Maybe. Whattaya mean?"

"You know that lake, the one closest to Quill, but opposite direction of Piwese?"

"About half a mile?"

"That's it. Kathryn, she swims there almost every day. Takes a bath, is what she does, and swims."

"How can she stand the cold water?"

"She just does. She's Norwegian. Used to it or something."

Kathryn was in her mid-thirties. Her husband, Olaf, raised wolf-mix huskies for a living. He sold them to a dealer who twice a year visited Quill, taking four or five dogs away with him on a private plane.

Tall, broad-shouldered, with dark blond hair, Kathryn's skin always seemed slightly sunburned. Her smell was a bewitching combination of sweat and fine soaps. Every year the plane delivered a package of soaps from Kathryn's mother in Oslo. Lilac, crushed orchid, oatmeal, the bars were individually wrapped in gilt paper, carefully fastened with a ribbon.

Kathryn spoke English with a thick accent. Around their house, she and Olaf spoke Norwegian. When I first met her I thought her manner was hard-edged, severe, but finally realized it was simply the way I interpreted her natural directness through my own shyness. Whenever she came to the house to cook with Hettie, I liked to sit in the kitchen. Though I stared at her when she was occupied with other things, I could hardly look at her when she spoke to me.

Pelly led me down an overgrown logging road, then down a footpath that ended at a small lake. While most northern lakes were edged with spruce and boulders, dropping off quickly and deeply, this one had an unusually wide, stony beach along a shallow inlet.

"Stay behind this boulder," Pelly whispered. He had a serious, warning look.

"Is she there?"

Pelly pointed to the far side of the inlet.

Kathryn had apparently just gotten to the lake. She unfolded a blanket and spread it out near the water. She set down a towel, then took off her shoes and socks. Crossing her arms and grasping the bottom of her sweater, she lifted it off, tossed it onto the blanket, facing toward us, revealing for a moment her breasts, which she covered then with crossed arms.

"If she takes off her sweater, I'll die," I said, hardly realizing in my awe that my exclamations had fallen behind Kathryn's actions.

She now stood at the edge of the lake, testing the water with her toe. Facing away from us, she took off her loose jeans and underwear, leaving them where they fell on the stones.

"She can see us," I whispered in alarm, though Kathryn had already been facing away from us several moments.

"Just shut up and watch," Pelly said, agitated.

Kathryn leaned back, holding her face to the sun, her hair falling down over her shoulders. She then bent down to her jeans, took from a pocket a bar of soap, unwrapped it, fastened her hair up with its ribbon. She touched the bar to the lake, stood up, and inhaled its fragrance. She placed the soap on top of her jeans. Holding her arms tight across her breasts again, she waded in.

"I've got to have that bar of soap," I said, totally serious.

"You'll want it more in a few minutes," Pelly said.

Waist deep now, Kathryn shouted something in Norwegian and slid into the water. Springing up, she shook her head back and forth; water flew from her hair, which was partly loosened from the ribbon. Though the water was frigid, she now actually seemed *used* to it. With graceful concentration she swam in a sidestroke. She returned to shore, picked up the soap, waded back in the water, and began to soap her arms, shoulders, breasts, belly, and legs. Holding the bar, she dove under, swam a moment, then returned to shore, taking a few running steps to the blanket. Sitting cross-legged, she patted herself dry with the towel, then lay on her back, her head resting on her clasped hands.

"I can't take this," I said.

"Get lost, then," Pelly said.

I started back to Quill, and Pelly stayed.

Where the footpath met the logging road, I saw Olaf. He was about forty, with a wide, blond-bearded face, sharp blue eyes, and a crooked front-top tooth that gave his speech a subtle whistle. He was tall and bulky, yet graceful. Most often Olaf could be found feeding, grooming, or exercising his huskies. They were kept in well-wrought pens in back of his cabin.

As I made my way down the road a few huskies bounded, barked, and leapt up on me and Olaf, then ran off toward the lake.

"Gone swimming?" Olaf said.

"Swimming," I said nervously. "You kidding? Too cold."

"How do you know? You try it?"

"Just looks cold," I said.

"You'd get used to it. Pick a day hotter than this. Give it a chance."

"Okay, maybe I will."

I ran down the road.

Kathryn visited our house about a week later. Pelly was out somewhere. Sam was in his shed. Kathryn knocked on the door. "Hettie," she called in, "look what Olaf caught. It's for you." She opened the door and held out a pickerel.

"Come in, Kathryn," Hettie said, pleased.

I sat at the table. Kathryn walked right past me without saying hello. Hettie seemed to notice this. They stood at the sink, where Hettie cheerfully began to clean the fish, while Kathryn gave her a recipe for fish soup. Hettie repeated each ingredient the way another person might jot it down. It struck me that Kathryn was taking an unusual length of time for this. She paused between each ingredient, and the pauses did not come from forgetfulness or for the sake of emphasis. During each pause, Kathryn looked over at me with an expression I could not decipher, making me more and more uncomfortable. Finally, she said, "Do you mind, Noah, if we speak—in private?"

Hettie did not look up from the fish. She merely repeated the recipe out loud again.

We went outside, and Kathryn immediately took my face in her hands. I could smell the fish. She held my face tightly. I could feel blood changing places under her hands, rushing behind my eyes and to the sides of my head. She looked directly into my face. "There someday might be, you discover a man watches your bathing wife and you will wish to break his neck. You're lucky, Noah—Pelly, too. Olaf, he held his temper and talked to Reverend Mackay instead. They had a good talk." She let go and walked away without another word.

By August I was homesick. I missed Mina and Charlotte. Each morning I felt I had made the wrong decision, yet by midday I was again firm in my resolve to stay on in Quill a little longer. It helped that Hettie and Sam were welcoming, well past their strong sense of privacy.

I had received two notes from Mina and a chatty letter from Charlotte, and had myself written a letter addressed to them both. Charlotte's letter read:

Dear Noah,

Since you have been in Quill I talk to myself a lot. I say things like, "Hi, dummy!" Just to keep in practice for when you get back. I had a long talk with Auntie about the times you used to knock me down in the snow and say nasty things. She said you did those things partly because you thought I was pretty and thought that you were funny looking. I said that you were right!

Then Auntie said not to tell you about our talk, because you

*would think we talked about you behind you behind your back.
I said, "Well, we do!"*

*Let's see, what else? Today Auntie washed my hair. We
worked on a lesson—arithmetic. You know what I say to arithmetic. I say Yuck. Then I worked on my handwriting. Here
are some t's. You can use them as examples:*

$$t \; t \; t \; t \; t \; t \; t \; t \; t \; t \; t \; t$$

*I was happy to hear about Pelly. He sounds nice. Maybe I
can meet him sometime. Maybe he can visit. Or we will visit
Quill. Auntie says let's just wait and see.*

*Auntie says this is the first time you and she have been apart
and that it takes some getting used to. She starts a lot of letters
to you, then puts them in the desk drawer. She has got the first
page of maybe ten letters in there, then something happens and
she gives up and starts a new letter. She says she was never ever
good at writing letters. She says it's not fair, though, and she
knows it, because she like to get letters so much!*

*We are doing fine, though. Auntie talks about the Ark now
and then, and sometimes I see her looking at the postcards.
Every night she writes on the calendar just before dark. So
things are about the same here, Noah, except that you are in
Quill. But we know you will be back here soon.*

> *Love,
> your cousin, Charlotte*

In her first note Mina had asked, "How is school?" and in
her second remarked, "I'm convinced you aren't attending
school because in your one letter you made no mention of it."
She was right, of course. What I also had not mentioned was
that from my first day in Quill, Pelly had campaigned against
it.

"That teacher," he said, scowling. "Calls himself *Reverend* J.
A. Mackay."

"Probably that's because it's his name," I said.

"Should be Reverend J. A. Asshole, if you ask me. I ever show you the drawings I did of him?"

"Nope. Let's see them."

We walked to the house, went into our bedroom, where Pelly reached under his bed and pulled out several stacks of drawings and paintings. Rummaging through them, he came up with two, which he handed to me. One showed Rev. Mackay being carried off by a giant crow, its eyes aflame, people in Quill pointing up. The other had Mackay fleeing a giant beaver in terror, each of its two front teeth bigger than Mackay himself.

"Not your usual portraits," I said. "So you think Mackay's scared of animals, or you wish the stuff you drew here'd happen to him?"

"Both."

"Guess you don't much like him."

"Not funny," Pelly said, frowning severely. "Me and him didn't get along. I won't go near that school of his. I tried a few times. Last summer."

"Mackay was here last summer?"

"Yeah, that was his first," Pelly said, looking over in the direction of the schoolhouse, narrowing his eyes. "I told Sam I wasn't going to class anymore."

"What'd he say to that?"

"Said, 'Who told you to go in the first place?' One day I raised my hand. Asked a question. So Mackay calls on me and I ask it. And he makes me feel stupid, not just for asking it but for not already knowing the answer. I just walked out. From day one we didn't get along, is what I'm trying to say here."

"I'm not raising my hand, then."

"What kind of school's that, where you got to feel that way? But you go ahead and try it if you want. It's mainly him just twisting Indian stories around, filling them with Bible people, or else making you scared of evil inside yourself. I don't like that stuff."

"Me either. I'm not going."

"Thought you promised."

"I did. I promised my mother I'd at least try it. But she don't know about the radio programs. They're like going to school."

"If I was you, I'd go and keep my promise. That way you won't have to lie to her."

"I wasn't gonna lie. Who said anything about lying?"

"I'm just saying, if you take in a class, you won't *have* to lie. That's all I'm saying."

I waited until late August to attend a class. I went with Paul Koivisto, whom I hardly knew but liked. He was as tall as Aki, and he resembled his father in almost every way, down to his deep voice and generous spirit. But also like his father Paul was occasionally given to sullen moods, and at thirteen to an enormous tolerance for drink.

Paul had attended class on a regular basis. He had a library of over a hundred books. Sam called him real thinker. "You'd just be talking with him," Sam said, "about any old thing, and he'd get this serious look. 'Let me ask you something,' he'd say. 'Picture this: You're lying in bed. No stars out. No moon. Pitch black. Now—is it darker with your eyes closed or open?'

" 'How do you think up questions like that?' I'd say.

" 'Can't help it,' he says. 'A lot of things come out of me as questions.' "

While appreciating his philosophical nature, Pelly tended to needle Paul Koivisto about it. I recall a time when we were fishing. Paul reeled in a pickerel. Pelly grabbed it, held its gasping face close to his own, and said, "Reverend, what is life?" then placed a fatal whack on the back of its head with the handle of his hunting knife. Paul knew what was going on.

"Lookit, Pelly," Paul Koivisto said, "I agree he's a jerk. He's the most mixed up of all the teachers I've seen. I keep going just to see what happens, you know?"

Pelly watched the fish's eyes glaze, dropped it on the ground, and in a deft radio announcer's voice said, "Lights out."

Chores done, a whole afternoon ahead of us, we'd meet in front of Paul's house, fall into our usual alignment—Pelly and Paul on either side of me—and set out. Pelly might have his jacket on. Maybe we would go to the landing strip, if it was hot enough, and step on tar bubbles. We could do that for hours! Just talking about girls or hunting, or jumping between subjects. Pelly might tie his jacket around his waist. Maybe we would go to the boulders on Paw River and watch the Cree boys work the rapids with their canoes, under the watchful eyes of their fathers. Maybe we would take our twenty-twos and try and flush ptarmigan or rabbits out in the open, never totally careless with the rifles, but sometimes taking halfhearted potshots at crows, knowing that if Sam and Aki found out, they would harshly reprimand us. Pelly would be walking slightly ahead of us, holding his jacket in one hand, his twenty-two in the other, snapping his jacket at blackflies along the logging road. Eventually Paul became distracted and said, "Got to get back."

"Books books books books books," Pelly would say. "Radio's much better." He knew Paul was going to go back home to read.

"Don't own one, remember?"

But Pelly considered the radio our private realm and never once invited Paul Koivisto to listen to our programs.

About seven-thirty one August morning, Paul came to get me. Pelly had set off somewhere. He did not want to be there when Paul arrived. The schoolroom held about twelve students, all Cree except for Paul Koivisto and myself. The Indians in attendance stood in separate groups at the back of the room near the windows, while Paul and I sat next to each other at desks in the back row. Rev. Mackay stood at the podium, his breathing loud and labored as if he had just returned from an arduous walk.

Gaining composure, Mackay wiped sweat from his brow with an enormous handkerchief. "We have a new classmate today," he announced, pointing at me. I sunk down in my seat. "And so I intend to welcome him with a story that occurred right here, in Quill, not so long ago."

He set aside his cardboard illustrations and put his lecture notes in a leather satchel, which he closed and placed on the floor next to the podium. His eyes seemed to squeeze closed. Opening them again, he said, "The world, children, is full of *temptations.*"

Mackay's words were administered with quivering exactitude. His finger was raised high in the air and his gaze charged with menace and certainty. He thought if he stared directly into a student's face, the words would be more forcefully imported into his or her heart. But for a Cree to look directly at the person he was speaking to was considered impolite. It was best to glance around, returning to a face only now and then. In this way the landscape was invited into the conversation. The Cree students in Mackay's class were constantly glancing away. I do not think he ever discovered, much to his exasperation, why they looked so distracted.

Now, in his most conspiratorial tone, Mackay divulged: "I shall now tell you something I have for weeks kept in my heart."

He paused, looked haggard, wild, burdened by a terrible secret.

"I was," he all but whispered, "tempted by land-otter girls."

A group of Cree boys got restless.

"This is what happened," he continued. "I was out on a walk. Walking, I was deep in meditation about our Lord. How He gave us such a beautiful country. The lakes, the forests, the animals. He gave us the faith to survive our difficult lives on earth. I was lost in my thoughts when, quite suddenly, out in front of me I saw a tiny person! Yes, a *Mamakwasew!*

"And this small creature said to me, 'I know two girls who need your help. They require your counsel. They are full of doubt and fear. They are lost souls.'

" 'Where are they?' I inquired of the dwarf.

" 'Follow me,' he said.

"How fortunate I felt. This is why I am here on earth, I said to myself.

"I followed the little *Mamakwasew* down the road that runs east from Quill."

There was a steady tapping at a window. Everyone turned and saw Samuel Bass's great-grandmother, Ruth. Mackay stopped talking. Ezekiel Bass, who was about ten, stood up and walked out the door. In a short while he returned, escorting his great-grandmother. He helped her into a chair directly in front of Mackay in the first row, then walked to the back of the room. Ruth Bass spoke only a few words of English, perhaps understood much more, I do not know. She was one of the oldest people in Quill.

Before he reached the back of the room, Ezekiel's father, Jason, appeared at the window waving for Ezekiel's attention. Ezekiel stopped, turned to Mackay, and said, "Have to go. Help my father set out a trap line, now." He walked out the door.

Throughout the previous summer and in June and July of the present one, Mackay had come to expect this kind of interruption. A relative's face at the window and a pupil abruptly gone to clean fish, attend a baby, set a trap line. When this occurred a look of displeasure crossed Mackay's face. He closed his eyes, and it looked as though he may have been cursing and counting to ten at the same time, his lips twitching.

"I followed and followed the *Mamakwasew*," Mackay went on, "until we came to a footpath. There the *Mamakwasew* beckoned me farther.

"We got to the end of the path, and suddenly the *Mamakwasew* ran off! Before me, just at the edge of a lake, there stood two beautiful girls. They were facing me and dressed only in God's splendor. Shamelessly they held out their arms to me.

" 'Oh, my dear children,' I said."

"Oh, my dear children," Albert Sandy, a Cree boy of about

fourteen, mimicked from the back of the room. Albert zipped down his trousers, thrust out his hips, opened his eyes wide, lolled out his tongue to one side of his mouth, and started in a greatly affected drunkenness to stumble toward two Cree girls across the room.

There was much laughter now. Mackay blushed and tensed his jaw. "Albert!" he said. "At least have the decency to allow me to continue."

There was a third appearance at the window. Albert zipped up his trousers and turned with everyone else to see his father, George Sandy, looking in. George was tracing out and winding tight a long piece of moose sinew. He held one end between a thumb and forefinger and the other end between his teeth. Albert turned to Mackay and said, "Got to help, making fishing line." Then he strutted out of the room, returning in a moment with *his* grandfather, a small, wrenlike man named John Sandy. John Sandy sat next to Ruth Bass. Again Mackay squeezed shut his eyes as if pierced by a headache, opened them, and stared at John Sandy. Albert again left the room.

" 'Oh, my dear children,' " Mackay said. " 'The *Mamakwa-sew* has deceived us all. It is summer. Geese are plentiful. Hearts are full. You should find yourself spouses to worship with, to love. I will marry you together. You will have many children. I will baptize them.' "

When another knocking was heard at the window, Mackay turned and retreated to his cot. He sat facing the room. Esther Mink, a woman of about twenty, had lifted up her baby girl to the glass. Seeing this, her little sister, Rose, stood up and apologetically said to Mackay, "My sister . . . uh, she . . . needing some help." Rose Mink left school. Shortly after, both Rose's grandmother Sarah and her grandfather William slowly walked in. William actually hobbled. He had poor knees and was thin and bent over. His face was wizened and he hardly ever spoke. He was close friends with John Sandy and sat down next to him. Mary sat at the desk to William's left, so that now all four Cree elders sat in a row right up front.

Most of the Cree children, at this point, filed out of the schoolhouse. In fact, there were just two Cree girls remaining, as well as Paul Koivisto and myself. John Sandy had nodded off to sleep.

Paul Koivisto leaned over and said, "I'm gone." He shrugged toward Mackay, stood up, and walked out.

Mackay sat another moment on his cot. Returning to the podium and perusing the room, he saw the two Cree girls looking out the window, and now both Ruth Bass and John Sandy were asleep at their desks.

"I will complete my story," Mackay said, fixing me with a glare that told me to stay put. "Then we'll adjourn until afternoon class."

John Sandy snored lightly. Ruth Bass rolled her head onto his shoulder. In contrast, both Sarah and William sat upright and alert, watching Mackay's every gesture.

"So the two beautiful women said, 'Come for a swim. Then you can baptize us.'

"I began to walk toward the girls, when suddenly they both turned away from me. And I saw they had tails! They were ottergirls! They were part of the trick being played on me by the little devil *Mamakwasew*!"

Hearing "*Mamakwasew*," Sarah and William looked at one another, then back to Mackay, and muttered something to each other in Cree.

"I shielded my eyes with my hands," Mackay said, demonstrating this to the remaining few. "Then I turned. It was nearly dark. I found my way back to the road. In the distance I saw the lanterns of our village. And so, without once looking back, I hurried toward home."

The two Cree girls at the back of the room now left. Mackay leaned forward on his podium and looked at the floor.

"Which lake?" William Mink asked.

Mackay wrinkled up his forehead and looked up at William Mink. "Which lake *what*?" he said.

"Otter girls," William Mink said. "Which lake? At which lake?"

Mackay pointed east. "The first lake you would come to," he said.

"That lake—no!" William Mink stated flatly. "Not that lake. That is where Kathryn goes in the water. Otter girls, they are in two more lakes, farther away. I seen them there, long time back."

Mackay returned to the cot. Sarah and William Mink left. John Sandy and Ruth Bass remained asleep. I went back to the house and found Pelly sitting at the table, listening to the radio. Hettie was sitting there as well. "How'd it go?" Pelly said.

"He talked about land-otter girls," I said.

"Did he meet any?" Hettie asked.

"He said he did. Said there were two of them, and they wanted to take him swimming."

"Did he go swim?" Hettie said.

"No," I said, shaking my head, "he didn't. He did not. He put his hands over his eyes, like this. Then he came back to Quill."

"Sam is right," Hettie said. "That reverend, is *fool*. Land-otter girls, they don't offer more than once a life, to swim with you."

Pelly put his hand on mine and, trying to keep a straight face, looked at me. "Lord be with you, my son," he said.

CHAPTER FOUR

Evidence of
Things Not Seen

By now, Pelly was gone, Anthony had flown east over hundreds of streams and rivers, whose waters had leveled since the spring flooding, the recently arrived flocks, the fields bright with wild flowers. I asked Mina if she thought Sam and Hettie might appreciate my spending the summer with them. "Then again," I said, "I might be the worst possible reminder of Pelly."

"I sincerely doubt that," Mina said. "Why not go, pay close attention, and stay or leave as you think fit."

So, once again, after saying good-bye to Charlotte and Mina, I flew in early June to Quill. Willie Savoie was now the pilot working the region. He was a short man with a thick mustache that made his thin face seem even thinner than it was. He was not unfriendly, exactly, more an observer and listener. When he did speak it was in mumbling staccato, mixed French and French-accented English.

My first week or two back in Quill I did not know what Sam and Hettie thought of my return. We had only tentative conversations but kept a close eye on one another, careful not to ask about the private ways each of us was adjusting to our common loss. But then one morning I went to talk to Sam in his shed. Without looking up, he said, "I never liked that saying, 'Time heals.' " He was working on a mallard, its head just coming into view. Shavings flew from the block of wood and scrolled up on the dirt floor. "It heals some things, but makes the rest worse just because they've gone on longer."

"Sure is strange sleeping in the room now. Listening to the radio by myself. Sometimes when I get up in the morning, I forget. I still expect Pelly to be waiting outside with the unicycle."

"It's a fine thing you did, coming to stay with us," Sam said. "She can't exactly show it now, but it means a lot to Hettie."

"Means a lot to me, too," I said.

In my few weeks back in Quill I had learned how grief attends each person differently. At Paduola Lake, when I heard the news of Pelly's drowning, I had been immediately solaced by Mina and Charlotte and even Anthony, who had said, "There's some comfort in knowing you spent as much time together as you did, son." But in my room that night and many nights after, I felt confused, torn. I fought grief by trying to keep myself awake all night, and when I did sleep my dreams were full of Pelly's unicycle routines, though they took place at the bottom of the pond, his hair wavering like seaweed, fish flicking through the spokes, his jacket floating away and Pelly riding after it.

In Quill, Hettie told me her hands felt crowded. "My hands," she said, looking at them, "no room, to hold things."

She often dropped the kettle. Sam said, "I've shown her time and again how to hold the damn thing. But she just can't get it right anymore."

Hettie's problem with the kettle shook Sam, but he did not know what to do about it. He thought only Job and Mary could help. But Hettie's parents would never speak about such serious matters in English, and Sam, in turn, could not speak Cree with the emotion and detail necessary to accurately portray Hettie's behavior. He worried that her real sorrow would get lost between languages.

"I'm considering the idea of Job and Mary spending a day in the house," Sam said, looking up from the decoy. "Just to watch. Maybe to see something I can't see."

"Why don't I go right now and get them," I offered, and Sam sent me off.

I told Job and Mary that we needed their help. Job put on his red flannel hat with earflaps, and he and Mary walked with me to our house.

Sam met us in the kitchen. He gestured for them to sit at the table. Mary sat down, but Job remained standing for a few moments. Then he sat down across from Mary.

Her name, *Walks,* was inspired by the rough, almost callused skin she had on the soles of her feet when she was born. Her mother, spent from dreams of endless walking, remarked upon seeing the feet of her daughter, "She's already done a lot of walking."

Aged now, Mary Walks had features exotic even in a village of striking Indian faces. Stout like Hettie, she had white hair streaked with gray, and even though it was cut unevenly, there were two meticulously woven braids atop her head. Her deep brown eyes were widely set under thick eyebrows. But it was the finely drawn structure of her face, its delicate bones and uncreased skin, that implied a resistance to time opposite that which a deeply weathered face would show.

She wore a print dress, slightly faded, which had been among the clothes sent by the Anglican Church in Winnipeg, and a sweater patterned with leaves. She sat very still, both hands on the table. Now and then she would glance at Job.

Both Job and Mary faced the woodstove. To its immediate right was Sam and Hettie's room; to its left, mine. Pelly's drawings and paintings were still under the bed.

"This," Job remarked, "is a good, table." He ran his hands over the top.

"It's a—good table," Mary said, "that Sam built here."

"That's right way, in English say it?" Job asked me.

"Exactly right," I said.

"Good," Mary said.

Hettie came out of the bedroom, surprised to see her parents.

"Did my father say it's, a good table?" Hettie asked.

"Yes," said Sam, who then sat down in a chair.

"And—my mother?" Hettie asked.

"Her too," I said.

Hettie appeared satisfied that, after all, certain things remained constant. We were to have tea with Carnation powdered milk in it. She set out cups and a loaf of bread. Then she dropped the kettle. Immediately she returned to her room, shut the door, and stayed out of sight for the rest of the morning.

Job reached down and picked up the kettle, replacing it on the stove. Sam went back to his shed. Job and Mary remained seated at the table the whole time between breakfast and lunch. I did a few odd chores, returning every so often to sit with them.

Then came lunch—smoked whitefish, cinnamon bread baked by Kathryn, tea with Carnation milk. Hettie appeared in her bedroom doorway, saying nothing. Sam, in from his shed, poured hot water into two cups, then placed the kettle back on the stove. He stoked it on purpose with a few logs. The water boiled up again. Job and Mary sipped their tea, not looking at the kettle. The kettle steamed and overflowed. Hissing like a geyser, it rattled, and finally the bottom scorched. Hettie stared at it, motionless. She went back into her room and closed the door.

Following a silent lunch, Sam returned to work. Job and Mary lay down on the two beds in my room and took naps. I had promised Einert Sohms I would help with his inventory, so I spent the afternoon in his store. When I returned, just after dark, supper was almost ready. Mary Walks had been cooking while Job slept. We were going to have rabbit stew without spices, coffee with Carnation milk and two spoonfuls of sugar in each cup, just the way Job and Mary most enjoyed it. Job knocked on the door, and Hettie emerged. Sam walked into the house, scrubbed the bottom of the kettle, and heated water for coffee. Everyone sat down but Hettie, who placed her chair near her bedroom and sat facing away from us.

"Jill and her sister live up the hill. Jill won't do it, but her sister will." Sam raised his coffee cup. "Here's to her sister."

Soon it became clear that only Sam and I would speak. Job and Mary ate without looking up, except to glance at Hettie, who also ate without looking up.

"That Einert Sohms," Sam said, pouring himself more coffee, "he's sure getting irritable these days. I brought over a decoy this morning, and he says, 'Already have enough here.'

" 'Jesus, Einert, I'm just showing it to you!' I say."

"He was complaining at me a lot, too," I said.

"Complaining at everyone lately," Sam said. "Maybe it's his bones bothering him again, aching up his hands—that's arthritis."

"Today—you know what happened?" I said.

"What's that?" Sam said.

"I put up two shelves full of sardines. Brunswicks, King Oscars, and Norwegian Crown Prince. All in nice, neat rows. Spent about an hour unpacking them and putting them up just right. So then, Einert's in the back room trying to fix his radio. I hear static coming in, and then nothing. Einert's back there cussing a blue streak. He comes out, walks right up and says, 'No, no. You got those sardines all wrong! Brunswicks go over here. Crown Princes go over there. King Oscars over there!'

"He's moving them around, switching their places. 'What's the difference?' I say.

" 'The difference,' he says, 'is that my way is right and your way is wrong!' "

"What's he paying you these days?"

"Three dollars fifty cents an afternoon."

"I'll have to talk with him. Got to send him to a doctor for his hands. Else he'll be losing his temper, throwing sardine cans all over the place and paying you a dollar a day, maybe less."

"Einert, his bad hands, still can hold—a kettle," Hettie suddenly cried out in frustration. She stood up, placed her plate on the chair, and disappeared into her room.

After supper Job and Mary returned to their house. They said nothing about what they had observed of Hettie's behavior. "They'll go home and talk it over," Sam said, rubbing his face with his hands. "Hettie's struggling. They saw that much. Guess I just wanted to feel less alone with the whole thing. Sitting here now, I can't say whether it worked or not."

The next morning Sam told me that the unicycle had bobbed up and washed ashore. "It was a few days before you got here," he said softly. He had stepped outside and was leaning against his shed, looking nervously toward the house as though any second Hettie might overhear. "I was getting wood by the pond. That's when I see it. Seat was rotted, could see the springs. It was all rusty."

"What'd you do with it?"

"Went to the shed, got a shovel, dug a hole, and buried it, simple as that."

I could tell that seeing the unicycle had been hard on him.

He went back into his shed, sat on his bench, and began work on the mallard. He was raising its eye by carefully carving a thin moat, then flattening out the wood around it.

"Sometimes when I think of him on that one-wheeled thing-amajig, it gets to me in ways I can't describe."

I watched as he began to paint on the duck's bright colors. It was as if he were embroidering his own grief on this object, which one day a hunter would float out on a marsh. I left Sam alone for the rest of the day.

Before supper he sat in Pelly's favorite cane-bottomed chair taking splinters from his hands with a tweezers. "My carving's grown careless," he said. "I'm falling behind in my work. Behind what, I don't know. Just behind."

Hettie was with her parents. She had taken to preparing supper, then visiting Job and Mary. She'd return after we had filled the kettle with water, made coffee, and begun eating.

Sam walked to the woodstove, lifted the top of the stew pot, leaned over and inhaled deeply, then covered the pot again. "Mind if we talk a while before eating?" he said.

"Nope."

He sat back down in the cane-bottomed chair. I sat at the table. "Job finally said something to me," Sam said. "What he said was, that Hettie's hands have got *wunikesis*. Something like that, I can't remember how to pronounce it exactly. Means "amnesia." Means, according to Job, Hettie's hands forgot how to hold things right. He says it's contagious. I told him sometimes me and Hettie hold hands while sleeping, and he nodded. He said that's why I'm getting so many splinters lately."

"Far as I can tell, you haven't forgot how to carve ducks, though, Sam."

"Maybe it works slowly, how do I know?"

"What can you do about it?"

"It's not just the splinters. It's not just the hands forgetting. It's the whole thing, Noah. The whole way Pelly being lost has worked on us. It changes things, you know. Changes everything. Take for instance that kettle. You see how Hettie won't go near the thing."

Sam leaned forward in the chair, hands cupped to his face, elbows on his knees. "And last night," he said, "I had this dream. All the splinters I've been getting? They gathered together and turned my hands into decoys! Don't tell this to Hettie, okay? Me and Hettie then—neither of us could hold the kettle. Frightened me a lot.

"When I woke up I knew right then something had to be done, and I thought back to when I first brought the new shortwave your dad gave me into the house. I remembered how I got dance music on it from the Hotel Fort Garry, down there in Winnipeg. I persuaded Hettie to dance with me. She caught on right away, even though I was a clumsy dancer. In fact, it seemed like the clumsiness was the part she liked most.

"So I turn to Hettie. We're laying in bed, and I say to her, 'How about if we have a dance?'

" 'You want *now*, to dance?' she says. And I'll tell you, Noah, I was pleased to hear a trace of humor from her.

" 'No,' I say, 'I meant a dance for everyone in Quill. There'd be plenty of food, and people would dress up, and your parents can come to it. . . .' I imagined the whole thing out loud for her.

"She sat right up and laughed a little. 'I dropped the radio before,' she says.

" 'It's not broken, though,' I say, because I'd tried it out.

"Now we've been married for thirty-five years, so I knew that she knew some of what I was thinking. She knew I wanted to try and cheer her up, cheer myself up, too.

"She thinks about it.

" 'We can try,' she says."

I stood up, put one hand on the back of the kitchen chair, looked at the far wall as though I were about to make a speech. "A dance," I said, "is a great idea."

Sam stood up and did a little dance, like a colt wobbling on spindly legs, jutting out his elbows like a fluttering rooster, then sat down for a brief moment in the cane-bottom and quickly slid over to his chair at the table. "We'll have to wait until next Sunday," he said. Sunday evenings CNG, a station in Winnipeg, broadcast its weekly dance concert from the ballroom of the Hotel Fort Garry. "That'd be July first. It's Monday today. Lot of work to do in between."

I dished up the stew, made tea, and we talked about the dance. Hettie came home a while later. She walked directly to the kettle, stared at it a moment, turned, and said, "Sam tell, about the dance?"

"Yes, he did," I said.

She ran her hand along the kettle's handle but did not lift it. Then she took up the ladle, put some stew on her plate, and sat down to eat.

"We'll personally do all the inviting," Sam said, getting up for a second helping. "Noah, you go over tomorrow and ask the Koivistos, the Montminys, and the Amundsons, okay?"

"If you don't mind," I said, "could you ask Kathryn and Olaf?"

Sam gave me a quizzical look. "Sure," he said, "that's fine with me."

"I'll tell Job and Mary."

"Already, I did," Hettie said.

"What's good is if Hettie comes along to the Cree homes," Sam said. "I need her to translate."

House to house, the next day, the dance was discussed. The consensus was that the porch of the Hudson's Bay Company store was easily large enough to hold everyone. Not only did Sohms agree, but he soon began to supervise with an enthusiasm that reminded everyone of how he acted on New Year's Eve. He put together a dance committee made up of himself, Sam, Isabel Montminy, and Marjorie Malraux. Isabel was put in charge of decorations.

The committee met for the next five afternoons, and after each meeting a new idea was circulated around Quill. A central table should be built and set out between the store and an arrangement of smaller tables. The store's rickety railings should be repaired and painted. Rupert Malraux should provide whirligigs. Isabel should wind ribbon around all the chairs and table legs and attach balloons to the porch ceiling with twine. Lanterns should be roosted high up out of the wind. A platform should be nailed up for Sam's shortwave.

On Thursday morning Rupert Malraux brought ten whirligigs to the porch, nailing them at evenly spaced intervals along the freshly painted railing. Einert Sohms had hired Paul Koivisto to paint it. The whirligigs included a race—an orange-and-white windmill caused the silhouettes of two jockeys on horseback to slide between two rails—and a witch. The witch whirligig had long black hair, black eyes, and red lips. She wore a pointed black hat trimmed in yellow, a short black coat, and high-buttoned black shoes. She was astride a black broomstick with frayed twigs at the rear end and a propeller with six black-and-red blades at the front.

There were buglers, woodsmen sawing logs braced over sawhorses, men working well-pump handles, young girls scrubbing clothes on washboards, a chef holding a wedding cake exactly the shape of his chef's hat, a ballerina, men in rowboats. There was an "early-bird-catches-the-worm" whirligig—four men played poker while another man, a tier above, judiciously polished a leather bridle; from his work table a wire extended, and bobbing at the end of the wire was a metal bird, a metal worm in its mouth.

Whenever the wind picked up, all the propellers whirred and the figures performed their various labors.

Everyone hoped that Sunday would be a night of clear radio air.

On Friday, while we were out hunting ptarmigan, which

Hettie had offered to cook into a stew, Sam and I stopped near a stream to talk.

"We've got two birds, is all," he said, looking at the plump quail held at the necks under his belt. "Let's try for one more at least, then go back. There'll be plenty of food, no problem with that."

He grew pensive, seemed nervous about something.

"You worried about how Hettie will hold up, what with the dance and all the people?" I said.

"It'll go fine, I hope," he said. "No, it's less that than a question I've been wanting to ask you."

"Ask away."

"Did you and Pelly ever talk about that hermit that's supposed to be living around here?"

"I heard Job mention a hermit. Aki, too. Couple of Cree kids said that their folks tell them, 'Don't wander around at night, or the hermit will get you.' Job said he knew where this hermit lived. Where his cabin was. Said he once heard strange music floating from it. Job said he'd never been in the cabin. Didn't know anyone who had, either. It kinda spooked me at the time, but I was younger then."

"All of ten or eleven," San said, laughing. "What I meant, though, was did Pelly say anything?"

"Nope."

"Well, Job is a good storyteller. And inside his stories there's always a kernel of truth," Sam said. "The strange thing is, I can personally guarantee he's out there."

We looked at each other, then both glanced away. Sam then told me that over the years, before any social event, rare as they were in Quill, a kind of ritual took place. Whatever the event, he said that an invitation *not to attend* would always be posted to the north and well outside of Quill. "It's for *his* benefit," Sam explained. "That way, he knows we're aware of him. Knows we've made the decision to leave him alone."

"Let me get this straight," I said. "You—"

But Sam, uneasy with the conversation, interrupted me. "Best not to think about it too much," he said. Then he checked the safety of his rifle, and we set out into the woods again.

As we searched out the next ptarmigan, I puzzled over a few things I had been told about the hermit. Not only had Job seen the hermit's cabin and heard unusual music coming from it, but Sam and others had communicated with him, if only through painted signs.

According to the stories I had heard, the hermit never harmed anyone. He did not look into night windows. No one ever seems to have seen him. Pelly left no drawings of him.

When I was five or six, Anthony showed me a map of the world as it was known in 1500. Patrolling the choppy waters of each unexplored sea was a grotesque beast billowing smoke from its nostrils, with flaring eyes and curved tusks. My imaginings about the hermit reminded me of those creatures. They both seemed to mean *Go no farther*—if only because confronting them, attempting to travel beyond them, meant you had to face your own fears.

Even the most contradictory anecdotes about the hermit had one thing in common, that he lived to the north. This made perfect sense to me. It had something to do, I now realize, with how a direction—in this case, *north*—took on a character in the imagination of people. The north seemed endless, timeless. Therefore it was hospitable to characters who either wandered ceaselessly or were fixed in one locale, tucked away into the vastness of the region. Cree stories described any number of hermits, ranging from benevolent spirits to the most horrific cannibal giants who isolated a victim and then devoured him. Entire hunting parties were said to have disappeared.

And everyone knew stories about men who had become so disillusioned with civilization (even in the smallest of villages) that they set out in the northerly direction, traveling for months or years.

"I feel lonely if I can't use my radio for a couple days," Einert Sohms once said. "I'd go stark raving if I was out there with just crows and my memories to talk with."

Sam and I shot three more ptarmigan and did not say a word to each other until we returned to Quill. Back at his stool, Sam painted a few invitations on square slats of shingle. He held out a hammer and nails to me.

"Why don't you post the signs?" he said.

"This is peculiar, Sam," I said. "Gives me the creeps."

"I can't argue with that," Sam said. "But it's something we've done now for years."

"Could he show up?"

"Hasn't before," Sam said. "This time the radio will sound out quite a ways, so even if he doesn't read the sign . . ."

"He'll know something's up."

Sam handed me the signs. "Just walk a ways," he said, "and nail them up on trees every hundred feet or so."

"Sounds easy enough."

"May be easy, but it's not simple," Sam said. "That is, if you start thinking too much about who you're talking to with these invitations. It's best, I think, to nail up the signs and come right back."

On Sunday evening the weather was warm and clear but windy, with clouds on the southern horizon, deep blue sky over the wetlands to the west, the sun crowning up the day's last light. In Quill, sequestered by spruce, darkness fell quickly.

Most everyone arrived, dressed in their finery, before dusk. Hettie wore a hand-sewn beige dress with a pattern of small flowers around the collar and cuffs, a button-up brown sweater, an apron with a design of umbrellas, wool socks loosely fallen over black tennis shoes. Sam wore a freshly laundered white cotton shirt, a black vest, khaki trousers, and newly polished brown shoes.

The children who attended were dressed up as well. Annie Malraux, for instance, had on a light green cotton dress with a white lace collar. She was ten years old. Paul Koivisto, who arrived with Aki and Hedda, wore a blue corduroy suit, a white shirt with a blue bowtie, and black shoes. "Going to church?" Sam teased him. "Too bad no preacher showed up this summer!"

Paul took the teasing well. "Mother said I should know this was an important occasion and dress properly for it," he said.

Sam held him by the shoulders. "You tell Hedda she's right, and that we appreciate it," he said. "You look just fine."

I had on my best clothes, too—light brown trousers, a white short-sleeved shirt buttoned up to the neck, and a herringbone jacket too heavy for summer.

The Cree families gathered to either side and sat in chairs on the porch. They wore their daily clothes—old denim trousers, housedresses, flannel shirts—but a special item, too: a fishbone ornament, a knot of dog hair fastened to their own, or some other decoration.

Each Indian family brought food: ptarmigan, pike, sturgeon, lake trout, hare, duck. The Mwoak family traveled in from across Piwese Lake in two canoes. There were three grandparents, two parents, and five children, ranging in age from three to fifteen. The dock on the Quill side resembled an enormous wooden xylophone with each of its slats slightly warped. The Mwoak family had trouble mooring. Even as they strenuously paddled, crosswinds caused them to drift. Finally they secured the dock, where they were met by Isaac Greys, a very large boy of twelve, who helped them from the canoes. Then Isaac escorted each of the grandparents in turn along the windswept dock to shore.

High atop its loft, Sam's shortwave picked up the broadcast. With swing music playing faintly in the background, the show's host, Reginald Stoppard, spoke into the microphone with a deep, bouncy megaphone voice.

"*Direct* from the stage of the ballroom in the *Hotel* Fort Garry in *down*town *Winn*ipeg, in the *won*derful *prov*ince of *Man*itoba, I'm your host, *Reg*inald *Stopp*ard, with tonight's live enter*tain*ment . . . *Maxie Elroy* and his *band* of *Snow*melters!"

A saxophonist came forth with a brief, soothing solo, then Stoppard returned to the microphone. "That was the man him-*self*, Mr. *Maxie Elroy*. The *Snow*melters are just back from a *whirl*wind tour of the provinces, where they played to *packed* houses in *Regina*, *Cal*gary, *Prince Al*bert, *Ed*monton, and *Van*-couver, British Co*lum*bia! And *now*, here's Maxie's ren*di*tion of the great hit, '*Sugar Blues*,' by Mr. Clyde McCoy!" Then the music came on again.

The popularity of the Big Bands had, in Canada, lingered into the late 1950s, and Sam and Einert Sohms could not have been happier. With each new song, they looked over at each other like members of a secret fan club.

The whirligigs worked in fine order, clacking and spinning along the railing. Isabel and Hedda brought food out—some brought by Cree families, as well as rabbit stews cooked by Kathryn, fish soups, wild berry pies, liquored and plain cider, and beer.

An hour or so went by. All the light was now coming from lanterns on the porch, candles on the tables, and the early stars floating in the new dark. What changed, too, was the encircling spruce. In the dusk their outlines had been sharpened, almost illuminated by fading light.

There seemed no hurry to dance. The radio would broadcast music until one A.M. People sat and talked, ate, milled around the tables. Hettie moved between the porch, where Job and Mary and other Cree friends and relatives were, and the table out front where Sam and I sat.

Sam poked me lightly with an elbow and nodded to our left. There was Einert Sohms combing his hair in Sam's truck mir-ror. He had placed a lantern on the hood. He was so fastidious in his combing that it was comical. He had to cock and tilt his head in order to locate, then keep an eye on, the least accessible spots. Looking straight on, he flicked up tiny waves on top, then moved the comb in smooth sweeps along the sides and back.

Unless he had been drinking, Sohms was usually very reserved. But now he walked right onto the porch and held out his arms as though they embraced a dance partner. Then he struck a formal pose and everyone quieted down. He reached up, turned off the radio, took a deep breath, and let it out. "As a boy I took dance lessons in Halifax," he said. "I remember Anna Tovee, a lovely girl. She was my partner." Then, arms around the invisible Anna, Sohms waltzed ceremoniously across the porch.

With that, the dance had truly begun. The porch filled with couples. Holding one another, they looked to Sohms, who turned the radio on again. A slow melody was in progress, featuring a muffled trombone. In all imaginable styles—steps newly invented for the evening, children in exaggerated amorous clinging, old with young, wives with husbands—the people of Quill danced.

My first dance was with Kathryn Amundson, who, to my amazement, had asked *me*. I took this to mean that she had forgiven me, or hoped that was true. Almost instantly I stepped on her foot. "You are doing fine, just fine," she said. Olaf was paying little attention to us; he was in an animated Norwegian conversation with his cousin Rolfe, who was visiting Quill. But Aki Koivisto was watching us.

At first I thought Aki did not approve. He stared at us for several minutes without much expression. Then this big, lighthearted man began to gesture obscenely in my direction. He ran his hands up under an imaginary dress, fondled a breast, rolled his eyes, and smirked in a way that made me laugh out loud. Kathryn took my laughter for nervousness, my attempt to turn her away from Aki as clumsiness. She stepped back to look at me, then clutched me tightly and swirled us around a few times, my face against her chest. I breathed in her perfume, which plagued me the rest of the night.

The song ended. I thanked her. "Bow and kiss my hand," she insisted, "like a true gentleman." I did as she asked and hurried over to Sam and sat next to him.

Aki immediately walked over and sat down on my other side. Sniffing my collar and inhaling deeply, he said, "Don't worry. Your time with a woman is close. Don't just now get a broken heart, or worse, about a smell. Dance with everyone."

I wanted to take his advice but could not. I did no more dancing. I sat there with Aki until he got drunk and fell asleep, head down on the table.

Looking at Aki, Sam said, "Well now, we can't have Hedda sitting out the whole evening of dances, can we?"

Sam got up from the table, walked over to Paul Koivisto near the porch, and whispered something to him. Paul then walked toward his mother, who was chatting with Kathryn at a separate table. Once Aki had begun to drink, she stayed away from him. Hedda was a tall, sad-faced yet oddly pretty woman, with light brown hair tied up in a bun, blue eyes, and a high flush to her cheeks. She was not well, but I did not know what, exactly, she suffered from, just that it sometimes kept her in bed several days in a row. Now Paul escorted Hedda to the porch. They danced slowly at arm's length without looking at each other. They merely held hands.

Other than Hettie, who had already danced a slow dance with Kathryn and one with Einert Sohms, no Cree people danced. They stood around the porch and watched the rickety and graceful movements alike, commenting among themselves. Out behind Sam's truck, the Indian children did imitations of the dancers. The Cree's own traditional dances were mostly aligned with luck. Luck in hunting. Luck in weather. To dance was a way of asking spirits and animals for luck. They figured when Pelly drowned it was a form of bad luck, and no amount of dancing could change that. Yet their attending the dance properly acknowledged Sam and Hettie's grief. Luck was a complicated thing—it carried from village to village, was deft at reversals, often occuring as swiftly as a boy dropping through the ice.

Now Sam and Hettie, too, were dancing, this time to a slow number. I saw Hettie look around the porch. I wondered if she might be thinking of Quill's other losses. There, leaning against the railing, were Abraham and Susie Voyageur. They had lost a young son in a toboggan accident. There, near the steps was Rosie Greys. Her son, Isaac, was her only family now. Years back her husband and daughter had died of scarlet fever brought to Quill by a fur trapper. I wanted badly for Hettie to believe what Sam had said—that people should not become their losses, just as they could never become their own fleeting luck.

Hettie fit her head to Sam's shoulders and closed her eyes.

When the song ended, Sam and Hettie walked over to my table and sat down.

Aki muttered in his stupor, "What, what?"

"Better get him home," Sam said, excusing himself to Hettie.

Hoisting Aki over our shoulders, we slowly maneuvered him toward his cabin, but it was not easy. He was a big man, and we kept falling with him. Sam and I began talking to distract ourselves from our burden.

"Doesn't seem you're enjoying yourself much," Sam said. "Thinking about Pelly?"

Aki shifted his weight toward me, and I all but went to my knees. Then he started up with one of his ballads, more sputtering than singing.

"Goddamn it, Aki," Sam said, "help us out here, will you?"

Aki looked blurry-eyed at Sam. "Sam," he said, "sing along with me, why don't you?" He snorted, then coughed and pulled us down again.

Once we had regained our balance, Sam said, "Look, I've been worrying about you. Maybe you should think about applying to one of those technical schools they've got in Winnipeg. Maybe Toronto. I thought of writing to Mina about this. I could help out with tuition. You're handy that way. You fixed the radio twice, just using the manual."

Lugging Aki, we neared his door. "There's experts that can fix a radio blindfolded," I said. "They just put an ear to the static and figure out what's wrong."

We got Aki to his living room couch and laid him down on it, took off his shoes, and covered him with a blanket. Within a moment he was snoring.

"Well," Sam said, "that way of thinking's pure ruin. Let's talk about this later. I don't want to leave Hettie alone too long."

He walked back to the store.

The stars were low and close, and a slight chill was in the air, so that Cree mothers tucked their babies under their sweaters, heads peeking out. Other children had fallen asleep in chairs and were covered by blankets or coats.

Reaching the table, Sam said, "Looks like we're running out of liquored cider. Why not go and get some more?"

"On its way," I said.

I walked up the porch steps. A few people were still in chairs along the railing. Einert Sohms was dancing with Annie Malraux, who even for the languorous melody playing had far more energy than Einert could muster this late in the evening. Across the porch, Sam and Hettie were dancing.

Hettie, peering over Sam's shoulder, got an expression of distress on her face. I caught this out of the corner of my eye and stopped near the door. The lines of her forehead deepened and she shouted at Einert, "Whose jacket is that?" She pushed away from Sam. Then, her voice wavering, she said, "Einert, where did you get, get it—Pelly's jacket? Why do you—have it on?"

This was a bewildering question. Not only had Hettie, long ago, packed away all of Pelly's clothes—summer clothes in one trunk, winter clothes in another, including his favorite jacket —but Einert was in shirt sleeves.

With a questioning look on his face, Sohms searched himself for the jacket with exaggerated movements of his hands, if only to demonstrate to Hettie his own confusion. Then, everyone hushed and watching, he held forth an imaginary jacket in hopes of appeasing Hettie, but this did not much alter the desperate look in her eye. She grabbed at Einert, then seemed to clutch the jacket to her chest.

She said loudly, "Where did you—" before moaning and collapsing into a chair. She bowed her head and held her own arms and would not meet anyone's eyes.

Sam, holding a hand near the top of Hettie's head but not quite daring to touch it, looked helpless. He said to Einert, "I think it's best we just go home now."

Sounds came back into the silence—crickets, the whirligigs. The radio music had ended. A light static was heard.

Without much talk people began to leave. Caps were put back on cider jars. Bowls of food were covered and taken home. Children were gently shaken awake and hoisted over their parents' shoulders, or else they meandered half-asleep down the road. Quick good-byes, "See you soon." What could be more true in Quill?

Sam, Hettie, Sohms, and I remained on the porch. Hettie took her hands from her face. She was trembling. "Dizzy," she said. "Tired."

Sam helped her from the chair. We set out walking, close together, toward our house. For some reason, just then I thought, *I've stayed with these people every summer since I was ten. I was fourteen when Pelly drowned. Now I'm fifteen.* Out of the chaos on the porch, I needed to hold on to things. Perhaps thinking in numbers would help. For the first time I was considering the possibility of continuing on in the world for more years than I had known Pelly. My head throbbed with the simple computation.

Farther down the road we turned to look back at the porch, bathed in waning lantern light. We watched the silhouette of Einert moving in and out, gathering empty glasses, smoking a cigarette, sweeping moths away from his hair.

Sam said, "I wonder if they're turning off the lights at the Hotel Fort Garry? Maybe I should take Hettie out there. Have some meals. Go to an adventure matinee. Stay in a hotel."

We walked Hettie home in the half-moon's light. She curled up on her bed and slept. Sam poured a cup of coffee and added whiskey to it. We sat down at the table. "Some evening," he said.

"No sleeping for me, that's for sure," I said.

"Probably not for me, either," he said.

"Was Pelly just in her head, and all of us got caught up in what she thought she saw?"

"It's real enough now," Sam said. "That's all I know. God-damn intentions for this dance turned out all wrong."

The next day and for many weeks, no one spoke about the dance at all, except perhaps inside their homes. "What happened, *happened*," Sam said. "Everyone'll have their own idea about just what that was."

Near the end of August Einert Sohms called a meeting. People lingered outside the store, hesitant, quiet. Then they went inside. For about five minutes no one said a word. They paid a lot of attention to their shoes or to the coffee they were drinking. Then Sam stood up and said, "You probably, each of you, have a notion about the dance. I agree with Einert that we should talk it out."

So the dance had surfaced again. But through the long hours of reminiscence, it was the incident with Pelly's jacket the meeting worked up to. Perhaps the intention was to hear everyone's version, so they could agree on one as the truth, but there were more opinions than I thought possible.

"I don't believe," Aki said, "Pelly is what I'd call a ghost. No one else has seen him, have they?"

"Hettie didn't actually see him, either," Einert said. "She just saw me wearing the jacket."

"*Ghost,*" Rupert said, scowling. "That's just a word. Your mind plays tricks. Out of misery or longing. It offers you something. You call it by a name."

"When I was a boy," Olaf said, "my father used to hang a saw and hammer from a branch, right in front of our house. He said if he didn't do that, trolls would come around. Trolls of doubt and lethargy. I asked him what they'd do. He said, 'They're so hideous, they don't have to do anything. They just sit in your kitchen. You go mad.' If I believed my father, then I must've believed in trolls."

"You both could've been wrong," Sam said.

"I doubt the whole country of Norway was, though," Kathryn said.

"Well," Sam said, "the whole country of Canada doesn't have to figure this thing out. Just us."

"My eldest brother," Einert said. "His name is Quantus. When we were boys, he saw a real ghost. It had a face and clothes. It knew the house. Walked around. We were told it was there when we first moved in. I myself never saw it. He said it was an ordinary woman in an ordinary dress. His description of her never varied. And Quantus never lied."

"You can practice describing something over and over," Rupert said, "until you're convinced. Doesn't mean that what you've described was truly there."

"If Hettie saw Pelly's jacket," Sam said, "then the jacket's true for her, isn't it?"

"Ghost for *her,* then," Aki said, "and not for the rest of us, is that what you mean?"

"Close to exactly," Sam said, nodding.

They talked long into the night through many cups of coffee and two loaves of Kathryn's cinnamon bread.

Finally Sohms said, "There's a Bible passage about evidence of things not seen."

He had offered this as proof that the very things that draw people closer or estrange them most severely cannot always be defined. Yet I had the feeling, as we left the store, that every person there took home the same conclusions they had arrived with, and that the dance would drift down into Quill's memory in all those varied interpretations.

=============CHAPTER FIVE=============

An Orchestra of One

September was a busy month in the store as Cree families prepared to leave for winter hunting camps. Each year a camp's locale was new, so as to let last year's territory rest—to allow the animals to replenish themselves. Indians came around to buy supplies: flour, ice-fishing poles, ammunition. The men examined maps with Sohms, marking their intended where-abouts. Sohms could then relay the locations to representatives of the Bay Company, who, once or twice a season, would fly in to purchase beaver, otter, lynx, muskrat, and other furs. At this time of year, because entire Cree families would appear at odd hours, Sohms took naps on a cot behind the counter. Three or four families might be in the store at three A.M.

September made almost four months since I had seen Mina and Charlotte, and I was growing anxious to get home. I had been kept up to date by long weekly letters from Charlotte but was ashamed of being such a poor correspondent myself. The more days that passed since her last letter arrived, the more self-conscious I got that I had not written, and when I did— only twice that summer—I spent much of each letter apologizing. In one letter Charlotte went so far as to comment on my being so apologetic. "If you spent more time gossiping or telling me your thoughts," she wrote, "than saying you're a dolt for not writing, well, then you'd have a real letter, wouldn't you?" Gently she prodded me to write what I really thought of life, of the people I spent time with, of Mina, of herself. She must have been frustrated that I was so closemouthed about so many things. Had I realized at the time what good letters would have been for her, I might have written more despite my reticence and outright laziness.

On September 5—I remember the date because I had written it on a number of inventory sheets while working in Sohms's store—a disturbing letter arrived.

Dear Noah,

Something happened to Auntie and she was laughing so hard telling it to me, that I got scared. I don't mean her usual laugh. It was another kind, that flew out of her right in the middle of a sentence. Her own laugh interrupted her, Noah. And that scared me. It was almost like a cackle, not at all like her beautiful laugh. She seemed surprised and even embarrassed by it.

Anyway, this is what happened. We had been sitting on our favorite boulder, fishing. You know which boulder. We were talking about this and that, about when you might be home. It got chilly out, so I said I was going back to the house to get sweaters. I walked to the outhouse first, then went into the house. I opened a drawer and took out our sweaters, and when I turned around, there was Auntie! "What are you doing here?" I said. But she didn't say anything. She just sat down on the couch. She was very nervous. Then she got up and went into the kitchen and sat at the table. I sat there with her. But I didn't say anything. I was holding our sweaters.

Finally, she said, "Charlotte, I saw the Ark. It was on the far side of the lake, and it wasn't like any of the postcards. It kept floating in and out of mist, so I couldn't make out the animals on deck, but I could see it was the Ark. It was coming to get me." She said that, Noah, with that laugh coming out every once in a while. Then she stopped talking and sat there.

So—what I'm thinking is that we've got to try and get Auntie to move us. Move us somewhere else, because if things were okay here, she wouldn't be seeing the Ark, right? What happened to her was too unusual to forget—she's talked about it every day since it happened, and won't sit on the boulder. When I come in from the boulder, she says, "Did you see it?" I take the question seriously, but I just shake my head no.

I don't know what else to tell you. Probably this is enough.

Love,
Your cousin, Charlotte

I never mentioned this letter to Sam or Hettie. But I knew that Charlotte was right. The years at Paduola Lake were taking their toll, and it was up to us to brainstorm a plan to get Mina away from there. It was useless to raise the subject with Anthony, and I had all but decided to broach it with Sam, when to my great surprise Charlotte and Mina showed up one day in Quill. Their plane arrived while Einert Sohms and I were having the following conversation:

"If there's anything you want to order," Sohms said, "you'd

better do it soon." He placed a stack of catalogs on a chair near the woodstove.

"I already ordered a new pen for Charlotte," I said.

"What about your mother?"

"I was thinking about a magazine."

"What sort?"

"Movie magazine of some kind. Do you know of any? Mother used to work for a movie theater, and she talks about it sometimes."

"Don't know of any such," Einert said. "There's a cinema-star calendar in one of those catalogs, though."

"She's got calendars. Bay Company ones."

"Not for next year already, I bet. Besides, maybe she doesn't want to be looking at people modeling Stanfield underwear at the top of every month for another whole year, you ever think of that?"

Einert stopped talking and turned toward his storage room. When a voice came through on the radio, he was like a coyote tilting its ears toward a distant sound. He immediately went in and closed the door. When he came out he said, "Just spoke with Willie Savoie. He's about to land. I'd go out to the plane if I was you."

"Willie was just here," I said.

"He's back," Einert said.

From the porch I saw Savoie's plane wheel around on the weedy strip, the first time I had seen a plane land there. When it stopped, Mina and Charlotte crouched out and arranged themselves a moment in the wind. The one whirligig left from the dance, the racehorse, clacked away on the railing. Savoie then jumped down and walked toward the shore. When he got to the porch, he said, "I say to your mother, take as much time as you weesh." He was opening and closing his fists, which made me think he had been gripping the wheel tightly, his plane buffeted by the winds.

"Willie," I said, "I see you landed on the strip. If you'd have come from Paduola Lake, you'd have had your floats on, right?"

"Is correct," Willie said. "I deed not come from zat way. I fly zem from Paduola Lake all ze way east to ze town of Thompson, where we land on ze pond. There I change to wheels. Mina, she is want to go from zere on ze train to Toronto. But jeest when I am preparing to leave, she say to me, Willie, I want you to take me to Queel. She pays me ze money and so here are we. Zat is what I know." Then he went into the store.

Dumbfounded, I slowly walked toward Mina and Charlotte. Halfway, I took in Mina's appearance. She had on a long green raincoat buttoned up all the way to her neck. She took off her raincoat, folding it across her arm. Charlotte, who had on a matching raincoat, did the same. Seeing them there, in Quill, made everything seem reversed. They had always met *my* plane.

Now, standing a few feet away, I said, "I'm happy you didn't go on to Toronto without seeing me first."

"Oh, Noah," Mina said, an expression of damaged trust on her face. "Please don't think we planned anything without you. It didn't happen like that at all. We just left so quickly. Isn't that odd? We spend years in a place, then leave forever in a matter of minutes. When we got to Thompson, I said to Charlotte, 'What have we done?' So I came to my senses and we flew right here."

"Charlotte wrote me about your seeing the Ark, Mother," I said.

"The Ark—well, yes," she said, fidgeting with the tie string of her raincoat, trying to act as if having a vision of the Ark had nothing to do with their hasty departure.

"I sure didn't expect to see you here," I managed.

"Noah," she said haltingly, "your father isn't coming back. We received a letter from him—oh, it said nothing, really. Nothing I shouldn't have expected. Just that he'd be away probably, it said *probably*, mind you—until next summer, but I expect he won't be back at all, you see."

"Something must've come up," I said.

"Another life came up," Mina said. "You see, I'm one hundred percent certain he is not coming back at all." She glanced at Charlotte, who was standing next to the plane. "I'll be honest with you, Noah," she said. "Charlotte is hoping you'll come with us. But I didn't think you would, not just yet, anyway, though I hope you will."

Charlotte drew back and looked away. Since I had last been home she looked older, her features more settled. Her fine black hair was braided up in tight ovals on each side of her head, held by red combs. Her nails, though, were bitten to the nub.

"I simply could not bear another day in the house," Mina said. "Try to understand."

"I do, Mother," I said. "It'll be all right."

"No, it won't be all right," she said, her voice trembling. "Not one more day I could stand . . ." She paused and wrung her hands. "Anthony'll never get on the Ark."

I looked over at Charlotte, who was scuffing the ground with the toe of her shoe.

"We're going to Toronto, as Mr. Savoie apparently told you," Mina said. "We'll stay in a hotel. Then we'll find a house or apartment. I've written to my family in Vancouver, and they've agreed to help out. If you don't want to come with us now, there's another plane in a month. Of course the schedules get less reliable as winter sets in."

I could see she was resigned to my staying in Quill, at least for a while.

"I've brought you a little money, and a few odds and ends, socks and things," she said, handing me a cardboard box tied with a string. "Charlotte's put several new items she's knitted for you in there as well."

Taking the box, I said, "Mother, don't you want to even look around? You've wanted to visit here for such a long time. At least meet Hettie and Sam."

"I had best not," Mina said. "It's best I don't."

"They'll be disappointed," I said. "I can guarantee you that."

"Please tell them I'll send money as often as I can, and that I'm deeply hoping they won't find it an awful imposition."

"I'll tell them all that," I said. "They won't mind anything. I'll explain things, okay?"

Then Charlotte said angrily, "I knew he wasn't coming with us."

"I'll see you soon," I said. "I promise."

Charlotte scowled and looked unforgiving. Her own doubts about going to Toronto must have been fierce.

Traveling between Paduola Lake and Quill, I had become accustomed to departure and to life having changed slightly in each place during my absence. But now a panic attended me.

"What's left in the house?" I said.

"In the house?" Mina said.

"Our house, what's in it? What *things* did you take? The wash basins?"

"Just a few things," Mina said, suddenly trying to calm *me*. "Clothes, photographs, very few things. You see, Charlotte and I had been debating this, Noah. We'd been speaking about leaving all the previous night, but we hadn't *done* anything about it. Then, when we heard Mr. Savoie's plane, we both looked at one another and the decision was made. There's never enough time to consider the consequences of leaving, and yet it seemed there was too much time to think about it. That's the catch, isn't it? The too much time and the not enough—they erase each other right out, and what do you have left? Holding still. Holding still and trying to convince yourself that somehow life will change anyway. When clearly it wasn't going to change, was it? It was damn well going to stay the same. Except for that radio. That's what Anthony called a change, I suppose."

Mina, who had begun to speak rapidly, faltered, then bit her lip. Taking a handkerchief from her raincoat pocket, she began to sob. Charlotte threw the hood of her raincoat up over her head and walked to the other side of the plane.

Mina wiped her eyes with the handkerchief. "Let me state it as clearly as I'm able," she said. "Anthony is not coming back. We made a decision to leave. Mr. Savoie's plane arrived. Charlotte left bread out for her crows. Now we're on our way."

Willie Savoie returned. Purposely not looking at any of us, he hoisted a mail sack—it would be an unscheduled delivery—into the rear compartment. He climbed up into his seat, and after folding back down the cramped passenger seats, he fastened himself in with cross-straps, looked straight ahead, and dangled a cigarette between his lips.

Mina wrapped her arms tightly around me. "I'll be fine," I said.

"I hope so, darling," she said. "And as soon as we can, we'll write our address, and then you'll come to live with us, and we'll all be together again. That sounds right, doesn't it?"

"Yes, it does, Mother," I said.

Mina and Charlotte got into the plane. Mina waved through the small oval window, but Charlotte looked out the opposite side. When the plane nosed up southward, veered east, and disappeared from view, I returned to the store. Sohms, who I knew had been watching through the window, pretended to be occupied with a box of wool socks. Then he looked over at me and said, "Why don't you take the rest of the day off. I've got things pretty much under control here. Willie Savoie took the main order. We can do the rest tomorrow."

"I'd rather work, Einert," I said. "I'll do anything. I'd just rather keep busy."

At supper that evening Sam asked, "What happened at the plane?"

"My mother—she and Charlotte are moving to Toronto," I said. "She didn't want to come and say hello. But she wanted to tell you she appreciated my being able to stay here."

"You stay," Hettie said. "But she's, your mother, eh? That Charlotte, she's like, a sister, too, so you think about going to them, eh?"

"I'm not hungry," I said, and went to my room. I listened to the radio a while, then turned it off. I lay awake in the dark. Fragments of memory were struggling to cohere, to form some conclusion about Anthony. I felt certain I would see Mina and Charlotte again. I knew I would. Anthony I was not so sure about.

By morning I had grown more obsessed than I could ever remember being, both disquieted by my obsession and lost in it. When my head cleared, I suddenly recalled Anthony poring over that *Dictionary of Musical Instruments.* Then Job Walks telling Pelly and me about strange music coming from the hermit's cabin. Then Anthony's inability to convince Mina, Charlotte, or myself that he was always where he said he was, out mapping.

It was true that he had given us money. I had seen government checks. However intermittently we received them, he had to have earned them somehow. And there were rolled-up maps and surveying equipment in the shed at Paduola Lake. Yet no amount of evidence could alter the persistent feeling that few things Anthony said were *wholly* true. Around dawn it had come to me, fitfully yet undeniably: Anthony was Quill's hermit! Then the force of the entire night's thinking carried me on to another revelation: my fear of seeing him was equal to my fear of never seeing him again.

The dread of betrayal came over me. Had Hettie and Sam known all along? Had Pelly? I could not believe he would have kept this from me.

I washed my face in the basin and walked out to Sam's shed, where I knew he would be. In one hand he held a ruddy duck decoy in front of him. He smoothed his other hand along its slightly curved back. Taking up a knife, he marked the borders between its wing feathers and underside.

"You must be out here this early for more than watching," he said. "It must've been a difficult thing, having Mina and

Charlotte leave that way. I've been thinking—you want me to teach you how to paint decoys? We could start with this ruddy."

He held the decoy toward me, but I refused to take it.

"I figured out who he is, Sam," I said. "Did you know the day I put the signs out for the dance? What if I'd run into him?"

Sam sighed deeply and looked at me. "It was bound to be hurtful, when you found out," he said. "To tell the truth, I'm glad you know. Maybe at the time of the dance I even hoped you'd run into him. Hettie and me could not bring ourselves to tell you. We didn't know our place."

"Pelly, too?"

"Afraid so, but that's a slightly different story. Of course, he and Anthony had met. Your father visited now and then. You knew that much. He brought the radio. I tried to explain some things to Pelly. Why it might not be best to bring up the subject of your father. So, he was caught between a rock and a hard place. You can see that, can't you?

"Anthony—he did his mapping work. But rumor had it he was difficult as hell. Sometimes he'd just leave in the middle of a job. He was a good surveyor, a good maker of maps, no doubt about that. If he wasn't, they'd have never taken him back each time. They didn't want to let him go. But the crews complained. This was over a number of years, mind you. They couldn't figure him out. Arguing with everybody. Sullen. All but impossible to work with.

"Then the murder happened—not in fact, though. No one was actually killed.

"A fight broke out—Anthony and another man. I heard it got very mean. The argument started out as a little bickering, and got worse. Until—and this is just what I heard. The other man, I guess, called him crazy, said he wasn't playing with a full deck, something like that. Insults were exchanged. Then fists —and Anthony, I'm afraid to say, took up a tripod and swung away. The other man went down bleeding from the head. Two others there, they couldn't revive him, and Anthony—he ran off."

"Ran off?"

"Correct. If he'd stayed, he would have seen the man come to. Just wobbled up to his feet, mumbled a while, and the next day he was back at work. But Anthony figured he killed a man, and nothing I could tell him later would convince him otherwise. From then on he was suspicious of everybody. Thought it was a trap—that we were all in on it. We didn't see him for a long time. Then slowly he'd come around again, realizing that if he was wanted for murder, the Mounties would've had him long since. But I think his proximity to the deed shook him beyond repair.

"I'll say this. I never once visited his cabin. He'd show up here, stay an hour or two, talk about music, listen to the radio awhile. Wouldn't take a meal with us. Job . . . well, you know this already. Job says he knows where Anthony's cabin is."

"I'll find it."

"Job won't take you, that's for sure. He just won't get involved that way."

"I don't need Job."

"Say you find him," Sam said. "What will you do, teach him a lesson? Just say here I am, so explain yourself! You figure it'll go like that? That some shame will wash over him and everything will be out in the open?"

"Don't take me for a fool, Sam. I'm fifteen. Maybe hearing him lie one last time will do the trick. It's better than nothing."

"I'd maybe argue with that," Sam said. "Did it ever occur to you that there might be things you don't *want* to know?"

"For instance?"

"Look, why not just let me take you down to Winnipeg? From there, I'll put you on a train to Toronto."

"For instance, what wouldn't I want to know?"

"I'll say it this way: you can feel abandoned by the same

person more than once. It can happen all sorts of ways throughout a life. It's not just what the truth actually is, but how it settles in your mind."

Sam stopped talking. My face must have been rejecting everything he was trying to say. "You'd better go over and tell Hettie your intentions about finding Anthony," he said.

Hettie was in the kitchen preparing a squirrel. She had already skinned it, removed the scent glands, and washed it off in a bucket. After cutting the squirrel into small pieces, she rubbed each piece with salt and dredged it in flour.

"Hettie," I said sharply, "please stop that for a minute, will you?"

Hettie sat down at the table, flour on her hands. "You sound . . . angry," she said. "Did Sam tell you, about your, father?"

"No—Sam didn't tell me. You didn't tell me. Pelly didn't tell me."

"Did Sam say go?"

"He didn't say one way or the other."

"Okay—okay. I say go, but take Sam with."

"No."

"If you find him—then Sam can leave, back for here."

"No, Hettie. I'm sorry."

I gathered a few things: a blanket, bread, tea, a small tin pot, a jacket. I stuffed it all into an old railroad pack of Sam's.

"What food you got, there," Hettie said, "good for two days, most."

I would not look at Hettie.

"Good-bye," she said.

"You should have told me," I said.

Half-blinded by my intent, I hardly saw the woods around me as I headed north. Then, calming a little, I slowed my pace, and when I came to a tributary creek I took a rest. It was a soothing place, with light filtering down through the spruces as it did. Up ahead, the creek fed into a wider stream that ran alongside a rutted logging road, which I then followed. The only sound was the occasional *kak-kak* of a raven. As I crossed a field of coarse grass, I was warmed by the early-morning sun, but soon I was back in the woods again. Then there were changes in terrain, a stretch of muskeg, marshes, more logging roads, and spruce as far as I could see.

I walked most of the day, swinging in wide arcs and veering off on dead-end trails, without seeing a single cabin or trapper's shack. Could I have missed Anthony's cabin? If he was in this region, he would have had to travel in quite a ways to have seen the signs for the dance. I wondered if he often stood among the trees at the edge of Quill and just watched.

Around dusk I set the railroad pack down by a small lake and decided to stop there for the night. I whittled kindling, made a small fire, and gathered more wood to use during the night. After taking out the blanket, I made a bedroll, using the pack as a pillow. Across the lake I could see where night had already arrived. I made tea and ate some bread with honey. Lying down on one blanket, I pulled the other over me, lost to fatigue.

It got colder than I had expected during the night. There was a chill wind off the lake. I woke with the blanket pulled over my head.

"Well, look who's here."

The voice came, it seemed, from both the well of sleep and a phantom calling down into it. Instead of turning over to look, I just closed my eyes, trying to echo that voice in my head so I might recognize it.

"I mean, son, you were never one to venture out overnight on your own. Let's have a look at you."

I rolled over to see Anthony peering down at me. He was thinner now, almost gaunt, and he wore a slate-colored great-coat. Pointing to a twitch in his cheek, he said, "This arrived about three months ago. Hops around on my face like a sparrow in a bush." His hair was longer, matted down with some kind of grease. As I stared at him he went for a fly that was buzzing near his face, an antic totally at odds with the moment. He then pretended to swallow it.

"I used to do that when you were a boy," he said. "Made you laugh every time."

"No, you didn't."

"You just don't remember."

We stared at each other.

"I figured it out," I said.

"You didn't figure anything out."

"Lie number one—"

"Wait a minute. Hold on."

"—out making maps . . . ,"

"True. That was partly true."

"Here and now, partly true is a lie."

"But partly true is what it is."

He rocked slightly on his heels, his hands in the greatcoat pockets.

"How's your mother?"

I waited, saying nothing.

"I think they've gone. I think they've finally gone. I knew they would eventually. Gone to Vancouver, most likely. Is that true?"

"You tell me."

"You've got your mother's tone."

"Probably because I got her way of thinking about you."

"Or maybe they went to Toronto," Anthony said, rubbing his chin absentmindedly. "She wanted to live there again."

Perhaps my silence verified his speculations. "Funny," he said, perusing the sky as if the invisible mail plane route helped him derive some understanding of Mina's whereabouts. "Willie Savoie's plane came *in* from the east, backward in its usual route." He glanced nervously about, occasionally detouring across my face. "I suppose it's all too complicated to explain," he said.

"That's your problem."

"Must have been yours, too, or else you wouldn't be out here. Look, certain decisions I've made haven't done too well by me."

"Not by some other people I can name, either. Where do you live?" I said, studying his face. "I mean *exactly*."

"I thought you had things all figured out."

"I mean, say the police were looking for you and someone had to draw them a map to your cabin."

"Know what?" he said, the pitch of his voice suddenly raised. "I'm considering going right into that lake there, up to my neck. It's getting to be a hot son-of-a-bitch day all of a sudden."

I was still cold, even with the blanket wrapped around me.

"I can't swim," he said. "You probably don't know that."

"How would I know."

He took off his shoes, threw his socks aside, then put his shoes back on. Before stepping into the water, he said, "I'm not going to take off this fine coat." He gritted his teeth and waded in deeper. The lake rimmed his neck. "Jesus, what fun!" he yelled. Then, with an almost bemused look on his face, the greatcoat flared out like a dark lily pad and he sank into it.

I fully expected him to be faking, or at worst his cruel joke had gone slightly awry. But after a few moments his head bobbed up, and with his arms flailing he spouted water. I could see he was in trouble.

"Stop waving your arms like that!" I shouted. "Just tread water and get back to shore!" But as I shouted instructions, he went under again. When he came up, he made the oddest sound I had ever heard a person make, something between the braying of a donkey and the wailing of a child.

I found a branch and held it out. "Try and grab this!" I called.

Up to the very moment he grabbed hold of the branch, I harbored some doubt deep inside, and I thought, He's fooling. I even thought, Well let's just *see;* if he wants to drown, let him. But as he struggled onto the bank, clutching at his throat, his face the color of a plum, a look of humiliation crossed his face. He groaned and rolled once, then turned toward me. "Go," he gasped. "Just—go back! Go!" He took a feeble swing at me with his fist. It missed but scared me and I fled.

After I had run a ways south, I stopped to catch my breath and sat down in a clearing between stands of spruce. I felt unconnected, lost between Quill and the lake Anthony had walked into. I couldn't think straight or hold still. I started back, north.

The grass was tamped down where he had been sprawled, but he was nowhere in sight. I took some bread from the pack, chewed it down, and thought: He didn't have any pack with him, so his cabin has to be fairly close by. Then I noticed a footpath and followed it until it tapered off into the trees. About a quarter mile into the trees I saw the cabin.

Its door was propped open with a bassoon stuck in the ground. A hacked-apart cello lay in the threshold. Chimney smoke billowed up into the sky.

I stood peering from behind a tree, listening for activity in the cabin or out back, but heard nothing except the crackling of the fire. "Anthony?" I shouted into the cabin, then stepped inside. Map tubes were lined up against the walls. There was a wooden cot, a few blankets on it, a desk, an axe, an iron pot, the soup ladle sticking out of it. A clarinet, an oboe, and a few string instruments were in the fireplace, smoke issuing from keyholes, heating the soup. Hung on the wall were a triangle and a trombone. An accordian was fanned out on the floor.

So Anthony had departed from his hermit's cabin, in a manner more haphazard than his departures from Paduola Lake. Perhaps he left as swiftly as the day he knocked down the surveyor. I imagined him zigzagging through the woods that very moment, to another cabin, another life I would know nothing about.

On the shelf was an empty bottle of whiskey. A second,

nearly full bottle was on the table, and I brought it over to the cot, where I sat, half sobbing amid the havoc of strewn instruments: "C for cello, Columbian lute, coronet . . . " And as I gulped the whiskey I saw myself sitting next to Anthony as he turned the pages, showing me the illustrations from his dictionary. The whiskey burned my throat.

I had drunk too fast. Slightly dizzy, my vision blurred, I went outside and gathered up pieces of the cello and used them to build up the fire. After finishing the bottle, I took up the clarinet. "Maxie and his . . . " I slurred, then tried to play, immediately splintering the reed with my teeth—the sounds were awful shrieks and sputterings. I threw the clarinet into the fireplace. Next I blew hard into the trombone, which bellowed, then nothing. "Where's the goddamned French horn?" I cried, then fell back onto the cot. That was the last thing I remember, except that in the middle of the night I retched up my guts and stumbled over a few instruments on my way back to the cot.

I woke early in the morning feeling ill, yet wanting to leave the cabin without delay. I tried to organize my thoughts away from how awful I felt, but the ravages of whiskey, the cold, and the rank smell of vomit and burned woodwinds all conspired against that. My head pounding, I picked out a broken souvenir of the night, the bassoon split halfway down its length, and fastened it to the railroad pack so that the whole arrangement resembled a tightrope walker's balance pole. It did not steady me all that much at first. Holding on to the bassoon with both hands, I stumbled along, backtracking toward Quill. But slowly, as I ate a little bread and drank from the cold lakes, I regained some strength and sense of direction.

Just after dusk I got back to Quill. I stood at the edge of the clearing and looked through our kitchen window. I saw Hettie leaning against a wall, her hands in her big dress pockets. Sam lifted the radio from the table and, holding it, turned to find me standing in the doorway.

Sam put the radio on the table. "You look like hell," he said.

As he took the railroad pack from me, the bassoon spilled onto the floor, splintering.

Hettie took a step forward. "What—is that?" she said, gently kicking the bassoon.

I picked it up and put it on the table.

"You're back, from angry," Hettie said.

"Yes, an angry place all right," I said.

"Where?" Sam said.

"It doesn't matter. I don't want to say."

"You hungry?" Hettie said.

"A little, but I'm feeling sick," I said. "I can't eat just yet."

I sat down. Sam nodded toward the kettle, and Hettie, reaching toward it almost in slow motion, picked the kettle up and poured a cup of tea, which she set before me on the table.

"You find him?" Sam asked.

"I don't know," I said. "I'll say what happened. Then you tell me if I did."

CHAPTER SIX

Cousin-Letters

October 15, 1959

Dear Noah,

I can't call Toronto home yet. But I guess now it is. It's very confusing. But Auntie says no matter how lost you feel you can still write letters. She says it's a lost art. She says, "No one can say Charlotte shut up, stop talking, will you?" In a letter you can tell just what I want. That's what I'm going to do. I'll start from when we first got here. We stayed in a hotel that had a small lobby. An elevator took us up to our room on the fourth floor. It was a small room but pretty. Every morning the maid put flowers in a vase on the table. Auntie always left her 25 cents. We stayed for six days.

When we left, Auntie took a pillowcase and a soap dish. Both have the name of the hotel on them, The Marion Arms. While we lived in the hotel I sat in the lobby and watched people come and go. Some live in the hotel permanently. Most just visit for a few days. There were ten clocks on the lobby wall. They told time in different cities. Paris, London, even Hong Kong. Anyway, Auntie says it's all right because most everyone who stays in a hotel ends up taking a little thing like a soap dish.

For five days we did nothing but look for a place to live. The newspapers have a section full of houses and apartments. We walked and walked. At first I thought, all these houses, this will be easy! But after trying and getting very tired, I thought, all these houses and none we like enough. My mind changed every minute. We walked some more and took busses. We had a map of the city. We ate sandwiches on the bus. When we got back to the hotel each night all we could do was eat crackers and go to sleep. Every morning we woke up with crumbs in the bed. We looked fifty places at least for a house to live in. Then we found one. We knew it was right for us. The address is 23 Olive Street. It's a light brown house with two stories. It's not too far from a place called Kensington Market. The market has all sorts of shops, food stores, also fish markets. Even early in the morning it's crowded. There's all kinds of fish, Noah. Ocean fish and lake fish. I remember going to fish markets with my mother in Halifax. Here they put the fish in bins and wheelbarrows outside. The fish are on ice. They have their eyes open. Since we have a refrigerator we can keep them frozen at home, too. Which brings me to tell you what else we have.

Okay, just pretend you walked in the door. Right away in the hallway is a silent butler. It's a wooden pole with metal hooks on it, to hang coats on. We had one in Halifax, too. Now I have my autumn jacket on it. Auntie has a blue coat on it. Now turn left. You're in the kitchen. It's a nice kitchen. You can probably guess the first thing Auntie bought. Right! Curtains. They are a lighter red than at Paduola Lake. There's plenty of cupboards. There's a table.

There's one window. The houses are very close together, which takes getting used to. When I lie in bed at night I can almost feel other houses touching ours. Now walk through the kitchen and stop in front of the bathroom on your left. Now look in. There's a bathtub. It has lion's feet! I'm not making that up, either. Now you're in the hallway. It has wallpaper. The wallpaper is tan with autumn leaves floating on it. Across from each other are two bedrooms, mine and Auntie's. At the end of the hallway is your room when you get here, hint, hint. Auntie's room has light green walls. Mine has white, but I can pick any color I want. Each of us has a bed, a table, a bureau, and a reading lamp. Your room has the same. On top of your bureau is a new hairbrush and comb.

Every week we're going to try and get new things. A rug or saucers, things like that. Soon the place will fill up. I miss certain things from Paduola Lake, but I know they are gone forever. I wonder if you think about our house there. I do. I think it must be lonely there now. I think that a place is lonelier when it once had people in it and now doesn't, than if people never lived there. I think that by now the crows know we are not coming back.

Oh, there's a room I forgot. The living room. It's got the largest window, two of them. They look onto Olive Street. Also, it's got the largest radiator. The heat comes out of radiators. Steam heat. Remember the accordian from the encyclopedia? A radiator looks something like that, except it's larger and made of iron. The ones in our apartment are silver color. They hiss and clank. If you hang a shirt or blouse near one on a hanger, the radiator will dry it. There's a radiator in every room. Also, the living room has two stuffed chairs and a sofa with wooden arms. Behind the sofa is a floor lamp. It's my favorite thing we own. It's got a lampshade with a pattern of housepainters, which makes me laugh. The housepainters are tumbling off ladders and different color paint is flying from their paint cans, and the ladders are going every which way.

I hope you can picture the apartment, but more I hope you see it soon. Are you working on your handwriting? I am here. It's easier to do my lessons because there's a library close by. I just walk to it. It's

*open every day except on Sundays. I know all five librarians there.
The one I know best is named Mrs. Gobey. She's the oldest. I told
her I was going to read every book. She said that nobody could, but
that it was a nice idea. She asked me what I wished to start with. I
said I didn't know. She said why not begin with travel books? China
and Africa. I said okay. She stacked some books in front of me. She
said, "The world is very unfriendly now. By the time you grow up
there may be places far too dangerous to visit. Reading about them
will have to do!" Then all of a sudden she got huffy. She said,
"Besides, certain people have a need to go everywhere! Constantly on
the move like convicts! Here and there, here and there. Jittery as
butterflies. They are just never satisfied at home ever! They'd rather
sit in a library in Tibet than right in their own neighborhood. Tsk
tsk. Well, to each his own." I don't know what got into her. Then
another librarian, Mrs. Pomeroy, came over and whispered to me,
"Don't mind Mrs. Gobey. She's really quite nice. She used to travel
a lot, and now her health won't allow it and she really misses it
terribly." Mrs. Gobey is always giving advice, but in a nice way, so
I listen. I'll just wait and see how good her advice turns out.*

*We have some money left, but not even enough to put me in public
school yet. Auntie says maybe next semester. That's only three
months away. But probably I'll have to wait until next September.
We keep our money in four places. Some is in the bank. Right now
we have $206 in there. Then, we keep coins in a jar in the cupboard.
That's for bus fare and to buy little things in the market. Then, we
have a bank shaped like a cow. It's on Auntie's dresser. When it fills
up, we just open a plug in its stomach and take money out. Then,
we both have purses. Mine is dark blue, Auntie's is black. We keep
a little money in those. Plus, there's one other place, I forgot. Remember the plastic combs I always have in my hair? Every day
Auntie tucks a five-dollar bill under one. She calls it emergency
funds, that I should use only if I'm lost. I should take a taxi, that's
a car you pay to ride in, with the driver's picture on the dashboard.
I should take a taxi directly home. Taxi drivers know every street.*

I know where the school is. Ten blocks from here. I've walked by it often. It's called Franklin Memorial. It's larger than the one I went to in Halifax by a lot of rooms. In front of the school is a statue of Franklin. Mrs. Gobey says he was an explorer and a tragic hero. He explored into the Northwest Territories. I don't know if you ever heard a radio program about him. In the statue he's taller than his shipmates, but all of them are stuck in the ice. Their ship, too. Even though he was an explorer and a hero, he has a lost look on his face. I said that to Mrs. Gobey. "Mrs. Gobey," I said, "Franklin looks lost." She got huffy again. "That's the sculptor's fault!" she said. If the weather is good at lunchtime, the students come out into the yard. They stand around and talk. I had the idea of finding a friend my own age there. So one day I went and stood in the yard. It was cold but sunny. The bell rang and students came out. Everyone was a student but me, except that deep down I remembered being a student in Halifax. Then a girl with dark red hair came up to me. She was a little older than me, I think. She asked if I was new here. I said I was just seeing if students at Franklin Memorial were nice and if they were smart enough for me to want to go there, too, but that I really had my choice of whatever school I wanted. I don't know why I said that. Pretty soon about ten girls are standing around looking at my shoes. They all had on beautiful shoes, but I didn't. Then I shouted that I wouldn't go to their school unless they all got nicer shoes! That just flew out of me. Then I felt so stupid. I ran home. Auntie said, "What's the matter?" I said nothing was.

Auntie says to tell you that we both know you have hard decisions to make. We know you have strong feelings about staying in Quill. We know they are extra strong because it's where your friend Pelly died. But you should think hard too about coming here. We're your family.

Well, here is my first letter. I'm not angry with you for staying, like I was by the airplane. Auntie talked to me all the way here. I understand a few things about Quill being a home, too. I love you.

Charlotte

October 24, 1959

Dear Charlotte,

Don't laugh at my handwriting. I am glad you found a place and that you sent a letter. Tell Mother that when I get there I am not going to attend school, so she should get used to the idea now so she will not bring it up later. I do not know when I will arrive in Toronto. I don't want to leave yet. I am working for Einert Sohms in his store. I work every day. I am learning the store business. If I want a job in a Hudson's Bay Company store, Einert said he will say a good word for me on my behalf.

Please tell Mother that I saw Anthony. Anthony is what I am going to call him from now on. Tell her I saw him near Quill and that it wasn't good and I don't want to talk about it.

You already know I listen to the radio a lot. Sometimes I listen all night. For instance, last night I was up in the middle of the night listening. I was tuning around 25M frequency and I got the London Orchestra. I listened to that for a while. Maybe for an hour. Then I fell asleep. When I woke up the radio was still on, except it was not London anymore, it was Halifax! That is how it works.

I'm learning another thing, too, but it will not do me much good in Toronto. Sam is teaching me to paint bird decoys. He is a good teacher. He's very patient. I am working in his shed. I have got a bench over to one side. How it works is, he sets out a model for me, a bird he has already painted. A duck or goose or some other one. This is the stage I am in now. Then I copy it. So both things I mentioned, working for Einert Sohms and painting decoys, make sense if I am going to stay up here, otherwise not much. But I am keeping busy. Plus I got a new radio repair manual and I am able to work on both Sam's and Einert Sohms's radio.

Please tell Mother that Einert is paying me by the week and I can send money to her. Not very much but some. Besides, I hardly spend any up here.

I hope you get in school soon. Kiss Mother for me. Kiss you, too.

Noah

November 2, 1959

Dear Noah,

Now here's something. We really needed money. We had run out. The cow bank was empty. So was the jar. So was the bank in the Kensington Market, except for $60. Auntie's family in Vancouver said they had to wait a while before they could send more money to us. This all added up to worry. Auntie said, "Don't you worry. It's not your job as a young lady to worry. It's my job." So Auntie found work. That's what I wanted to tell you. You'll never guess where! It's the exact same movie theater she worked at when she was young. Do you remember the one she talked so much about? The Northern Lights. It's still called that! Of course now there's a new owner. Auntie told me his name is Gus Wallant.

This is what happened. Auntie went to have a look at the theater, just to see if it was still there. She went by herself. She didn't plan on going in. But when she got there she did. She walked right in. It was late afternoon. I was wandering around in the market, which I like to do. We were going to meet back at the apartment and have supper. I had my five dollars but didn't spend any of it. Anyway, Auntie said, "I have to walk and think hard about what to do." The doors were open to the movie theater and Auntie stood in the lobby. That's when Gus Wallant walks out and says, "What are you doing here?" They started talking. Auntie told him that she used to work there a long time ago. They talked a while and it came out that Auntie was looking for work. Gus Wallant said, "I don't suppose you'd want to work here again?" Auntie said that before she knew *what happened she said yes she would. She told Gus Wallant that she'd do almost any kind of work except stand behind the refreshment counter. But Gus Wallant shook his head. He said there wasn't all that much else available. He ran the projector and a girl sold tickets. She sits in a glass booth out front. Plus there's another girl who stands by the door and takes people's tickets before they go in to watch the movie. She tears their tickets in half and gives them half a ticket to keep. But Gus had recently fired the girl who sold refreshments for stealing. Money or candy or what, Auntie didn't tell me. So finally Auntie said okay. Then Gus Wallant said to her, "This is a steady job. We never run out of movies or people who want to see movies. On your day off you can see the movie for free. Your niece can see it for free on any night. If a customer asks you what you thought of a movie, just say, 'Wonderful!' but try and say it in a way that means both the movie and the question were wonderful. Act as if you're flattered to be asked."*

Auntie said already she could tell that Gus Wallant was going to be difficult to work for. She said she felt old. She said that maybe she shouldn't work in that theater in particular, because not only will it make her feel old but it will make her feel like nothing's changed. "It's been over twenty years!" she said. Then she said she wasn't going to think about it too much, not now, that we needed the money and that it was difficult enough to start out again as an unemployed woman at her age.

So Auntie has been working there every night a week except one. She can choose the night she wants off. She has to tell Gus Wallant three days ahead of time, though, which night it is, and it can't be Saturday. Auntie said, "I'll change it every week." We had a talk. Auntie doesn't like us being apart most every night. I said I'd be okay. I can't tell yet if that's true. So far it's not too bad. I promised Auntie that if I go out, I'd be back in the apartment by eight o'clock. Sometimes I'm back by then, sometimes I'm not. Sometimes I go to the movie. I work at my lessons. I read. I read a lot of library books. Mostly I read books about different countries. But also I get some at the magazine store. First, I go in and look at the covers. Then I write down the title of one on a piece of paper. Then I come back the next day and hand the paper to the clerk. I say, "My aunt wants this book. Do you have it?" Then he goes to the revolving rack and finds it. They're books Auntie doesn't allow. I sneak them to my room. The one I'm reading now is called Strangers When We Meet. *It's about a man who's in love with a woman who's not his wife. There's one part where they're brushing their teeth in the bathroom, standing right next to each other! Auntie says such books are "steamy," but when she found one under my pillow, later I saw her reading it. I have a bunch of them hidden under some clothes in a box way in the back of my closet.*

I walk in the market. I know all the shopkeepers. One of them is Mr. Dalton. He's old, and he's got an ice-cream shop. He's short so he stands on a bench behind the ice-cream bins. Each bin has a different flavor. So far my favorite is chocolate mint. Mr. Dalton has very thick eyeglasses that steam up when he leans over to scoop up some ice cream. He always says, "Darling." "Darling, what flavor?" "Darling, that's fifteen cents." "Darling, whip cream or no?" One day I walk in and he's sitting at a table without his glasses or apron on, eating ice cream! I hardly recognized him!

Now I want to say that with the Ark and the Flood and all that, Auntie is about the same. She's got all her postcard collection up on her bedroom wall in rows. She used up a whole roll of tape.

Please write me another letter soon.

> *Love,*
> *Charlotte*

November 30, 1959

Dear Charlotte,

Here is $50, which you should give to Mother. When I read what you wrote about The Northern Lights, *I thought of all the times*

Mother talked about that place. I do not know what to say except that I hope it turns out to be a good thing, her working there. I told Sam and he said, "She has to pay the rent, doesn't she?" Maybe I will go to a movie whenever I get there.

I am a regular news reporter now. I listen to the radio news and then I go over to the store and tell it to whoever comes in. "You know what is going on in Japan?" I say, then I tell what is going on in Japan. It is funny, but I thought the other day how I can know the news in almost every city but that the opposite is never true. What I mean is, Quill in unknown to people in those cities, except for you and Mother in Toronto. Quill could disappear and who would care? I told this thought to Aki Koivisto, and he said, "That's exactly why we live here. We can just live our lives and be left alone." Well, as you can see I am still listening to the radio a lot.

My days are spent working in the store and painting decoys, and also thinking a lot about what I am going to do. Sam and Hettie are being very nice, and they like me to be here, and like it when I read your letters out loud. I hope you don't mind. They don't mention the letters to anyone else.

One other thing. You know all the drawings that my friend Pelly did, paintings, too? They were stacked up under his bed and I had not looked at them since he died. Then I spent half a night looking at them one by one. There were pictures of mail plane pilots. There were pictures of almost everybody in Quill, which I knew he was doing all the time. He had some drawings of a big circus tent, with him riding his unicycle in front of a big audience and me holding a megaphone. Some I had seen before, but some I had not, including two of me. So I send them for you and mother to remember me by until I get there. Kiss Mother for me.

Love,
Noah

December 13, 1959

Dear Noah,

Two days ago Auntie bought new copies of the same record albums we had at Paduola Lake. After Auntie bought the albums she rented a phonograph. When she got home she put the Stravinsky on. She sat next to it and listened. It was on just a few minutes when her face scrunched up. She took the album off. Then she sat with her face in her hands crying. She said, "What a mistake. A terrible, terrible mistake." That's all I could make out because she was mumbling.

The next morning she said, "You know what? Today I'm going to get new, different albums!" This perked her right up. "But let's give these two away first," she said. So I said, to who? Auntie says, "To our next-door neighbor."

We walked to the building next door. Auntie knocks on the door. This very old woman opens it up right away. She must've been standing right next to the door! "Yes?" she says. It was the first time I ever heard "yes" as a question. It made me laugh a little. She was bent over. We had seen on her mailbox that her name was Iona Aumerle. She's about a thousand years old.

"We're your new neighbors," Auntie says. "I'm Mina, and this is my niece, Charlotte. We live next door, at number twenty-three Olive Street. We wanted you to have these." Then Auntie holds out the albums. She had them wrapped up like a present.

"Yes?" says Iona. We stood on her porch for a while. Iona was holding the albums to her chest. Auntie and I were looking around, into her house. Then Auntie says, "May we come in for a moment, or is it too much trouble just now?"

"Oh, forgive me, yes," says Iona. Then she steps aside and shows us in.

We were standing in her dining room. There were empty vases all around. A few vases did have dried flowers in them, and a few had new flowers. But most were empty. "Are they antique?" says Auntie.

"Why, yes, I am," says Iona. "I am."

That's when we finally realized that Iona was nearly stone deaf. When she turned around to put the albums on a table, Auntie looked at me and pointed to her own ear and opened and closed her mouth like she was talking except that no words came out. Then we knew, too, that Iona surely didn't own a phonograph.

"Yes, you are what?" Auntie asks, real loud next to Iona.

"Oh, forgive me," Iona says. "I meant, I am a florist. That is, I am a retired florist. I had a shop in the market. Would you like tea?"

"Yes, that would be nice," says Auntie.

So we sit down. Iona makes us some tea. We each have a cup and saucer on our laps. Iona spilled her tea a lot. She'd pour it back from the saucer into her cup. She and Auntie were talking. Then, right out of the blue Iona says, "Please don't go down into the basement." Auntie and I looked at each other. We couldn't figure it out. Iona just blurted out about her basement, and I just started to laugh, and Auntie gave me a look.

"Why shouldn't we go down into your basement?" Auntie says. She's still speaking loudly.

"Oh, I don't have a pirate treasure down there," says Iona. "It's simply that we had rainstorms at the end of the summer this year. My basement was flooded. An awful mess. There was water knee deep."

"Did you call in someone to help?" says Auntie.

"Oh, my goodness, no!" says Iona. "Once I stood on the stairs and saw all of that water, I couldn't bear the thought of anyone else seeing it. And I haven't been back down there since. If there's more rain—or more likely it'll be snow, don't you think?—if more water gathers there, if the water reaches up one more step, why, I'll simply sell this house!"

"You can't mean that, Iona," says Auntie loudly.

"I most certainly can," says Iona, "and I do. One evening when I was already in bed, just about to take out my hearing aid, which I sometimes wear, I heard vases bumping together down there."

"Vases?" says Auntie.

"Why, yes," Iona says. "I had so many vases when I retired, ones I couldn't possibly part with, they were like old friends. I was in the business forty years, you see. But I couldn't keep them all upstairs. So, I'd put some in the basement. That night, I heard water bumping them around. I took out my hearing aid right away. The next morning I did phone a plumber. He said that sooner or later the water should subside. He said it would leave by the same routes, such as cracks in the floor, by which it may have seeped in. But that hasn't happened yet."

"That's just awful," says Auntie.

Then Auntie leans close to Iona and says, "Iona, if you're going to sell your house, let us know and we'll buy it."

Boy, oh, boy, that one shocked me. Here I am thinking how we have no money and Auntie is offering to buy a house with a flooded basement.

She must have been thinking about the Ark again.

We stayed with Iona a while longer, then we said good-bye and went home. Auntie says, "It's interesting having neighbors again, don't you think?"

"Yes, I do," I said.

"Did you like Iona?" Auntie says.

"Yes, I did."

"So did I," says Auntie. "She struck me as someone who might go out and buy a phonograph simply because we gave her the albums, and in case we should visit again."

I'll mail this now. Don't worry that no one knows about Quill. We do. We think and talk about you every day.

Today is the first real snow. It's been falling all day long. I have a new coat and gloves. You should see them! What are you doing? Auntie says, "How is your health?" I hope fine. I love you.

Charlotte

148

December 20, 1959

Dear Noah,   *worry*

No letter from you in a long time, dummy. Maybe one will get here today or tomorrow.

Gus Wallant has been here almost every evening before the movie begins. He gets here about five o'clock. Then we eat supper. Sometimes I cook. After supper Gus and Auntie leave for The Northern Lights. I know this is difficult for you to picture, since you've never seen the street we live on, or the theater, or Gus Wallant. Here's what he looks like: He's tall with hair that's turning gray and thick sideburns. I'd guess he's about ten years older than Auntie. He's around fifty-five, I think. He's got a big face. When I said that to Auntie, she said I was harsh. She said Gus Wallant's face was only big as it needs to be, and that he couldn't help it, just like everybody else couldn't help what their face was like. I said that I didn't think it needed to be that big. Anyway, he's not exactly fat, but he reminds me of a bear, the way he walks, and he hugs me like he's going to smother me. No matter what I complain about Gus, Auntie says he means well. He's friendly, that's true. I don't say much at supper. Neither does Gus or Auntie. They hardly look at each other. Gus has a little carved box he keeps toothpicks in. Once in a while I say things, just to find something out. For instance, the other night I said, "Auntie said that you're not the easiest man to work for, why is that?" But he just laughs, and the table shakes a little and he looks at Auntie, and Auntie says, "I just don't know what gets into her!" I guess you could say that Gus is nice to me. He's always bringing presents. You know the new coat and gloves I wrote you about? Gus brought me that, a watch, a stocking cap, mittens, and last night he brought me a round paperweight. It's made of glass, and inside it is a miniature village, and when you turn it upside down snow falls, and you quickly turn it right side up again, so that snow is falling on the village. Gus is always bringing gifts for Auntie, too. Last time he brought her a jewel that was shaped like a turtle. Right away Auntie *pins it to her sleeve. Gus says, "Of course it's not a real ruby or diamond, but then it's not a real turtle, either!" He was laughing. Otherwise he usually brings flowers or sweets.*

But listen to this. One night Gus comes back after the movie. It's late and the movie is over and they come in whispering. They sit on the living room couch. I'm in my room and I have my light off. I hear Auntie say, "Ssshh, you'll wake Charlotte." Except I'm already awake. Either she knows that or she doesn't. I'm listening at my door. Then I hear Auntie say, "Gus, don't. Don't, please. It's absolutely wrong. You're married. I'm married."

Gus Wallant says, "Only legally."

Then Auntie says, "Look Gus, I enjoy having supper with you, but I don't like lies."

"What lies?" says Gus.

"Oh, come on, Gus!" Auntie says. "You mean to say that you tell your wife every night that you sit by yourself and eat a sandwich at the theater, and she believes that? And what about now, tonight? Working late? Be reasonable, Gus."

"She doesn't care," says Gus.

"You're my employer!" says Auntie.

I can hear Gus moving around on the couch. Then Auntie says, "Don't, Mr. Wallant. I asked you—don't."

This went on for a while. That was the first night I snuck out. I got on my clothes and I walked down the hallway in the dark to the silent butler, and I put on my coat and went right outside. Either they didn't hear me or pretended they didn't because they were perfectly quiet. I was outside then. So I walked to the market, because where else was I going to go? Then I see a familiar restaurant, though I had never been in it. The sign says it's open 24 hours a day. So I go in. I've got my five dollars. I sit down at a table. There's tables and a counter, and at the counter there's round red seats that spin. I saw a man get up from eating at the counter, and he spun his seat around on purpose with his finger. Behind the counter there's spigots. And there's two waitresses. Now I'm the only customer in there. One waitress is about Auntie's age—Martha. The other one is a little younger, that's Berenice. Berenice starts talking to me, just to find out what I'm doing in there by myself at night. I say that my aunt didn't want me at home just then. I don't think I meant it, but it was what I first thought to say.

"Well, you just sit here and look at the menu, and when you've decided, I'll bring you something to eat," says Berenice.

So I read the menu and I say that I want a sandwich. A cheese sandwich and a soda. I took a very long time to eat the sandwich. I was taking tiny bites. They were watching me, but they didn't say anything. I even ate the crusts and took tiny bites of them, too, and the crusts made me think about the crows at Paduola Lake. Then I was done, but I didn't want to leave, only I didn't know what else to do. So I ordered another sandwich and soda, plus a piece of sponge cake. I ate those slowly. Then I was done again, and I ordered a third sandwich! But do you know what? I forgot the amount the sandwich cost! It was $.85. The sponge cake was $.45. A soda was $.25. So it all came to:

$$
\begin{array}{r}
\$ \ .25 \\
.25 \\
.85 \\
.85 \\
.85 \\
\underline{.45} \\
\$3.50
\end{array}
$$

That left me with just $1.50 to my name! But by the time I figured that out on a napkin, it was too late because here comes Berenice with the sandwich and soda. She says, "Some appetite." Then she sees my five-dollar bill on the table. "Is that all you have?" she says. I said yes. "Well, honey, you've almost spent it all." Then I just started crying, right in front of them both, but right away I stopped.

Now both Martha and Berenice sit down across from me. Martha says, "Okay, sweetheart, let's just sit here and find out a thing or two, and get to be friends, okay?"

I said okay. I told them about Gus and Auntie. Maybe I shouldn't have, but I did. They said if Auntie should ever come with me into the restaurant they wouldn't say a word I told them. "We keep a good secret," Martha said. Then she put her finger to her mouth and pretended to zip it shut. Like I said, I told them about Auntie and Gus on the couch. They listened to it all. They had both been to The Northern Lights. They heard the whole story.

"Next time, why not put a pillow over your head and try not to listen," said Martha. I said I'd hear things anyway.

Then Berenice says, "Well your aunt has got a life of her own, which doesn't sound all that good right now, and she's just trying to live it. But it's awful to feel you have to sneak out of your own house, too. Are you in school?" No, I said.

"Well, once you're in school," says Martha, "you'll have other friends."

Then Martha tells me a story about when she was my age in school. "I wish I'd have paid closer attention in school and done all my homework," she said. "I was always scheming to get out of work. One time, I had a take-home examination. That's when you have a subject, and you have blue notebooks and you go home and write and write everything you've learned about that subject. Such as history or biology. The next day everyone hands in their notebooks. So, this particular time I took home just one blue notebook. I only wrote on the first two pages of it. On the first page I started halfway through a sentence, like it was the end of an essay. Then on the notebook cover I put a big 3, right next to my name. I handed that in. A few days later the teacher hands back the notebooks and asks to see me after class. He says, 'This terrible thing has happened, the first two notebooks somehow were misplaced, and I only have notebook number three!'

"I cried out, 'Oh, no! Oh, no!' and I go into a fit and make a big to-do. I say how hard I had worked, and that I know that in the past I've been lazy, but this time I was up all night writing in the other

two notebooks. You know, to tell the truth I don't remember what happened, it was so long ago. I think he just got fed up and gave me a grade and that was that."

Her story cheered me up, and before I know it I'm having a nice time. Both Martha and Berenice say to come back any time I want, and then Berenice says, "Look!" We look and the plate's empty, because Martha had got so excited in telling her story she ate the cheese sandwich. So there's no problem about the bill. This made us all laugh.

"Come back just to sit and talk if you want," Martha said. "I mean it, too."

Then I left, and when I got home Gus Wallant was gone and Auntie was asleep. Which makes me think she didn't hear me leave in the first place. Or else she would've come out looking for me. I peeked in and she was sleeping.

At breakfast I didn't ask, and Auntie and I started to talk about other things. What would I like to do today? Things like that. Then Auntie says, "What did you hear last night?" Nothing, I said. Then she says, "I'm terribly sorry that you have to lie, because I know that you heard something." Auntie says she loves me very much. I say that I know she does. She says that she's very confused right now. She says for me to try not be angry or upset. I say I'll try. "The thing is," Auntie says, "that I keep having the odd feeling that Anthony is here. Not just in my memory, either. In Toronto. I can't put my finger on it, but the feeling's there all the same."

Since that night, it has happened more times, where Auntie and Gus are on the couch and I end up in the restaurant. I'm getting to be good friends with Martha and Berenice. I told them about you. During the day Auntie and I walk and take busses. We shop. We spend time together like always, except when I'm in the library. We've been to the zoo. We've been to museums. So, you can see from all this why I like daytimes best.

I hope that you're thinking of us. We think of you every day.

I love you,
Charlotte

January 1, 1960

Dear Charlotte,

Happy New Year! Kiss and say Happy New Year to Mother, too, please. I'm sorry I did not hear from you at the store on New Year's Eve. Einert said only a few calls came through. It was very bad weather. I know you tried.

It is hard for me to hear some of the things you write to me about, but I am glad you write them anyway. I should know.

On New Year's Eve Einert Sohms had his regular party, and Hettie and Sam went, but I did not. Instead, do you know what I did? I took Sam's shortwave radio completely apart and put it together again without looking at the manual once. Something had gotten into me. I did not want to be with people. I wanted just to feel like I knew how to do something. It was New Year's. I was feeling sorry for myself, I guess. I thought this: that I did not live at Paduola Lake anymore, that I would be in Quill probably only a little while longer, and that I did not know what it would be like in Toronto. Very philosophical, huh?

I thought a lot, and all my thinking just added up to me not wanting to even leave the kitchen. I got out the screwdrivers and took the radio apart. There were tubes and wires all over the table. It took me a few hours. Then Hettie's father, Job, I told you a lot about him, he knocks at the door. When I let him in he says, "I saw lanterns on." He sits down and we play a long game of checkers, then he leaves. Then I wrote this letter, but I will not send it until January 15 because that is when the next plane is due to be here.

Happy New Year and kisses to Mother and to you.

Love,
Noah

January 10, 1960

Dear Noah,

Happy New Year! We tried to reach Quill but couldn't. I hope
the scarf arrived that we sent you for Christmas. So you see I'm still
knitting.

Auntie brought home some blue pears. They aren't real pears.
They're made of hard wax. A few days later she brought home two
wax apples and a bunch of wax grapes. All of it is in a bowl on the
kitchen table. That's the newest thing in the house.

Last week Auntie said, "Let's sit down and talk." So we did. She
said she didn't like me being alone so much. She said she'd like me
to be with her at night. She said, "How would you like to help earn
a little money toward school?" How? I said. "You could work with
me at The Northern Lights," she said. "Gus said it was fine with
him. He needs an usher. We already have Nan, to take tickets at
the door. Or maybe you and she could alternate selling tickets and
tearing them at the door. You'd have a flashlight and you'd show
people to their seats. Basically, that would be your job. Sometimes
people arrive late, the movie's already begun, the theater is dark, and
you'd have your flashlight. Now there's a law that keeps you from
receiving a paycheck at your age, but Gus will add your wages to
mine. How does that sound?" I just said okay to everything.

So now Gus comes over for supper, we eat supper, and then all
three of us go to the theater. Gus and I don't get along very well.
He's bossy. He snaps at me. He tells me to sit way in the back and
watch the people, not the movie. He says when I see somebody with
their feet up on the seat in front of them, I have to walk over right
away and shine the flashlight in their face and say, "Please!" Then
I have to shine the flashlight onto their feet.

Gus seldom comes into the theater itself during a movie. He stays
in his office until the movie's almost done, then he goes up to the
projection booth. If there's any trouble, I go get him. As to how he
treats me, Auntie says that the worse she and Gus quarrel, the worse

he takes it out on me the next day. Auntie told me, "Don't worry, you'll never see Gus Wallant sitting at our breakfast table."

But do you know what? I've been in Gus's office. Don't tell anyone this. I snuck in there once. I looked all around. The drawers and closets are filled with empty bottles, liquor bottles. I bet Auntie knows this. Here's something else. One night a customer was talking loud. He was in a seat about halfway down the aisle. It sounded like he was arguing with someone. I took a deep breath and walked down there. He was saying things to the woman next to him, maybe it was his wife. She was staring straight ahead, all embarrassed. Well, here it goes, I said to myself, and I shined the flashlight on his face. "Please," I said. "Please stop talking so loud, you're disturbing the other customers."

He glares at me and he says very loud, "I'm only talking when they aren't!" He's pointing to the actors on the screen!

"Go get the manager," somebody says.

So I run up the aisle and I knock on Gus's door. "Gus, Gus," I say. I hear a groan. So I go ahead and open his door.

Gus is sitting in a chair. Ticket stubs are all over the place, on his lap and on the floor. He growls at me. "What do you want?" he says.

I say that there's a man talking loudly. I tell Gus that I shined the flashlight on him, and that I'm too scared, so that's why I came to get him.

So then Gus gets up in a way that's even more scary than the man in the seats. He looks around his office. He sees a bottle and picks it up and he breaks the end off it on his desk!

Then I say, "Forget about it, Gus. It's okay. I'll go and shine the light on him again, I'm sure it'll work." But Gus is already wobbling mad out the door. "It's okay, Gus," I say, and I'm trying to push him back into his office. I'm pushing on his stomach. "You just go back to sleep in your chair," I say.

But he shoves past me and walks into the theater. He stands there at the top of the aisle. Auntie is watching this from behind the counter. *She's got a very, very worried look on her face. Gus is listening, and he hears the man talking loudly. I say to Gus that he's not talking as loudly as before, but Gus hears somebody else ask the man to shut up. That's exactly what he heard, too—"Shut up!" That did it. I'm thinking, Oh, no, Gus is going to clobber the man with the bottle. Why did I ever tell him? I'm following Gus down the aisle with the flashlight. Then Gus grabs the flashlight away from me. First he shines it right into the loud man's face. And then he holds the flashlight right under his own chin so that his face is just like the man in the moon! Then you'll never guess what. Gus cuts himself! Right on his own cheek with the bottle on purpose! It was awful, and he says to the man, "Get out of my theater!"*

So right away the man stands up and turns in the opposite direction of Gus, "Excuse me, excuse me," all the way past a lot of people pulling their knees back. They don't know what's going on. About twenty people get up and leave.

Then Gus goes back up the aisle and right into his office. Auntie sees him bleeding and goes in, too. In there Gus pours some liquor on his face and Auntie says she'll get a first-aid kit, that the cut is not very deep, but it's bleeding a lot. Oh, boy, I'm telling you, Noah, that was some night.

The next morning Auntie says that if Gus behaves badly again, he's going to ruin his reputation more than it has been already. He's going to lose his license to operate The Northern Lights, and he might lose the theater all together, permanently. Auntie says that now we're in a real bind. That's because we need the work to pay our rent and buy groceries and all of that, plus save for school. If Gus loses the theater, there's no guarantee it will open again or that we can go on working there even if it does. Auntie says that Gus is a drunk partly because she won't be in love with him. It's complicated, she says, but the result might be very simple, that we'll lose our jobs. So what do we do? That's what I asked. Auntie says that Gus has been warned by the city before about poor behavior, she wouldn't say exactly what. Maybe this time will shake some sense into him, she says. Maybe Gus will act properly. She says that I should just be polite and do my ushering job well, and to keep an eye on Gus, and stay out of his way. She says, "I'll try and stay friends with him, but I doubt that it will be as easy as that sounds. We're in a bind."

Now it's been a week since all of this happened, and Gus has been acting okay. But each night we hold our breath. I sit in the back row like always. There's different couples who sit back there and kiss. One couple I recognize. The boy has his hair slicked back and his sleeves rolled up and a pack of cigarettes tucked in one. I can hear him breathing, but it's as if the girl isn't breathing. I never hear her. I know her perfume, though. And once I saw her combing her hair and straightening up her blouse in the ladies' washroom. She is sort of pretty, but she snarled at me. I was staring at her. She said, "Pervert!" So I just said the same word back and ran out. They just ignore me, even if I'm sitting right next to them. They do whatever they please. Sometimes I can hear them kiss! Once in a while I look, I can't help it, and at first I like it and then it's like I shouldn't be there, so I get up and move to another seat.

Anyway, Gus has acted calmer. I said to Auntie that things seem better, don't they? Auntie just said, "We'll see what happens."

We love you and miss you and wish you were here. We have Pelly's paintings of you up in nice frames.

Love,
Charlotte

February 8, 1960

Dear Charlotte,

I showed Sam your last letter and he said, "Somebody ought to kick that Gus Wallant's ass across the river, and if nobody else does, I'll do it myself." He was really riled up. I believe that Sam would do what he says, too. It all made me think that I should be there with you, to help out. Sam says that Gus could harm you or Mother, do you think that might be true? Ask Mother and then write me and tell me what she says—promise! It has been so cold here. You know how cold it can get! These days, outside it is best to cover everything except my eyes. You remember. The Indians rub a little black grease just under their eyes, to absorb the sun. The glare off the snow hurts. Out ice-fishing, almost the minute you pull out a pickerel, it is frozen, and you can stick it straight into the snow next to you, then carry the whole bunch back like firewood. It seems like I spend half my time cutting and bringing in firewood.

There is not all that much work to do in the store these days, so I spend more time painting decoys. Also, I go out hunting with that fellow, Paul Koivisto. We get along fine. He is quiet. He does not say much. Other than Hettie, Sam, and Hettie's parents, he is the only one I see regularly, which may strike you as strange for such a small place. Of course I see people at their work, like Olaf taking care of his huskies, and we chat for a minute or two. Sometimes, after he tells me what to do in the store, Einert just keeps to himself all afternoon.

Lately at night I tune in on stations that broadcast in languages I cannot understand. There's music, then talk, and even when they play no music I keep listening. According to my channel guide, they are Asian and Indonesian. Paul Koivisto brings over his encyclopedias and we look up the locations.

Kathryn Amundson is going to have a baby any day now, Hettie says. The doctor should have arrived by now from Winnipeg, but he has not. The weather has been bad, and two planes have turned back. Hettie's sister, Edna Blackduck, is a midwife, so Hettie is not worried. But Olaf wants a doctor here, and every couple of hours he comes to the store and asks Einert to call in about the weather and a doctor. He's got the doctor's room all ready for him at his house.

Do not forget to tell me what Mother says about Gus Wallant, if she thinks he is harmful or not. Kiss Mother for me. I miss you, too.

Noah

February 27, 1960

Dear Noah,

I asked Auntie what you wanted me to, and she said, "No, Gus is disturbed and quite unhappy, but I sincerely do not think he would hurt anyone, except, perhaps, himself. So please put Noah at ease on that subject." That's exactly what she said, I wrote it down right afterward.

Two days ago was my thirteenth birthday. So Happy Birthday to me! You always forget.

We had a party and a cake. The party was not at home. It was at The Northern Lights. When I was just about to blow out the candles —this is jumping ahead a little. When I was just going to blow, Auntie called out, "Make a wish!" I closed my eyes tight, but didn't make a wish. Everyone probably thought I did, but I didn't. Do you think there's something wrong with me because I couldn't think of a wish? Later I thought I should have wished for Noah to be here and for a million dollars to fall from the sky so Auntie could quit her job. Even five thousand!

Anyway, the party was in the afternoon. Gus ordered a movie especially. It was called The Mummy. It was very scary. It was about some archaeologists who go to Egypt, which you can find in Paul Koivisto's encyclopedia, and dig up the sacred tomb of Princess Ananka and what kinds of scary, awful things happen to them when they find the tomb. I was really scared. I wouldn't look around.

I invited Berenice and Martha, from the restaurant. Auntie invited old Iona Aumerle, from next door. Of course Gus was there. Plus Shelley, who sells tickets in the glass booth, she's seventeen. First, we had a cake that Auntie baked. It was chocolate with white frosting, and my name was written in chocolate letters on top. There was punch that Gus had poured a lot of rum into. He goes up and starts the movie. It's dark in the theater in the middle of the afternoon. Gus comes back down and soon he's drunk so much punch that he's wobbling up the aisle. He falls asleep near the back. He's sitting up asleep, snoring away. Iona goes and sits right in the front row because she forgot her glasses. That was funny to me, Iona sitting so close watching The Mummy. I saw her fiddling with her hearing aid.

After the movie I opened my presents. Here's what I got: Auntie gave me a pair of black, open-toe dress-up shoes. Plus a flower box that I can plant seeds in now and place outside the window in the spring. And a photograph. The photograph is of Auntie standing in front of The Northern Lights, only it was taken when she was twenty-five! She looked so pretty!

Shelley gave me a charm bracelet and a little booklet called 142 Ways to Be Popular, which she said she reads all the time. "This will help you when you get into school," she said. There's three sections. One is for both boys and girls. Some of the things in that section are: 1. Record your laugh on tape and play it back. If it sounds awful, change it. 2. Don't become a twosome hermit. Even if you are going steady, continue to see your other friends. 3. Be friendly. Smile at people even if you don't have a reason to. 4. Give yourself a snappy new nickname like "Smoke," "Speed," or "Atom." 5. Visit people in the hospital but not so often that you become a pest. 6. Keep your nose out of the upper atmosphere. 7. Don't crack your knuckles. 8. Don't "make out" just because you're too dull to think of anything else to do. 9. Learn to play a musical instrument. 10. Don't be afraid to start a fad—someone has to. 11. Think up unusual parties, like going to the county fair or picnicking after swimming or having a hobo party. 12. Don't take foolish dares. 13. Act as if you're having a good time even if you're not. 14. Don't laugh at someone trying to learn to water-ski.

Those are just the general ones! I'd never tell this to Shelley, but I'll say it to you. I think just the complete opposite way. These things are stupid! (I hope you're laughing, Noah.)

Now, here's some listed "Especially for Girls": 1. Learn all about sports and cars. 2. If he apologizes for his dancing, compliment him on his natural rhythm. 3. Don't suspect a boy of being up to no good *if he runs out of gas—give him the benefit of the doubt unless it happens all the time. 4. If you are fond of an egghead, ask him to help you with your homework. 5. Offer your services as waterboy to the football team. 6. Be the first one to wear new hairdos. 7. Develop a perfume that smells of ham and eggs to wear in the morning. The boys will love it. 8. Start a charm class for shy boys and then date your best pupils. 9. Don't wear too tight clothing.*

There's a section called "Especially for Boys." I'll put the booklet on your bureau so you can read it when you get here—I know you'll love it—ha! ha!

Let's see, what else? Gus Wallant gave me a hand-sewn change purse with twenty dollars in it! Iona gave me a vase. Martha and Berenice pitched in together for a bracelet, plus some perfume. The perfume is called Le Kiss. There's a romantic picture on the box that reminds me of the couple kissing in the back row.

Everyone was drinking punch and talking and having a nice time. Berenice and Martha were really funny. They were tipsy and were telling funny stories. Then each of them took the perfume bottle and turned it upside down, except that the top was still on. They pretended to put perfume on their fingertips and then dab some behind their ears. They were saying, "Ooh, ooh," and then started talking about men they once knew.

Martha said, "When I went out with Stuart Mattison, now there was a dish! You remember him, don't you, Bernie? The lawyer? Well, he'd ring my doorbell and I'd put a little touch of perfume, ever so little, right . . . just like that. . . ." And she pretended to dab some right on her thighs!

Auntie was really laughing hard, but suddenly she acts upset and says, "Martha! Charlotte is only thirteen!"

But then Berenice says, "Yeah, but Martha was only twelve when she went out with that lawyer!"

Then Martha and Berenice and Auntie too almost fell on the floor laughing. We each had a second piece of cake. Gus was still asleep in his seat.

I hardly remember what happened next. The first thing I know I'm looking around and everyone's asleep. Shelley is asleep off by herself down the aisle. Iona is asleep in the front row. I'm awake, though. I'm sitting next to Auntie. I'm in the aisle seat. And that's when I suddenly sense somebody crawling down the aisle. It gives me a creepy feeling. So I close my eyes and put my head on Auntie's shoulder and pretend I'm asleep. Then I realize it's Gus, because I know how he breathes when he's drunk. He's feeling his way along the aisle. He's on hands and knees. He can't see it's me in the aisle seat. He thinks it's Auntie. He stops right there next to me. He starts babbling, "Mina, please, please. If you abandon me now, I'll kill myself. I'll drive my car out on a bridge over some river and get out and jump."

Then I don't know what got into me, Noah. I say to Gus, "Gus, when I abandon you I'm gonna take your car first."

Then he realizes. He looks up and sees it's me, and he gets very upset and confused. "Smart ass," he says. "Don't you dare tell Mina what I said, do you understand?" He was holding my wrist tight. I say yes, I understand.

Then Gus goes up to his office and pretty soon I heard some bottles. I wake up Auntie and I say that Gus is in his office. She says, "We'd better go home and freshen up a little before work tonight."

Auntie wakes up Iona. She's startled and says, "The mummy!" like she'd been dreaming about it, and that cracked us up. We just leave Shelley and Martha and Berenice there asleep. They're all out like a light.

We took the bus home. Iona says she had a wonderful time. I say thanks for the vase. Then upstairs at home right away I tell Auntie what happened with Gus. I tell her everything. She says, "You poor thing. How did this all happen? We live in a little world again, between the apartment and the theater. Noah is hundreds of miles away. Anthony . . . God knows. And now this pitiable creature, crawling on his hands and knees grabbing your wrist. I'm so, so sorry. I bring so much on us. . . . " She was both laughing and crying. Then she looks up and smiles and says, "But the party was great fun, wasn't it. Did you have a good time?" I said I did, which was true.

So Happy Birthday to me, Noah. Send a letter soon. We miss you.

Love,
Charlotte

March 10, 1960

Dear Charlotte,

I talked things over with Sam and Hettie for many days, and I have thought hard, and I decided to come to Toronto two planes from now. I asked Einert and he said that if the schedule runs smoothly, I can leave Quill on April 2nd. Willie Savoie will fly me all the way to Flin Flon. I will get a train from there to Winnipeg, then to Toronto. I should arrive in Toronto on April 15th, around three o'clock if everything goes all right. You can check on the schedule there, too.

I did not forget your birthday, I just forgot to mention it.

Kathryn had a baby girl, which they named Marit Elizabeth. It was a difficult birth. The weather stayed bad and the doctor could not arrive. So when it was time, things were set up in Einert Sohms's home in back of the store. He had the doctor on the radio, who was giving instructions to Hedda Koivisto, who had some experience as a nurse years ago, and to Marjorie Malraux. Also Edna Blackduck was in the room. I waited in the main room of the store near the woodstove and kept a supply of hot water ready. Aki, Olaf, Sam, and me were there. It was rough going, especially because the doctor's voice kept fading. Hettie later said that Edna could have delivered the baby easily and did not need any radio, but she was not asked.

But Kathryn said Edna helped a lot anyway. From the store we could hear the instructions being given and Einert repeating them, trying to keep his voice clear and calm. We could hear Kathryn moaning and calling out. And finally we heard the baby crying. It was quite a time! Kathryn was not doing too well for a few days, but she is very strong and recovered just fine, and the baby is beautiful and healthy. As for me, it is a small thing, but I secretly felt happy that I had recently fixed Einert's radio and had it in good working order. Hettie said that Edna told her that Hedda Koivisto and Marjorie did some things wrong, but that it turned out fine. They will talk about it for a long time, I am sure!

I am thinking about going to an electronics school in Toronto but do not tell that to Mother, in case I change my mind.

I do not know how I will say good-bye to Sam, Hettie, and the others, but I think I will just say it and say I will be back soon, which might or might not be true. They already know that, I think.

So, Charlotte, I will see you soon. Kiss Mother for me.

wisdom

Love,
Noah

P. S. Your letter (Feb. 27) just arrived today!

March 11, 1960

Dear Noah,

I knew it, I just knew that something bad was going to happen at The Northern Lights. Auntie and I stopped talking about it altogether. But Gus had been acting up again. There were more complaints. Then one night two things happened. He'd been in his office drinking again. I was selling tickets in the booth out front. Then about eight o'clock, which is when the movie begins, Gus walks out into the lobby and walks right up to Nan—she's the girl taking tickets *at the door. Nan is short for Nancy. She is sixteen. Gus grabs a ticket right from the customer who's about to give the ticket to Nan! He holds the ticket right up close to Nan, who's frightened. Gus is talking in a mean voice. He tears the ticket exactly in half. Auntie is watching from behind the counter, shaking her head back and forth. Gus says, "Exactly* down the middle. I mean exactly. It's an equal exchange in my theater. The customers give us something, we give them something, even Steven. Understand?"*

Poor Nan bursts into tears and runs out the front door. She's not coming back, either, I knew that right away. So then Gus takes her place at the door, taking tickets. He's tearing each one slowly in half. One lady in line says, "We've heard about you, Mr. Wallant."

I wish that's all there is, but it isn't. The movie is going for a while. Things are quiet. I'm sitting in the back row again. Then all of a sudden a flashlight beam is going over the audience! From up in the projection booth! It had to be Gus. I hurried and got Auntie. She was adding butter to popcorn in the vat. We both stood at the back of the theater. Then right on the screen some words appear. See, sometimes there's an emergency phone call, from a baby-sitter or a relative for someone in the audience. When that happens, Gus is able to request that a customer call home. He places the words in front of the projector in a certain way, in the machine actually, I think. I don't know exactly how it works. The words show up on the screen in the bottom center. But this time wasn't an emergency. Auntie would smack me if she knew I was using this language, but what Gus put on the screen was this: GODDAMN FILTHY FEET OFF MY SEATS! Auntie and I run up the stairs. Auntie knocks hard on the door. "Gus, Gus!" she's shouting. No use, so we go back downstairs. Customers are leaving left and right. But a lot of people stay, once the words are off the screen. Things get calmed down again.

The movie is going along. Then on the screen is a love scene. A man and woman are kissing, and right while they're kissing Gus makes an arrow point to each one. Right above the man it says GUS and right above the woman it says MINA.

"That's the last straw," Auntie says. "He's going to lose the theater." She goes back upstairs and knocks again, but Gus wouldn't come out. Downstairs I could hear her shouting.

By this time most everybody's leaving. Now I see Gus wobbling at the top of the stairs. He makes it downstairs into the lobby. He sees everybody leaving and calls out, "What's the problem here?" Then he falls flat on his face. Right down on the carpet. Customers are stepping over him on their way out. Then everyone is gone except for Auntie and Gus and myself.

"This is the last straw," Auntie says. She's looking down at Gus. "He's got a good heart, but he is a hopeless wreck."

Then I'm splashing paper cups full of water onto Gus, but he's out cold. "We can't just leave him here," I say.

Auntie says, "Yes we can." She goes and gets a blanket from the office and covers Gus up with it. Then she goes back to the office and telephones Gus's wife, but there's no answer. Auntie went upstairs and turned off the projector. Then we turned off the lobby lights and locked the front doors. Then we went home. Auntie didn't say one word on the bus. When we got home she just said, "I'm so tired."

So like they say at the end of the radio romance programs here, Stay tuned for the next episode.

We miss you,
Charlotte

March 22, 1960

Dear Noah,

Your letter just got here today. We are so happy you will be here soon! I hope this reaches you before you leave Quill.

You should know that Gus Wallant is giving up The Northern Lights. I think he has to. I think people are making him. Auntie doesn't say it like that, but I think it's true.

Auntie said, *"Gus has offered the theater to me. This could be a stroke of luck, a fine opportunity, no matter that it's come about in so painful a way." She says she'll beg, borrow, or steal. She made a phone call to her family in Vancouver, and they said they could help some. Then Auntie went to a bank and is getting a small loan.*

So now we really need you to help out!

Auntie and I talk about you so much. Sometimes I even ask her what you might be thinking about. Auntie said that maybe one of the reasons you had to stay in Quill was as a way of coming to grips with what happened to Pelly, your friend. Auntie said it takes a long time, that there's a lot for you to figure out. Things about Pelly, things about Uncle Anthony, things about Paduola Lake. Just a lot of things. Auntie, as usual, says, "You'll understand more when you've had more life." Can't you just hear her saying that? I think I understand a lot of what she told me about you right now.

Now here's my own thoughts. I don't want to make up a family. I tried that when I first got to Paduola Lake. I never told you this. I tried to think that my mom and dad were just away somewhere. But now I think that who's ever right in front of me, that's who my family is. That's why I'm glad you'll be here soon.

Sometimes in my dreams Mom and Dad float by. This I never told you, either. Usually they have their eyes closed, sometimes they don't. Once I dreamed them in the cannery, in Halifax. The walls were falling on them. The thing is, that they are gone now. I cry always whenever I think of them. I know I won't see them again. So I asked myself, who's my family now? Then I say that it's Noah and Auntie Mina. Then I say that's something! Maybe I taught myself to think this way. I don't always like the way I think, but when it comes to you and Auntie I like it.

I heard a program on the radio here. You'll love it, Noah, because there's all sorts of radio programs. So many! There's one where people telephone in and give their opinions. It's on late at night. Auntie says that's because so many people need the whole day to practice how to say what they think. Also, a lot of people can't listen to the radio during the day. Also, because it's on late at night you can just turn the program off and go right to sleep. I have a little transistor radio that I listen to in bed.

Anyway, this one night I heard people talking about the afterlife, they called it. It was about people's ideas of heaven and hell, and about where they thought friends and relatives who died had gone. People gave their opinions. There was a Catholic priest, a Jewish rabbi, and a minister of some kind, all listening, and they also gave their opinions. And I thought, If I called in, I'd say that my mother and father sometimes floated by with their eyes closed. To me, whenever they float by, I know where they are, the rest of the time I don't. That's what I would have said on the radio. I haven't even told Auntie this, but I'm glad I told you.

Now these letters can stop, because you're going to be here soon. We can hardly wait!

Love,
Charlotte

============CHAPTER SEVEN============

The Northern
Lights

While waiting with Sam and Hettie for Willie Savoie's plane, Sam gave me a watch. It was on a gold chain and had a flip-up top shielding the glass. Black roman numerals were set against a white background, and there was a tiny hole so you could glimpse the mechanism. "It's a gentleman's watch," Sam said, "but anyone can tell time by it." He showed me how to wind it, how to clip the chain to my belt.

I had tried to concentrate on the landscape—the wetlands, the spruce—but as we heard the muffled whine of Savoie's plane, I felt a tightening inside. Hands in my pockets, shoulders hunched, I drew into myself. We saw the plane lower from a cloudbank, tilting, rebalancing, setting down, then leaving a widening rift of water as it circled back on Piwese Lake. About fifty yards from shore, Savoie anchored. He then rowed a pontoon to the rocks. "I am ready when you are," he said.

I looked at Sam and Hettie. "Okay—good-bye," I said. Hettie checked the rope securing my suitcase, adjusting it to no useful purpose except to show her affection for me. She turned away, took a few steps, stopped, and looked at the house. Sam, placing an arm around my shoulder but not looking at me, said, "Yes, good-bye, Noah. You're doing the right thing. You thought hard, worked your options down to one—your family. And that takes courage."

"I don't feel courageous," I said.

"No matter," he said. "You're acting as such."

Sam pulled me close and said, "Don't forget. We're your second home." He then joined Hettie, and they walked toward the house, not looking back.

In the plane tears covered my face. Uneasy at this, Willie Savoie kept up a radio conversation with Einert. "Want to say anyteeng to Meester Einert Sohms?" Savoie asked.

"No thanks," I said. "Nothing."

"Let's get to Fleen Flon, then," he said.

"I'll say good-bye to you now, Willie," I said. "Might as well get the good-byes over with all at once."

On the Muskeg Express—eight passenger cars, two locomotives back to back, a caboose—I slept fitfully. Woke, slept again. The next afternoon in Winnipeg, I changed trains. Between Winnipeg and Toronto, the cars grew crowded. I kept near my suitcase, which was dark blue with gold buttons along its leather strapping and borders. Dinner was announced. In the dining car, a porter said, "You'll have to leave the suitcase above your seat." I preferred to buy sandwiches in the snack car, eat them in my seat, leave the suitcase on the luggage rack. Again during the night hours it was difficult to sleep; porters jostled by, their walkie-talkies crackling messages, people boarding or detraining at small stations, sometimes at a stop where there was no station at all. In their seats, other passengers slept in as many contortions as an alphabet. At one point, a lanky, red-haired woman, with keen, glancing eyes and a kind, almost apologetic smile, stood up across the aisle from me. She set out a quilt, two blankets, and a pillow on the luggage rack and hoisted her daughter up onto this makeshift bed. The little girl, who had the exact same color hair and who wore cotton pajamas with feet, slept soundly. The woman adjusted her chair, looked at me, and whispered, "Where are you from?"

For a moment I drew a blank. "Speak *English?*" she tried.

This made me laugh, and I said, "Well, I'm from two places," thinking of Quill *and* Paduola Lake.

"That can't be," she said. "You had to be born somewhere, eh?"

"Then—Toronto," I said.

"Is that one of the original two, or a third altogether?" she said.

"Third," I admitted. "The other two are up north."

"I thought so," she said. "By your suitcase. I visited up north once. I saw a lot of suitcases like yours. Don't take it wrong, I mean it admiringly, the way you can admire many things of another century, for instance." She took out a Whitman's Sampler box, opened it, offered me a piece of candy. "The top row's chewy inside, the middle ones are nuts, the bottom rows have sweet fruity middles," she said. She showed me the inside lid of the box, which had a guide to the candies. I chose a nut candy, bit into it, embarrassed at how loud it was.

"My name's Millie," she said. "I'm divorced. Millicent— that's my name, really. But it's an old lady's name. So is Millie, but not quite as old. I have earplugs, but I left my extra pair at home—that's Winnipeg. Otherwise I'd loan them to you. I'm bringing the girl, upstairs there"—she pointed to the luggage rack—"to see her father. I stay in a hotel. He comes to get her.

Two days later—and this is a monthly thing—he . . . brings her back. It works out. Know how we eased things for the girl? We got rid of the 'mommy' and 'daddy' words. We just said, 'Call us Millie and Frank.' It worked."

"How do you know?" I said.

"Parents *know*," she said. "They just do."

She leaned back, closed her eyes, and dozed off, the candy box open on her lap. I took two more pieces during the night, holding myself back from taking a third.

According to my watch, and the schedule that I had studied, the train arrived at Union Station an hour early. So I had to wait for Mina and Charlotte. The vastness of the station, its cathedral acoustics, the bustle of people, the cafe, the bakery, shops, all made it seem like my idea of a city. Walking toward the front doors, I found that life took on a dreamlike quality; colors blurred, the loudspeaker voice (*"Now boarding for Montreal, Quebec City, Halifax . . ."*) drifted to the upper halls, the rafters. It seemed to take forever to get to the street. Now, venturing outside, I could smell the water of Toronto Harbor, could hear the keening of invisible gulls. Across the street, beyond considerable traffic, was a bus. When it shifted moaning gears and moved on, I saw people's heads gliding back and forth, bobbing in and out of view. Clutching my suitcase, I made my way up to the railing. Tall, gun-metal lamps—like thin trees bent to the shape of catapults by heavy snows—surrounded a frozen pond. Green slat benches bordered the ice.

On the pond, old, young, novices, show-offs, men in business suits, silk scarves trailing from their necks, wobbly couples who grasped at each other for balance, laughing and a little afraid, all skated to waltzes that played over a loudspeaker. A young woman in jeans and a turtleneck sweater and white skates fell hard and immediately looked around, embarrassed. At the far side was a booth with a sign that read SKATE RENTAL. Behind its counter was a hive, similar to Einert Sohms's, though with larger compartments full of skates, each labeled by size. The booth was attended by a thin, elderly man with tousled hair and octagonal spectacles. He wore a uniform of black galoshes, dark green trousers, and a short-sleeve shirt, a cloth badge on his breast pocket. His gloves were gray and had flared bottoms and thin red stripes like a railroad worker's, and he ate a sandwich without removing them, chatting with a skater. A wide, black-bristled broom leaned against the booth; the attendent, I thought, must be the custodian of the rink as well. He must walk out in his galoshes and sweep the shards of ice to the rim. I wondered if the skaters had to wait off the ice as he swept or if he swept around them.

As I leaned against the railing, travel fatigue engulfed me. I could barely move. The turns and spins of the skaters repeated Pelly's acrobatics over and over again in my mind. I was hundreds of miles away, yet still in Quill.

Finally, I returned to the station. I recognized Mina and Charlotte from behind. They stared up at the schedule board, with its white letters and numerals clicking in arrivals and departures. I set down my suitcase. "Mother, Charlotte!" I shouted. My voice echoed.

They turned and held still. I ran halfway to them, then remembered my suitcase. I saw that a man holding a dozen or so oranges had placed several oranges on the suitcase. I ran back. Seeing alarm on my face, he clumsily took up the oranges, shrugged apologetically, and said, "I was just resting. Haven't seen a cardboard one like that in years. Looks in good shape, too. I know an antique dealer. He has a shop on Ulster Street, near the university. Pretty sure he'd be interested."

"No, thanks," I said, panting. "I need it for my clothes."

I ran back to find Mina and Charlotte in such a state of awkward excitement that they were hugging each other. "Oh, Noah," Mina said, "are you happy to be here?"

"I'm happy to see you both," I said. I held Charlotte's hand and tentatively kissed Mina on her cheek. It had been six months since I had seen them. We kept stealing glances, registering changes. Mina looked tired, yet her eyes were as alert as ever. She wore a simple checkered blouse, black pants. A light green sweater was tied around her shoulders, and she held a black clutch purse. Charlotte was thinner and she seemed older. Her hair was shorter, with bangs across her forehead. She had on blue jeans, a fresh white blouse, and red tennis shoes. Adjusting her yellow plastic sunglasses, she spun around and said, "Glamorous city girl, huh?"

"They look very nice on you," I said.

Standing there, talk zigzagging between us, Mina was in high spirits, proud that The Northern Lights was hers. "The bank loan came through," she said. "The family in Vancouver has sent money, too. Gus Wallant agreed on installment terms. We had to put five thousand dollars as a down payment."

"Have you ever *heard* of that much?" Charlotte said, shaking her head back and forth.

"It's ours now," Mina said. "Yours, Charlotte's, mine. We're in it together."

Two short bus rides later we stood in front of the cinema. The marquee read CLOSED FOR RENOVATIONS. The name THE NORTHERN LIGHTS was formed by white bulbs on a wooden background. "Finally, I get to see this place," I said.

"It's changed since I was a young woman, Noah. I can hardly tell you," Mina said, and swept her hand in front of her. "This is College Street," she said. "The theater number is four fifteen. Toronto University's down the street. Olive Street's not too far away, either."

"And the market," Charlotte said.

Mina unlocked the wide glass doors. "Might as well jump right in, Noah," she said. "If you're going to help, you'll be here every night."

As we entered the dusky, midday lobby, Mina said, "Let's have a look around."

Charlotte flicked on the lights. "Over there," she said, acting as tour guide, "is the concession stand. We keep the light on over the candy bars all night. It's a small light, so it doesn't melt them. There's candy, popcorn—see the vat? You pour butter right down the funnel. And there's spigots for soda pop. Grape, orange, and Coca-Cola. In the winter we'll have hot chocolate. The prices are listed on a piece of paper. It's taped to the cash register, which I'll teach you how to work. Auntie will sell refreshments and I'll sell tickets. We've got it all figured out."

"Slow down, darling," Mina said. "Don't worry, Noah, you'll catch on. Fifteen, nearly sixteen, in a month. My, my—well, that's quite old enough for the job. And it's a very good thing to start out in the city *with* a job."

I looked around. Just inside was a ticket booth with an oval opening in its window and a roll of tickets on its marble counter. A black corkboard hung at the top of the window, with the words NOW SHOWING strung up in white plastic letters. But no movie was listed. Below, it read 8 P.M. A pale red carpet covered the lobby floor. Framed movie posters decorated the walls. Among them were *Gone With the Wind; Little Caesar; Lady on a Train; Dance, Fools, Dance;* and *Trouble in Paradise.* A plush red couch was on each side of the inside door. A metal ashtray atop a wooden stand stood next to each couch. Waist-high metal stanchions, with thick maroon velvet ropes loosely stretched between them, formed a corridor leading to the tall wooden box with its ticket slot.

"At first," Mina said, "your duties will be simple, Noah. You'll have your own office."

Mina pointed to a closed door to the left of the concession stand. Its sign read OFFICE.

"You'll see that employees get to work on time," she added.

"But that's just me, Charlotte, and you," I said. "Right?"

"For a while, that's correct," she said. "And a projectionist, when we hire one. But soon, if business is as good as it was when the theater closed, we'll hire a ticket seller, and maybe someone to tear tickets at the door. And even an usher. But in the meantime, we'll distribute those chores among us. You'll sign paychecks, soon as you're sixteen, that is. You'll answer the telephone. You've not used a telephone; that's a treat. 'Hello, The Northern Lights Theatre,' you'll say. 'Can I help you?' What could anyone want, besides the time the movie begins, the name of it, perhaps a general idea of what it's about?"

"I've never seen a movie, Mother," I said. "I'll sound stupid."

"The office is filled with catalog descriptions," she said. "You can even tape a paragraph that describes the movie we're showing to the telephone. Simply read it to whoever asks."

"I'll do that," I said.

"Sometimes," Mina continued, "a customer will hate a movie, even be offended by it. Leave in a huff. You can never tell why. I've experienced this. They might complain out loud, demand their money back. The worst wait until the movie is almost over, then come complaining out into the lobby. 'I'd like to speak to the manager,' they say. I'm afraid, Noah, you'll have to deal with that. You can say—and be firm, businesslike—'Look, we did *not make* this movie, we're only *showing* it.'

"But as you'll see, the plaster on the ceiling is loose. The ceiling is in poor condition. So, if plaster falls on someone, we are indeed responsible. Twice since I've worked here we had to pay cleaning bills to get plaster dust from someone's clothes. We need to get the ceiling dome repaired as well. I've telephoned several places, and it's just too expensive right now. Besides, we'll need an artist, not just a carpenter or ceiling painter."

"An artist?" I said.

"Yes, like Michelangelo," Mina said.

As if on cue Charlotte walked to the wall just inside the actual theater and turned on the dome light.

I looked up at the dome, which was severely faded and

chipped, with gaping white holes of plaster showing through. A mural, a circle of human figures, surrounded the center, each group illustrating a chapter of early Canadian history. Going clockwise: Indians in ceremonial dress held a feast; a deer was tethered upside down as several men built up a fire; two lumberjacks wearing identical logging boots, checkered shirts with suspenders snapped to black trousers, worked a crosscut saw into a log; a missionary in a black robe held out a gold cross to a family of kneeling Indians; a frontier family stacked logs near a cabin sequestered by tall firs; an Eskimo paddled a kayak, a seal draped across its bow, icebergs floating past; a lone fisherman, rubber boots up to his waist, on the deck of a small boat hauled in a net full of fish; an explorer dressed in buckskin stood atop a ridge, scanning a riverine valley. Most of the figures, even the kneeling Indians, gazed skyward, so that the cumulative effect was a worshipful moment of awe at the display of aurora borealis on the dome.

"It's always night up on the dome, huh?" I said.

Slightly irritated, Mina tried to educate me. "The idea, Noah," she said, "is to show that the lights are eternal. Inspiring. It's like a church. Sometimes I sit here alone, just looking at the dome and imagining the audience under the protection of heaven."

"Well, I'll have to think about that one, Mother," I said. I picked up a shard of blue plaster from an aisle seat. "Looks like that one man, with the blue shirt—see him, in that family? Looks like he's falling apart."

"Every few days," Charlotte said, "we have to use the sweeper on the seats. Plaster dust gets in your mouth."

"It smells kind of musty in here," I said.

Charlotte ran to the wooden proscenium, then walked up three stairs to the stage. "It's the curtain!" she shouted. Behind her was an enormous velvet curtain as wide as the stage, with folds as deep as storm waves. White, tassled cords hung at either side.

"The curtains once worked electronically," Mina said. "But now that circuit is broken. You'll have to work it by hand."

Charlotte ran back up the aisle. Catching her breath, her face flushed, she said, "If you have to open it, wear a clothespin over your nose. I've been right up next to it, Noah. Auntie says we'll get somebody to clean it. But they'll have to kill it first!"

"Charlotte!" Mina said. "We *will* hire someone. They'll use the proper shampoo and cleaning tools."

Mina raised her hand toward the dome. "It is quite remarkable, don't you think, Noah?" she said dreamily.

Then she turned to more practical matters. "I've put a notice up," she said. "At the Adelaine Electronics School. I've advertised for a projectionist. I'm sure you could easily run the projector, Noah, but I'll need you in the office." She grew contemplative. "I'm just wondering . . . yes. Why don't you take a bus to the electronics school, Noah? It's been ten days since I placed that notice. No applicants have telephoned. You can ask in person. Use your good judgment. Perhaps you'll have some luck. We want to reopen on May first. So we must soon find a projectionist. I've already ordered the movie. It's upstairs. It's called *The Magnificent Seven*."

"Never heard of it," I said.

"You can read about it in the catalog," Mina said. "It's very popular in the U.S. Anyway, it's time you explore a little. It will do you good not to hesitate, to plunge right into the city."

"I've already been on busses," I said. "Been in Toronto less than two hours, and I already rode two busses."

"Yes, you have, haven't you?" Mina said patiently. "I have an excellent street map. It's at home."

"I'll look at it," I said. "I promise."

"Oh, yes," Mina said. "One more thing. I have an announcement of the reopening. I was up half a night working on it. You could take it to the newspaper office."

Mina went into the office and returned with the advertisement, which she handed to me. She had drawn a reasonable facsimile of the front of the theater and placed on it a glamorous silhouette of a dancing couple. "I found the couple in an advertisement from nineteen forty-five," she said, admiring it.

"Okay," I said. "I'll go to the newspaper first. Then to the school. I'll explore, like you say. Mark the places on the map for me, will you?"

"No," Mina said. "Perhaps tomorrow you should look up the locations in the phone book. Take your time. Ride the busses. Acquaint yourself with the city. No matter, Noah, if you get a little lost."

"Let's go home now," Charlotte said.

"Yes, let's," Mina said. "We'll see the upstairs tomorrow."

Mina hugged me and said, "This will work out just fine."

She locked the front door behind us, and we walked a block. Both Charlotte and I held my suitcase handle. We took a bus down College to Palmerston Avenue and from there walked to a corner market. Mina brought lettuce and red peppers. Then we walked to Olive Street.

"There it is," Charlotte said, pointing to number twenty-three.

We walked up the stairs, across the porch, and Mina opened the door. In the hallway was the silent butler. I hung my jacket on it. Glancing into the kitchen, the living room, then down the hallway to where my room was, I said, "I want to see the lion's-feet bathtub you wrote me about."

Charlotte took me by the hand and led me down the hallway. "There," she said, pointing to the tub.

"I need to sit in it a long time," I said. "I about broke my neck trying to find a way to sleep on those trains. I feel achy, too."

"Maybe you're coming down with something," Mina said. "Here, let me see." She placed her palm on my forehead and closed her eyes as though listening. "Perhaps one degree. Not a real fever. It could be from fatigue. Charlotte, please run some hot water for Noah."

Charlotte placed the rubber stopper in the drain and turned on the hot-water spigot. "There's suds in that blue bottle there," she said.

"I don't want *suds*," I said. "Where's the soap?"

"It's in that dish on the shelf," Charlotte said. "See it? The dish shaped like a turtle."

I lifted up the soap dish and examined it. "Didn't I see one just like this next to the kitchen sink?" I said.

Charlotte shut the bathroom door, turned the spigot open farther, and whispered close, "Auntie has two of each trinket like that. She's got two giraffe candle holders; the candles go into their backs. She's got two dish towels with swans on them. She's got two ashtrays with elephant decals. Look around, you'll see what I mean."

"There's only one lion bathtub, though," I joked.

"I never mention *that*," Charlotte said, biting her hand so as not to laugh. She opened the door. "Want to see your room while the tub's filling?" she asked.

"No," I said. "I think I'll take a bath and go in there myself."

Charlotte looked at the suitcase, which was near my feet. "If you can bear to be away from this," she said, "I'll take it to your room."

"Just set it on the bed," I said.

Charlotte left and I closed the door, took off my clothes, and sat in the tub as it filled.

"I'm making a special dish," Mina called in, knocking at the same time. "It'll be about an hour."

My skin was chafed from the changes in air over the past few days—from the clear, chill air of Quill to the dry, stuffy air of the trains, the passengers' cigarette smoke. If the air had confused my skin, the density of people on the street, objects in store windows, had confused my eyes. Trying to take everything in left me with a terrible headache.

I turned off the faucet, eased down in the tub, and placed my feet against the high drain to keep the water in. In the tile-

and-porcelain quiet I rubbed the sides of my head and thought how silence had never been a burden between Pelly and me. We would often sit on the porch and say nothing, an easiness between us, our thoughts settling with their true weight and comfort. I needed that silence now and tried to hold the memory of it as long as I could. But the memory fed my exhaustion, as if I had actually traveled back to Quill. I fell asleep, propped up in the bath, and briefly dreamed of that very thing: Pelly and me sitting on the porch. Until something he said—I could not catch exactly what it was, but his expression was characteristically somber, and the timing of his words, subtle and hilarious —woke me up with my own laughter. I heard Mina puttering around the kitchen. I stood up, toweled myself dry, wrapped the towel around me, and walked to my room. I shut the door and went to the bureau, where I found pajamas and the new comb and brush Charlotte had written me about. By habit I combed my hair back. Then I crawled under the sheet and blankets, drawing them up to my chin, and fell into a deep sleep.

When I woke it was dark outside. I remembered leaving my clothes piled on the bathroom floor, but they were now neatly stacked on the chair near my bed. A plastic nightlight shaped like an owl was plugged into a socket near the door. I knew there was a twin light somewhere in the house. In its vague illumination I saw, on the wall to my right, the two portraits of me, newly framed, that Pelly had done. The pictures were perfectly aligned.

Mina had unpacked my suitcase, folded my shirts, which were stacked on top of the bureau so that I would be able to choose which drawer I wanted them in. The suitcase was in the open closet, where my jacket hung on a wooden hanger. I felt a familiar comfort in Mina's fastidiousness. After looking at the portraits a long time, I got up, dressed, and walked into the kitchen.

Charlotte and Mina sat at the table. Looking at me, Mina said, "I expect you'll want some tea."

"Guess I missed supper," I said apologetically.

Dishes were stacked near the sink. A mushroom-and-onion pie was in a tin on the ledge, a few wedges gone. Some lettuce-and-pepper salad was in a big wooden bowl.

"Sit down, darling," Mina said.

Charlotte stood and brought the pie and salad to the table, where my place had been set.

"I'm hungry," I said.

"You should be," Mina said. "You haven't eaten since break-fast on the train, I imagine."

"It's delicious," I said. "I missed your mushroom pie, Mother. When I smelled it from the bedroom, I remembered when the mail plane used to land, and the pilot would deliver food, and I'd always hope to find mushrooms, because then I'd know we'd have mushroom pie."

"I learned the recipe in Vancouver," Mina said. "As a young girl. And Anthony loved it."

Her voice stalled, and she stared at the tablecloth. After a moment of nervous hesitation, she said, "Noah, I was hoping to wait to ask this. But I know I have to ask it now, or else it'd do bad things inside me until I did ask. I don't wish to know about Anthony. Charlotte showed me your letter where you said that you preferred not to talk about when you last saw him. That's as it should be. But answer one simple question, will you?"

"If I can," I said.

"Do you suppose," Mina said, "that Samuel Bay would tell your father where we are? That is, if Anthony asked him directly, might Samuel say, 'They're in Toronto,' even if that's all he said?"

I swallowed a piece of pie and thought a moment. "It's like this," I said, looking first at Charlotte, then at Mina. "If Anthony asked Sam, Sam wouldn't lie. If he said, 'Do you know where they are?' Sam would feel obliged to say that he did. Which would be the truth. Then if Anthony worded it right— if he said, 'Are they in Toronto?'—because it's surely one of the places you often said you'd like to live in again, Mother— then Sam would probably say, 'Yes, they are.'

"I think Sam would figure that Anthony had the right to try and find us, even if he'd gone and left us like he did. I'm pretty sure that Sam would think to himself, Well, my lying isn't going to make a difference, except that from now on I'd think of myself as a liar. Sam would think straight at it like that, I'd bet."

"I see," Mina said. "It makes sense. Thank you for telling me, Noah."

"Charlotte wrote that you had the feeling Anthony was here, Mother," I said.

Mina fidgeted with the corner of the tablecloth. "It's just a feeling."

"I can say this much," I added. "Sam claimed Anthony wasn't working on the mapping crew anymore. Said he's gotten into some deep trouble, and he wasn't mapping."

"Noah, please—enough," Mina said, raking her fingers through her hair. "I'm tired. I'm going to bed now. Charlotte, you'll finish up with the dishes, please."

"Okay, Auntie," Charlotte said.

Mina stood up and walked around behind me. She kissed the top of my head. "So happy you're here," she said. "*So* happy, darling." Then she walked to her room, shutting the door behind her.

Charlotte tried to spice up the conversation. "I've got a tutor," she said, "who comes in twice a week. She's preparing me for school."

"What's she teach you?"

"She's catching me up. Geography, math, biology. But she says that Auntie did a fine job."

"Did you tell her that?"

"Of *course* I did, Noah," Charlotte said.

Charlotte washed the plates and silverware. Drying the dishes with a towel, she placed them as neatly as Mina would in a plastic drainer with a rubber mat underneath. "I'm going to bed now, too," she said. "Noah, I've got lots to show you here. The market, everything. You glad you'll be working at the cinema?"

"Just a lot to get used to, is all," I said. "You went through it. I know that you still are going through it. Of course I'm happy to be here. Don't be a dummy."

"Good night, Noah," she said, walking to her room, not turning around.

The next morning we sat together and had a breakfast of hot cereal, orange juice, and toast. Mina had two cups of coffee. "What kind of cereal is this?" I said.

"Cream of Wheat," Mina said.

Charlotte stood up from the table.

"Don't you *dare,*" Mina said, obviously sensing what Charlotte had in mind.

But Charlotte could not be stopped. She went straight to a cupboard, held open its door, and said, "Ta-da!" like a ringmaster.

The cupboard was crammed with cereal boxes. "There's Cream of Wheat," Charlotte said, "oatmeal, Rice Krispies, Cheerios, Wheaties, the breakfast of champions; there's—"

"That's quite enough," Mina said. "Perhaps I went a little to excess in my cereal shopping." She tightened her mouth, lowered her face as if trying to force a serious expression, to distract me from her blush of embarrassment.

Charlotte opened a lower cupboard and it, too, was filled with cereals.

"Mother," I said, "what could you have been thinking about? All those!"

"They're not all for eating," Charlotte said.

"Charlotte!" Mina said sternly. "I'll explain to Noah in due time."

"Explain what? Mother, what's wrong with the cereals?"

"Only eat the cereals in the upper cupboard," Charlotte instructed, opening yet a third cupboard above the sink, filled with boxes. "The others have wadded-up dollar bills in them. Some—the Wheaties—have five-dollar bills. The oatmeal has tens. See?"

"I don't get it," I said. "I thought you had a bank account."

"We do," Mina said. "You don't have to *understand* this, Noah. You just have to know that if anything should happen to me . . . if there's an emergency of any sort—listen, now. There's money in the boxes. The bank can't know about it. They can't know I've saved this, or else our monthly loan on the theater will be raised. That's what you have to know, and you'll tell no one. And that's that."

As if looking for money, I slowly poured more Cream of Wheat from the saucer into my bowl, which made even Mina smile a little. Charlotte then noticed the pamphlet, *142 Ways to Be Popular,* in my shirt pocket. Pointing to it, she said, "Did you read any of it?"

"Yes, I did," I said. I took the pamphlet out and placed it on the table. "And right now, before I have to go out into the *city,* I want to read the things I've marked to help me make my way."

Charlotte gobbled her toast, wanting to pay total attention. She folded her hands together and said, "Can't wait."

"All right then," I said, "here they are." I smoothed out the pamphlet with my palm, then showed Charlotte how I had marked in red pencil certain entries under the heading "Especially for Boys." "Number ninety-six: On a date don't be too stingy with money, but don't be too extravagant, either. Number ninety-nine: paint your car purple or bright red or yellow. Number one hundred: Get a sports jacket to match it."

Charlotte was giggling. "Number 101," I said. "Whistle at girls, but be different—whistle symphonies."

"Oh, God," Charlotte said "Now I *know* you can do that!"

"You bet I can," I said, and whistled a few bars of *The Rite of Spring*. "Okay," I continued, "now, there's 102: Make the best grades you possibly can—girls are impressed by men with brains."

"I can't imagine being impressed by a man without a brain," Mina joined in.

"Number 108: Spread the rumor you are a woman hater. It will work in reverse. Now, get this one. Number 112: If your girlfriend wears braces on her teeth, get a set for yourself."

That set Mina laughing to tears.

"Wait, Mother," I said, "there's a list here, 'How to be Popular with Your Parents.' "

"Read a few, Noah," Mina said. "Then we've got things to do."

"Okay," I said, talking faster now. "Number 120: Be interested in the things your father does at his job. Number 133: Try to understand the kind of music your parents like. Number 134: Don't play them out of your house with one particular record. Number 135: If you've done something wrong, be ready to take your punishment. Don't lie your way out of it."

"That's fine, Noah," Mina said, "that's quite enough." All trace of hilarity had drained from her face.

"Number 142. Listen to this one, Charlotte."

"Noah!" Mina said, taking the pamphlet from me and and folding it up.

"Number 142: Indian wrestle with your father and let him win."

We sat in silence a few moments. Then, with a burst of enthusiasm, I said, "Well, I'm going to look up the newspaper and electronics school now. *The Toronto Star*, right?"

"That's correct," Mina said, carrying the dishes to the sink. "I've put the telephone book on the couch, the street map next to it."

I looked up the addresses and jotted them down in the border of the map. Putting on my jacket, I announced, "This is it! Courageous Franklin defies death in the city." Charlotte laughed: Franklin was the famous doomed explorer she wrote me about, whose statue was in front of the school.

"Try and find a reliable person for a projectionist," Mina said. "Time is of the essence, Noah. We'll be at the theater from noon on, all afternoon. You meet us there. We'll be putting stain on the baseboards today. We'll no doubt work into the evening. We'll get something for supper near the theater. All right, darling? Don't forget your key. Did you take the twenty dollars I left on your bureau?"

I checked my pocket, felt the key, the bill, the loose change. "Yes," I said. I clipped the watch to my belt. "So long."

"Don't be shy to ask directions," Mina shouted after me. "Or which bus to take."

While I waited for the bus at Bloor and Palmerston, I saw a mailman unlocking the side door of an iron mailbox. Crouching, he shoveled mail into a gray canvas sack with his hand. I wondered if this was the box Charlotte had mailed her letters from. Though three others waited at the bus stop—a man dressed in work clothes, keys at his hip, a woman clutching a physics textbook, and an older woman holding a leather briefcase—I was suddenly convinced that the mailman was the person I could trust with directions. He must, I figured, have the whole city memorized. He could tell me which bus to take. I waited for him on the sidewalk in front of a florist's. "Excuse me," I said. He stopped halfway between me and the shop, took off his sunglasses, and said nothing. "I need to get to King Street. *The Toronto Star*," I said.

"Sorry," he said with a slight British accent, which I recognized from radio characters. He adjusted the leather strap on his shoulder. "Ask me from Queen's Park to Bickford Ravine,

I'd know every crack in the bloody sidewalk. Every hydrant. Why not ask a cabbie? Or a bus driver?"

"Thanks anyway," I said.

I returned to the stop. When the number 3 bus arrived, I stepped to the back of the short queue and got on, not knowing if it was the right bus. I rode through its entire route, looking out the window, not budging from my seat. I tried to learn the street names: Howland, Albany, Brunswick, Dalton, there were dozens. After an hour we returned to Bloor and Palmerston. The driver turned and looked down the aisle. "This isn't a merry-go-round," he said.

"I'm looking for *The Toronto Star*," I said.

"That's out at King Street. Number eighty, I think. Transfer at St. Joseph's Hospital, then ride down King. I'll call it out."

I sat upright, trying to notch his directions into my memory, following them to save my life: it kept me from feeling totally disoriented. I transferred buses, got off a block from the newspaper, jaywalked across King Street, and went in.

At the information desk, I was directed to the advertising office. In a room full of desks a young woman glanced over. "May I help you?" she said.

She was a year or two older than I, I guessed. She seemed young to be working in such an important, bustling place; I guess that's how it works here, I thought. She had dark brown hair, pale green eyes, and a pleasant, serious tone to her voice. When I said, "I'd like to place an advertisement," she detected I was not from Toronto.

"Are you from the plains or something?" she said. "Saskatchewan?"

"No, Manitoba," I said

"Not Winnipeg," she said, sure of her assessment. "Not the city."

"You're right," I said. "Far north of there. Paduola Lake, Quill."

"Never heard of either," she said. "Well, let me see what you've got there," she said, walking to the counter, her eyes on me the entire time. She turned Mina's artwork toward her. After reading the advertisement she said, "I didn't know The Northern Lights had even closed. There wasn't a fire, was there?"

"Fire? No," I said. "New management. Me. My family, I mean." She was so pretty it made me nervous. "Have you been there? The cinema?"

"Many times," she said, preoccupied with the advertisement, lining it up on a mock-up sheet.

"You don't sit in the back row, do you?" I said, recalling Charlotte's letter describing couples in the back row, kissing. She looked puzzled. I had just met her, and here I had probably insulted her.

"What I meant was," I said haltingly, no doubt making things worse, "I see that you don't wear eyeglasses. So you probably have good eyes and can sit way in the back."

She leaned close. She had pale lipstick on, and I inhaled her light perfume, and my stomach knotted. "I do *not* sit in back," she said, "because girls who sit there are *whores*. At least that's what my mother says." She had a slightly mocking tone now. "I have friends who sit in back. As for me, I like to sit in an aisle seat. I don't like to feel too crowded in."

"You have a lot of ideas about it, I guess."

"Anywhere you sit, there's a chance of having at least three people around you. In front. In back. Next to you. Unless the theater's not crowded. Then it's no problem."

"Unless the theater's not crowded, right."

"See!" she said, stepping back. "Your voice. That's what I mean. The way you say it—the*ater*. Say it."

"Theater," I said obediently.

"See? That's definitely not a city boy talking."

"Guess not."

"You must've seen a lot of movies, being a manager."

"I've never seen one."

She scrutinized my face to see if I might be kidding.

"I'll read the catalog descriptions, though," I said. "In fact, I read one this morning."

She blinked rapidly a few times, gave a short sigh, and said, "Whatever you say." She looked back to the advertisement. "Well, this looks fine." After counting up the words she closed her eyes, mumbled some multiplication, and said, "That'll be six dollars thirty cents a day. How many days do your want it in the paper?"

"Let's see," I said. "Today is April sixteenth. We want to reopen on May first."

"In that case, I suggest you place an ad just a week before. That would be on April twenty-three. It'd be close enough to the opening date that people wouldn't forget. They'll like this ad. It'll catch their eye."

I filled in the amount on a check that Mina had signed and given me, placing it on the counter. Taking the check, she looked at it closely. "By the way," she said, "did the catalog description you read this morning happen to be of the movie"—she looked at the ad—"*The Magnificent Seven?*"

"Yes it was."

"So, what's it about?"

I thought back to the catalog. "Paid gunslingers try to route bandits out of a Mexican town that they're terrorizing."

"How do they do that?"

"I'm not sure. They just know how."

"Okay, that's good enough for me. I'll go."

She kept looking at me. I hesitated, then said, "I have a free ticket. It's called complimentary." I reached into my pocket and dug it out.

She did not say a word.

"What I meant was," I said, "it doesn't have to be for *The Magnificent Seven*. This ticket's good for any night, for a year."

"Want me to find someone to offer it to?" she said flatly, looking around at the people in her office, then back at me.

"No!" I said. "No—no, here's two tickets. Two complimentary tickets."

"No thanks," she said. She shook her head slowly back and forth and sighed. "One will be fine, thanks." She plucked the ticket from my hand.

"That's okay. You're welcome."

"You have to sign the receipt for the ad," she said.

I signed it. Turning the receipt toward her, she read it. "Noah Krainik," she said. "Well, pleased to meet you. I've never met a manager of a cinema before. My name's Mariya Ludovic."

We quickly shook hands. "Where's your name from?" I said.

"It's Yugoslav. Mariya was my great-aunt's name. Family favorite."

"I heard a Yugoslav soccer game once. Over the radio. Yugoslavia versus England."

"And?"

"And what?"

"Who won?"

"I forget. Some static erased it, I think."

Mariya looked disappointed.

"But Yugoslavia was ahead three goals."

She half frowned, turned away, and said over her shoulder, "Good-bye, Mr. Krainik." She sat at her desk and began typing.

Back on the street I walked to the bus stop, then boarded a bus for Bloor Street, transferring according to the map at Dupont. Some blocks down Dupont, I got off at Harbord and walked to a district of quonset hut warehouses, binderies, and leatherworks near Central Technical School. On Croft, above the door of a wooden building with a sheet metal roof, a sign read ADELAINE SCHOOL OF ELECTRONICS, founded 1925, and had a painting of a man working the wiring of a house, a leather pouch full of screwdrivers attached to his belt. Chimes went off when I opened the door. Inside was a vacant receptionist's desk. In a haphazard pile of papers, I saw Mina's notice:

PROJECTIONIST WANTED
THE NORTHERN LIGHTS THEATRE
(call afternoons)
863-1320

No wonder the notice had gone unanswered, I thought. I tacked it up on a bulletin board full of other job notices and events.

I walked down the corridor and looked into the first room. Four metal cabinets, their lowest drawers open, were to my right. In their compartments were some items I recognized from studying catalogs: tumbler switches, sockets, voltmeters, fuses. On three walls were pegboards holding pincers, pliers, and electrician's scissors. Two metal-topped tables had radios on them, in various states of repair. A class had probably been in session. Metal-legged stools surrounded the tables. A green chalkboard was covered with equations and diagrams. I walked to a table, took up a thick manual, and began paging through it.

"Lunchtime, now," someone said from the doorway in familiar clipped speech. "Nobody, is here."

I turned and saw a man in a black T-shirt, denim jacket, jeans, and western boots, a pack of cigarettes in his breast pocket, eating a doughnut. He was not tall, but solidly built, and he stood in that stiff posture, looking sideways and down, in a manner I had seen in so many Cree men. His black hair was combed up and back, greased on the sides, tied back in a small ponytail.

"What you doing?" he said, glancing about. "Want, to be a *student?*"

"No. Looking for a projectionist. My family owns a movie theater. Called The Northern Lights."

"Ain't been."

"We're opening it up on May first."

"Never been to a movie. My wife, either. My daughters, them, either. We don't go. How much is it?"

"Fifty cents. How old are your daughters?"

"One's seven, one's just past two."

"Two-year-old gets in free."

"Seven-year-old, if she'd get in free, I'd take us."

"She can't."

"Then screw it, nobody goes."

"Well, think about it."

"I won't."

We stood looking at each other a moment. "Are you Cree?" I said.

"Cree—right," he said. "Right. Name is Levon Makowisite."

I thought hard, trying to hear Hettie's voice in my mind. "Means something like uses two hands?" I said.

Levon held out his hands, turning them slowly, showing his palms, then making fists. "Uses both, each good as each," he said.

"Ambidextrous, it's called," I said. "You must be good with tools."

"I got the name 'cause I was clumsy. Parents hoped it'd help, eh? Now, I'm learning, wiring. They'd laugh, maybe, 'cept they're dead."

"Sorry . . . well, my name's Noah. Noah Krainik."

"Noah," Levon said, mulling the name over. "He's the one, took a bunch of animals, out on a boat, eh? Had a lot of 'em to eat. Ate some he'd never ate before. More went out on his boat, than came back. Ate two of each. Even ate snake. Wandered a long time, long time."

"Is that how you heard it?"

"Yeah, my grandmother. She got it from, some preacher, the story. Is how she told it."

"I heard it a different way. But yours makes better sense."

"Where you from, that you know some language?"

"Quill—north Manitoba."

"Me—I'm from North Knife. Was."

"I know where it is."

"Yeah? Was."

He finished eating his doughnut. "Need coffee," he said. "The machine." He turned and disappeared into the corridor. I followed, past five more classrooms on either side, and saw Levon putting a coin in the machine at the end of the corridor. He pressed the button that indicated Black, then one that indicated Sugar. The coffee poured from a plastic spout into a paper cup. "Got to hold these fuckin' things right, at the rim," he said. "Else fingers'll burn. Spill it. I done that, few times."

Levon blew into the coffee and took a sip. "Projection, what?" he said.

"Projectionist," I said. "It's what throws the movie onto the screen."

"That's projector. I read about it. Studied it. I could, fix one. Could run one. I'll take it."

"Take what?"

"The job."

"Wait a second, Levon. Did you ever run a projector?"

"Could fix one," he said, gulping down his coffee, wincing from how hot it was. "So, could run it easy. I accept. When do I start?"

"You ever seen a projector?"

"It's got parts, don't it? Got a place to put, the movie in. Got a light, don't it? Can you run it?"

"I haven't tried."

"So, how you know then, maybe you can. Shee-it, ever think of that?" He turned back to the machine. He pounded his fist against it, then kicked it. Then he pounded it with one fist and at the same time pressed the coin-return lever with his other hand. A few coins jangled down. Levon turned to me and grinned. "Ambidextrous," he said. Turning back to the machine, he inserted a coin, punched the Black and Sugar buttons again, and watched the new cup fill.

"Tell you what," I said. "You come with me to the cinema. You meet my mother. Her name's Mina. Tell her you want to work the projector. See what she says. That's the best I can do."

"That's good enough," Levon said. He took out a cigarette, lit it with a metal lighter, took two quick draws, then offered it to me.

"No, thanks," I said. Then, "Okay—" I took one deep draw, exhaled, coughed a few times.

He extinguished it against the machine, then returned it to his jacket pocket.

"Let's go, then," I said.

"Can't now. More work here, to do, eh? So, I'll be there, when?"

"Tomorrow. In the afternoon. How about that?"

"Sometime, after twelve o'clock, eh?"

"Right."

"Northern Lights, okay."

"You want to know where it is?"

"Somewhere, in town, right?"

"Yeah."

"I'll get there."

"See you then."

I walked down the corridor and when I got near the receptionist's desk turned to look back. Levon was standing with one hand outstretched against the machine, waiting for a third cup.

The next afternoon Mina, Charlotte, and I were at work, staining the baseboards near the concession stand. On newspaper we slid along a can of stain and some rags. Each of us used a thin brush. Charlotte had her transistor radio tuned to a rock-and-roll station. Just after three o'clock there was a knock on the door. "I'll see who it is," I said. I had mentioned to Mina that someone interested in the job might stop by.

Out in the lobby four people stood on the street side of the door: Levon, an Indian woman of similar age, and two Indian girls—this had to be his family. Several bulging canvas laundry sacks, a large suitcase, and a smaller one were on the sidewalk. Levon held an electric hotplate, its cord dangling.

"Is that our prospect?" Mina called.

"Yes, it is," I said. "Charlotte, turn down the radio, will you?"

I opened the door and Levon's family walked in, luggage and all, but stayed near the door. The girls clung to their mother's legs, shyly pressing faces to her jeans. Levon's wife had long, smooth black hair, a somewhat angular face with striking black eyes, deeply brown skin. "This, is Philomene," Levon said. "That there, is Rosie." He touched the top of the older girl's head. Rosie was thin, with short hair clipped straight across her forehead, lighter-skinned than Philomene, but darker than her sister, who now began wandering around the lobby, finally sitting on the floor next to a couch, looking at us. "That's Sandy," Levon said.

Sandy, a chubby, round-faced girl, then stood up and walked to Charlotte and Mina, who stood out in the lobby now, staring at Levon. Sandy had on a pair of jeans, a sweat shirt, and for some reason pink rain galoshes. She then walked to the can of stain, stuck her entire left hand into it, and held it to the wall.

"No!" Mina yelled.

Sandy froze, but did not cry. Using a cloth, Mina wiped her hand clean. When Mina lifted her, she started to cry. Mina delivered her to Philomene, and Sandy clutched her mother's leg again.

"Noah, would you mind explaining?" Mina said sharply, keeping her eyes set on Levon's family. "Who, may I ask, are these people?"

"Levon, Philomene, Sandy, Rosie, I'd like you to meet my mother, Mina. That's my cousin, Charlotte. Mother, Levon's who I said is interested in the job. I met him at the electronics school."

Philomene was obviously going through difficulties of comprehension. I think she was translating, English to Cree, to herself. Her face showed perceptions and responses. Once those things registered, were actually absorbed, she took on an expression of tranquillity, as if a more profound thought blossomed in her mind. Rosie, now racing around the lobby, peering in at the candies, running in and out of the bathrooms, twice detoured back to Philomene, touching her knees like in a game of tag, as if to be reassured by Philomene's upright posture.

"Okay, so now I know everyone's name," Mina said. She was not harsh, just bewildered. "Why the four of them, Noah? Why the luggage? Are they on the way to the train? Going to visit relatives?"

"You got coffee, here?" Levon asked politely. He looked around the lobby.

"No, we don't," Mina said. "Noah, will you please answer my question?"

"The thing is, Mother," I said. Now both girls were again huddled against Philomene's leg. "I said that Levon could meet you. He knows how to work a projector. That's about all I know."

"Hot water, what about that?" Levon asked. "I got coffee, in my bag here. If you can just—you drink tea, eh?" Levon lifted up the hotplate.

"We have water," Charlotte offered.

"Good," Levon said. "Good thing for that."

Levon walked behind the concession stand and plugged in the

hotplate. Rosie opened a suitcase, taking out a kettle, which she handed to Charlotte. Charlotte filled the kettle, returned, and handed it to Levon. Levon placed the kettle on the hotplate, then stood next to Philomene. Sandy wandered off again, this time down the aisle toward the screen.

"I work here," Levon said, "you have to, get me a percolator, eh?"

"Look," Mina said pointing, "are these all your worldly belongings?"

"Can't say *worldly*."

"This morning," Mina said, "were these things in your house?"

"Can't say it was exactly, a house. One room. A sink."

"So, you've been out looking for a new home, and you thought you'd stop by to interview for the job, right?"

"You need a projectionist," Levon said, carefully enunciating each word. "To work the movie, projector, eh? I can do that. I can work it good. Now, you don't got to look, no more. Know what I mean?"

"No, what?" Mina said, tapping her foot rapidly. "What else can you tell me?"

"I don't want money, for the job."

"I see," Mina said. "Noah, did you hear what your friend said? He doesn't wish to be paid. Quite unusual, don't you think?" she said with some suspicion.

"Sounds interesting, doesn't it?"

"Continue," Mina said.

"I ain't seen it, yet," Levon said. "But I figure, the room that got the projector in it, got to be bigger than what we been living in, eh? Can't hardly be smaller."

The kettle whistled. Philomene, holding both her daughters' hands, walked to it.

"Paper cups are in the cupboard under the counter," Charlotte said.

Philomene located a cup, poured hot water into it. She reached into her black purse, drawing out a paper bag. Opening the bag, she emptied some coffee into a cup, stirring it with a pencil that had been lying on the counter. She then carried the cup to Levon. Levon reached into his back pocket, took out a packet of sugar, which he tore open and emptied into the cup. Now, taking the cup from Philomene, he looked at Mina. "I figure it out, this way," he said. "It don't cost you—nothing. I notice you got a ladder, out back."

"The fire escape?" Mina said.

"Yeah, it. We can come and go, up the ladder. Don't have to bother nobody. Nobody, has to see us. No customers, come to watch a movie, eh?"

"What you're suggesting," Mina said. "Correct me if I'm wrong. What you intend to do is live, with your entire family, in the projection room. Eat and sleep there."

"What else?" Philomene said matter-of-factly. It was the first time she had spoken. "What else to do, in a home?"

"This is ridiculous," Mina said. "Who's asking the questions here? Who's interviewing whom? Noah?"

"It could work, Mother."

"Absolutely not."

"No problem," Levon said. "None."

"It can't possibly work," Mina said. "There's city codes. There's proper housing and improper housing."

"Where we were," Philomene said. "Tiny room, all of us in it. That's improper house. Upstairs, here, we sleep, we eat. Will be quiet. Don't disturb the movie, when it's going on."

"Noah," Mina pleaded, "could you kindly explain to your friends here—"

"Show me the machine," Levon said.

Philomene, again trailed by her daughters, went to refill Levon's cup. "Up them stairs, eh?" Levon said.

"Yeah, upstairs," Charlotte said. "Let's go!" I could tell Charlotte already was taken by the idea of Levon's family living in the projection room. This irked Mina, who grimaced at me but said nothing.

Then Mina said, "I have nameless feelings about this, Noah. Nameless because if I named them, you'd hear words you don't want to hear. I'm holding you responsible."

"Let's go up," I said, hurrying toward the stairs to the left of the theater door.

Mina climbed the steps behind me, and when I got to the top I turned around to find her stopped, with Philomene close behind, balancing the steaming cup in front of her. "Good children, you got," Philomene said.

Mina seemed disarmed. "Thank you," she said, "they are indeed." She turned and saw me at the top of the stairs. "Noah, this has gone quite far enough."

"Let's see what happens."

In the projection room Rosie was scuffing her foot over the rug, a large rectangle of carpet left over from the lobby. She then touched static to Sandy's nose. "Stop," Philomene said, entering the room just after Mina. "She can catch, fire. Hold still now." Both girls stood still a moment, then sat down on folding chairs, looking at the floor. Philomene handed the coffee to Levon.

Levon began to inspect the projector. Mina leaned against a wall. Charlotte stood next to Levon, looking at the inside of the machine. About ten feet behind the projector was a table equipped for rewinding film. Philomene hoisted Sandy up and, making a pillow from her jacket, laid her down to take a nap. Meanwhile, Levon, repair manual in one hand, coffee in the other, took a mumbled inventory of the projector's parts, moving through them all with the precision of a watchmaker. "Picture gate," he said knowingly, which did not convince Mina, who stood shaking her head with an expression of grave doubt. "Yeah, there, it is," Levon said, putting the cup on top of the machine. "It's projector lens."

"Congratulations," Mina said.

"Take-off spindle," Levon said. "Deflecting roller with control." He was reading from the manual, double-checking parts.

"Now that you've named things," Mina said, "can you work it? The film is in that container, next to your daughter on the desk."

"No problem."

He got the case, lifted out the film on its spool, which he then attached to the sprocket. Meticulously following the manual, he threaded the film through the machine, finally attaching it to the empty take-up reel. "Turn out lights," he said.

"Hold on," Mina said. "The curtain is closed."

"I'll get that," I volunteered.

"Hold your nose," Charlotte said.

I hurried out of the room, down the stairs, and into the theater. At the end of the center aisle, I turned right and walked up onto the stage. I located the curtain rope. The curtain smelled like a ten-thousand-year-old moose hide. I kicked it and dust burst out, making me cough. I pulled the cord, and it creaked the curtain along its runners. The curtain was heavy, and I had to lean back, one foot against the proscenium wall. Finally the curtain was open, the huge screen revealed.

"Okay!" I shouted toward the projection room. "Ready!"

I walked down from the stage and sat in the front row. In a few seconds the picture appeared. There was dramatic music, then the title, *The Magnificent Seven*, in bold letters. Then the actors' names: Yul Brynner, Steve McQueen, Robert Vaughn, Eli Wallach . . .

But just as I settled to watch, the machine shut off and the screen went white.

I ran back up the aisle, then upstairs to the projection room.

"Now," Mina said, "we've seen that Levon can work the projector. Fine. That's fine. But this is not a rooming house. This is a cinema. A respectable business."

The room was silent. Everyone looked at Mina, who glanced

along our faces. She turned her lips in on themselves, sighed deeply, then said, "Levon, tell me, how did you make a living? How have you been living?"

"Saved up, is all," Levon said, and cast a challenging look.

"All right," Mina said. "All right—" She hesitated. "Is it possible I'm about to say what I'm about to say?" She closed her eyes.

"Look," Levon said, "we don't want no handouts." He held a firm pose, feet planted wide apart. "It's a good deal, eh? We live here. Work the machine. Don't cost you, nothing. Real quiet life, up here, that's it. Save you lots of money, eh? Plus—we use them stairs, out back."

"I'll agree to this," Mina said, "on a *temporary* basis. But—" She turned toward me. "I am decidedly *not* convinced."

"Tell you, what," Levon said. "I'm gonna offer, help out *even* more." He looked out the fire escape window. "This goddamn city, like to kill you in ways, if you let it. So I—"

"Levon!" Mina said. "Your language . . . "

Levon stopped talking, wrinkled his brow in annoyance, stared at Mina. "Your son here," he said, "I can already hear, that he talks like you. Sounds like you. Same with me. I talk, just like my mother."

He took out his partially smoked cigarette, lit it, took a few puffs, offered it around the room. Only Philomene had a brief smoke. Extinguishing the cigarette, he returned it to its pack. "This room," he said, "it's 'bout I guess three times the size that place we had. All we got to do, maybe buy some cots. Kids can use toilets downstairs. Take baths in the sinks. You know, after customers, they go home. Or, before they get here. Got all day for kids to wash up, eh? Keep it nice and clean."

"You were saying," Mina said, "about helping out."

"Right," Levon said. "I don't know sure, but I guess that Noah ain't been here too long. I take it on me, to show him around. Once we move in, even before we get cots, or get a percolator."

"I'll contribute that," Mina said, blushing at her own acquiescence.

"Soon as we get set up," Levon said. "Can do that in a couple hours, eh? After supper, I take Noah out."

Philomene, who had made three trips downstairs while we talked, was already unpacking. Rosie began to rearrange items in the room, clearing a space for cots, moving a small table over near the desk. It was as if they'd had a lot of practice.

"I suppose it's an equal exchange," Mina said. "Your work for the room."

"Equal, yeah. No problem," Levon said, turning to help Philomene with the clothes, which she was stacking neatly in a corner. "We get set up here, eh? Don't want to disturb your work, downstairs."

Mina, Charlotte, and I left the room, walked downstairs, and finished staining the baseboards without a word. By the time Levon and his family came down, we had worked our way to the other side of the lobby. Both girls were dressed in patched-up nightgowns. Rosie held a bar of soap and two towels. Sandy rubbed her eyes from sleep.

"She must have been tired," Mina said.

"I'm gonna get them baths, now," Philomene said. "Which room, sinks?"

"The ladies' room," Mina said. "That one, over there." Philomene and the girls went in.

"We're set up," Levon said. "Maybe get cots, tomorrow."

Charlotte said, "We're getting take-out sandwiches for supper. Want some? We're going to eat here, then finish up."

"No," Levon said. "I'll get some supper, get it someplace else."

"It's fine, Levon," Mina said. "We won't make it a practice, but this time, as you've only just moved in, it will be fine if we provide supper. The girls are in their nightgowns. You don't want to go out to eat. . . . "

"No problem," Levon said. "Getting food, some other place, eh? Maybe Noah wants, to go with me, eh? Show him around."

"When are you going?" I said.

"A while."

"Mother," I said, "I think I'll go with Levon. Meet you back home."

Mina looked skeptical. But she had said that I should explore the city, so not wanting to contradict herself, she said, "Fine. Yes, it would be nice if you showed Noah around. Where were you thinking of going? The market? Downtown?"

Levon thought about it, then said, "Parks."

"Parks," Mina said. "I see. The skating rink?"

"I was more, thinking—Humbert Marshes. Then, High Park. Grendadier Pond, maybe."

Disquieted, Mina said, "I understand, Levon, certain places in the parks may not be safe at night. Is that your understanding?"

"We ain't going to *them* places, no way," Levon said emphatically. "No way, not going nowhere police find us in trouble."

"That's reassuring," Mina said, smiling wanly. "Well, then. Noah, it sounds like you'll have a nice time. In the parks."

When Philomene appeared with her daughters, the whole family went back upstairs.

"Perhaps Charlotte and I will have a chance to talk with Philomene a bit," Mina said.

"Well, yeah," Levon said. "The thing is, Philomene, she don't much like. To talk. But she can listen, if *you* wanna talk. She don't talk much, though. 'Specially at night. Both her parents, they were like that. Brother, him, too. Sister, her, too."

"We'll simply leave her alone, then," Mina said. "If Philomene or your daughters want to be sociable, fine. If not, fine, too."

The moment Levon and his family were gone, Mina whispered through clenched teeth, "This is not an orphanage. If there's one single bit of trouble, Noah, they'll have to leave. Is that understood?"

"Got it," I said, feigning a casual manner. "But look, they've already moved in. We've got Levon now, and we save money, not having to pay him."

"*That* I don't like, either," Mina said. "One could begin to feel responsible. To feel obligations toward them. We know so little about them, Noah. Besides, if a person works, he should be paid. I'll work out a wage. Perhaps for my own benefit more than Levon's, I don't know. Still, I won't ask them rent."

"I know it's unusual," I said, "but it might just work out better than you think."

"Charlotte," Mina said, "would you go and fetch sandwiches, potato salad, and lemonade, and some plastic forks, over at Delano's grocery?" She handed Charlotte some money, and Charlotte walked to the street.

Back in about fifteen minutes, Charlotte set the food on one of the couches. She got paper cups, then poured lemonade into each. We ate the sandwiches, potato salad, and marble cakes, which Charlotte had chosen for dessert.

After dark, about 9:30 P.M., Levon walked in the front door. Mina said, "When we're here, Levon, and there's no customers, it's perfectly all right to use the inside stairs."

"I like, the fire escape," he said. "Noah, you 'bout ready?"

I stood up and said, "See you at home."

It was my first night out in the city, and Levon and I walked out to College Street. But Levon was not interested in taking in the sights. He walked fast. Past shops. Past store windows, mannequins. Apartment buildings with tall entranceways. I fell a few steps behind and did not protest.

On a block of almost identical Tudor houses, he suddenly stopped. "Look at them houses," he said, somewhat derisively. "Plenty room, to walk around. Meals, in one room. Sleeping, in another room. Talking, in another, eh?"

We walked at least half an hour through residential blocks without exchanging a word. We turned down Wright St. toward High Park, where we found a padlocked iron gate with a sign reading PARK CLOSED 10:00 P.M. I checked my watch, which read 10:30. When I looked up, Levon was deftly negotiating the spiked top of the gate, then vaulted down to the other side. I did the same, but slower, and caught my jacket on a spike, clumsily ripped it loose, and thudded hard to the cement, barely keeping balance. I recalled High Park as a green area on the map, which I took out of my pocket. "Just want to see where we are," I said.

"Don't need no map," Levon snapped. He pointed to his forehead. "Got it all in here."

The entrance sidewalk, rimmed with antique gaslights flickering shadows, was met by several dirt paths with manicured edges that wound over brief lawns into the trees. "This one," Levon said, and veered down the second left-hand path, walking fast. A tree or bush gave off a damp, sweet odor, which made me notice that some of the trees had plaques with Latin names. The familiar smell of spruce was in the air as well. A tar bicycle route ran parallel to the path a while, then wound off through birch and beech.

We arrived without seeing another soul at Grendadier Pond. At one end was a trickling creek, which we followed into yet another woods. There we came to a bench. "Sit," Levon said. We both sat down. "There's a footbridge," he said. "Other side of them trees."

"Yeah?"

"Listen for the planks."

"Planks?"

207

"Two are loose."

"Then what?"

"Then, get into the trees."

"Who is it?"

"Park cop, bastard, knows my face. Caught me once. One night."

"Doing what?"

"Same as we're doing now."

We sat looking through a clearing at the steamy pond, until we heard the planks rattle under heels. Levon was up and gone, and I crouched and followed his shape behind some manicured bushes. A policeman, whose face I could barely discern through the maze of twigs and tiny leaves, appeared near a bench. He propped a foot up, flicked a match across his heel, and lit a cigarette. I saw the end glow and disappear. My blood beat fast with the tension in the air; it was as if a fierce, silent argument transpired between Levon and this anonymous figure. Levon made two fists and was breathing unevenly. I felt in all of this like Levon's younger brother, one he had little patience with, one he was stuck with.

"What'd he do when he caught you?" I whispered.

"No fuckin' talk," he said, his voice strained.

The policeman disappeared back over the bridge. We heard his heels again on the planks.

Silently Levon stood up, assessing the darkness in the direction of the footbridge. "Gone," he said.

I followed as he threaded his way along the creek until it reached a small pond. Flat stones led up from the water. Crouching at the edge, Levon counted, "One, two," going along the stones. "Three . . ." He lifted the third stone; under it, a length of black fishing line was staked to a twig. He tugged the line, lifting out a small, fat fish. "These kind," he said, "go for bread dough." He removed the hook from a bony lip. "Good fish to nightline. See, if it's caught, it don't thrash around. Just stays still, dumb like."

"What kind is it?" It was light gold with white splotches, bulged eyes, delicate fins and tail, gills pumping.

Levon laid it on the ground, securing it with his foot. "Don't know," he said. He took out a jackknife, sharpening it on a stone. Then, in a quick, expert way he cut off the fish's head. Its mouth puckered, bubbled, locked open. Levon took a plastic bag from his satchel, put the fish body in it, and put the bag back in the satchel, which was lined with newspaper. "Clean the guts out later," he said.

"How do these taste?"

"Like liver," Levon said, curling back his upper lip in harsh disapproval. "Don't know what people here feed 'em."

He baited the hook with a tightly rolled piece of dough. Then he punctured the fish eyes with the knife, rubbed its fluid on the dough, and put the fish head in a second bag, which also went into the satchel. Lightly tossing the line into the pond, he said, "Let's go."

We hurried farther into the woods, emerging at a meadow with a baseball diamond at the far end. One light shone from the backstop fence onto the infield, but the outfield was mostly dark. For a while we stood among the trees, just listening. Then Levon led me across to the fence, which arced the entire width of the outfield. He opened his satchel, taking out a mousetrap with a spring-lock bar thick as a belt buckle. He baited the trap with cheese stuck into dough, set it near the fence, sifting crushed peanuts all around the trap. "This don't usually take a whole night," he said. "Them ground squirrels. Chipmunks, they call 'em, here. Lots of 'em. This place, the Spediva Ravine, everywhere."

Levon repeated the trapping procedure at four different fenceposts.

"That way," he said.

We walked over to the dugout and stepped down into it. It stank of leather oil and urine. Levon sat down on the bench, reached into his satchel again, taking out a thermos. He unscrewed the top, then filled it with coffee. Sipping, he looked at me. "Want some?"

"Not now," I said.

He looked out at the field. "Movie popcorn," he said. "Them hard little kernels. Be real good for chipmunks. And them bigger squirrels, at the ravine." Levon nodded to himself and poured more coffee.

"How can you drink so much coffee?" I said. "Doesn't it make you nervous or something?"

"Makes me calm," he said, taking two deep gulps, then closing his eyes. "Now," he said. "Listen for them chipmunks."

"You *hear* them?" I said.

"Only if nobody's talking."

The field rang with crickets, and every so often a night bird called in an odd arrangement of notes followed by a brief, slurred whistle.

"Look, you offered to bring me here."

"Probably a mistake, eh?"

I looked at Levon, who appeared to be sleeping. His eyes were closed, his breathing steady, his head nodded slightly to one side. But then, talking slowly, like a somnambulist, he said, "They make these little screams."

"The chipmunks."

"Good thinking."

An hour went by, then another. Trying to get comfortable on the bench reminded me of the nights on the train. Shifting slightly, straightening up, Levon finished the coffee.

"Did you come direct from North Knife?"

"You're talking," Levon said.

"That's right, talking."

"You want to talk, okay. No—didn't. Not direct. We lived in cars, a while. In between places. North Knife, Flin Flon. I fixed up junk cars, engines, eh? Pretty good mechanic. Fixed up a Buick once, fixed it up fine. Big car, that one. Lived a

summer in it. Drove it, too. Then Philomene, she says, either
we drive it back north, or drive it south."

Levon fell silent again. Then, bolting upright, he said.
"That's it."

"What?"

He shot me a dismissive look of pity, placed the thermos in
his satchel, and ran from the dugout to the fence, me close on
his heels. Starting on his left, he checked the traps. At the last
one he stopped and said, "Got one." Moving quickly, he removed it from the trap. "Hold it," he ordered.

It was warm, and blood beaded at its mouth. The bar had
broken its neck. Levon returned the trap to his satchel, then
collected the other traps, carefully unsetting each one. Without
speaking he set out running across the infield again, back toward the path leading to the park gate. I caught up with him at
the gate. "Let's get to Humbert Marshes," he said. He tossed
his satchel over the gate, onto the grass. We both climbed over.
"Can't be long, there. Philomene, the girls, in a new place, eh?
First—we get a duck."

"Duck?"

"Yeah, you heard of 'em, right?"

"Matter of fact, Levon, I have. Seen plenty. Eaten plenty.
Even made decoys."

"Look—I ain't enjoying this *talk*."

After another hour's walking, I said, "You angry at me or
something? What'd I do? I got you a job, didn't I?"

"I had a job, to give," Levon snapped. "We met up with each
other, is what happened. You keep thinking of it as a *favor*, you
keep thinking of it wrong. You know that private shit, you asked
me about before? Where I'm from? Down the line, some weeks,
maybe I tell you something. Might talk with you. But I don't
owe you facts about me, eh? You ain't family. In North Knife,
I was already a person closed up, and the city here, it closed me
up more. Tell you what. Just make up whatever you want to

think, about me, about Philomene, all of us. Consider what you make up, the truth. Got it? Made-up truth's better than not any, 'specially if it's all you got."

Touring me through his nighttime haunts—his territories— was a basic reciprocity, an exchange between families. Come daylight that obligation would be taken care of. And it would not surprise me if Levon's family kept their thoughts, their sufferings, entirely to themselves in the projection room. I supposed that going on that way, our families working in the same building but having little other contact, was better than any false encouragement about friendship, better than not knowing where one stood. After all, Indian-white relations in Quill had been much like that. I would have to draw my understanding of their travails from the dozens of stories I heard up north about Indian life in the cities. Men on alcoholic jags, some ending in death. Or suicide. Few able to find work. Indian kids growing up not speaking any language well. Families crammed into tenements. Cut off from home. Not able to go back; sometimes not welcome back. Other times coming home and finding the readjustment equally impossible. Foundering between worlds, no-man's-land.

Humbert Marshes were a series of weed-choked lily ponds rimmed with cattails among several large, open ponds. There was a ravine to one side, a scenic lookout with a bench, drinking fountain, and pay telescope, which Levon led me to. "Got a quarter?" he said. I searched in my pocket, came up with one, and handed it to him. He slid it into the telescope slot. Focusing the scope, he located the dock, which was lit by two lights covered by tinted glass. "That's it," he said. "Duck pond. Take a look."

Through the scope, in the hazy light of the dock, I saw a sign that read: PADDLE WHEEL RIDES $2.00 PER HOUR. A number of paddle-wheel boats, with slat seats and oval shells with huge clown faces, were moored there.

When I looked up, Levon had already dug his heels in, leaned back on his hands, and begun sliding down the rocky incline. I followed suit, scraping my hands, finally near the bottom just letting go entirely, tumbling hard to a stop. Levon did not help me up. His mind was on the ducks. "Best," he said, "to come at 'em from in the water."

The pond smelled of rotten weeds, and a breeze brought in fumes of boat oil and gasoline, though we could not see any motorboats, and heard only the mutter and throaty clicking of ducks. As we approached, they stirred, moving in clusters among the paddleboats.

Taking off his shoes, pants, and shirt, Levon said, "You wait in a boat. Count—to fifty. Then knock on the bottom of the boat, eh? It'll make the ducks, come over for a look."

"Yeah, but listen. Let me get this duck, okay?"

"If you miss," he said, "my family's got what? Fuckin' liver-tasting fish, a bony fuckin' chipmunk. Ain't got no refrigerator, like you, eh?"

Removed as we were from the north, I still remembered how my acquaintance, Johnny Makinaw, showed Pelly and me how to ambush ducks. One way was to get them curious but stay out of sight. Now it was I who stripped off my clothes. Levon dressed again and slid into a paddleboat. He lay flat and said, "Okay—go ahead."

I slipped into the water and made my way through ankle-deep muck to a place I could crouch under the dock. Holding my breath, I dipped down, emerging under the dock, where I breathed air thick with wood rot. Moving sideways, I went under again, coming up behind a gathering of ducks, who were between the boat and me. In a moment Levon was tapping the side of the boat and scraping it with the heel of his hand, making a sandpaper noise. At first the ducks squabbled, some furiously paddling out from the dock. But as Levon kept up the noises, a few grew curious and maneuvered close. Soon two mallards were nuzzling the bow, inspecting it. I moved closer, only my head above water. From a few feet away, I slid under and shot up, actually lifting one duck on my shoulder, which flapped away squawking, while gripping the other by a scaly leg.

It went berserk. I tried clutching its neck, but its thrashing made that impossible. Suddenly I saw Levon on the dock. He leaned out and, grabbing the duck from me, twisted its neck hard three times until it became still.

At the dock's end was chaos, ducks skittering across the water, flapping away, an outburst of duck noises. Levon ran back to the trees and sat panting against one. Mud-soaked, I joined him, drying myself as best I could with my jacket.

"Cops don't come down, here much," he said as I got back into my clothes. "Good thing for that. That there, was 'bout the worst I ever seen it done. Next time, I'm here by myself, eh?"

I was ashamed and found little humor in it, but I recalled what Job Walks once told me and said it out loud to Levon: "A person who has bad luck in hunting gets to eat right along with everyone else."

For the first time Levon smiled, even started to laugh. "You remember just what you need to, eh? From up in Quill." Rubbing his eyes, he said, "Okay, come back—you're invited."

We made the long walk to The Northern Lights in silence, a chill in the air, me holding a muddy jacket, Levon with the fish, ground squirrel, and duck in his satchel. We walked in the shadows of apartment buildings, under the glare of streetlights, police cars slowing down to have a look, then moving on, empty streets, walked up a fire-escape stairway into a room above a movie theater, where two sleepy-eyed Cree girls were warming their hands over the coiled heat of a hotplate.

At the sight of her father, Rosie hopped up and down. Even though we weren't over the dome, when the floor shook I wondered from which mural figure plaster had loosened.

"He's here, for supper," Levon said.

Philomene just nodded, taking the satchel from him. She set the satchel on the table, opened it, and Rosie and Sandy crowded around it. I had seen this so many times in Quill: men pulling beaver over the snow by ropes attached to pegs through the animals' noses. A satchel full of cold-stiffened hare. Sleds packed with moose meat. The Cree children crowding around, excited. The women lifting enormous pickerel and lake trout by the gills, carrying them to a cleaning place by the fire. Talking. Laughing. A big meal in the works.

Levon looked at me. "Make up what you want," he said. "But what we got—it's right in front of you. No problem."

While Philomene began expertly to shear the duck, I saw by my watch that it was 3:30 A.M. A bus heaved by, and I was startled that they ran so late. And then the phone rang downstairs. "Been ringing, for half the night," Philomene said.

Clearly, she'd had no intention or interest in answering it. The ringing was an intrusion to her, so I ran down to the office two steps at a time. "Hello?"

"I was about to call the police." Mina's angry voice trembled.

"I'm here," I said. "Things just—I was out walking. With Levon. And I just got back, and now I'm going to have some supper. I'm okay, Mother. Fine. Can't believe it, but I'm really hungry. Guess I'll sleep on a couch, okay?"

There was a silence on the line. "Noah," Mina finally said, "we highly disapprove. We were worried sick."

"Then we've all got a problem here, Mother. Let's talk about it later, okay?"

"You've spent all of two nights in our house."

"I'm afraid to ride a bus this time of night."

"Fine, stay there. Two nights at home, one night there. Fine. It's your decision, Noah." She hung up.

CHAPTER EIGHT

The Pond over which a Radio Voice Glides

To *the sound of menacing music, a sombreroed band of Mexican outlaws, ammunition belts strapped over sweat-stained shirts, enters a sun-scorched village. Horse nostrils flare. Resident dirt farmers huddle in doorways. Men, women, and children scatter from the town square. Other men, hats in hands, eyes cast to the ground as though afraid to look . . .*

Sitting in a center seat of The Northern Lights, I watched the opening scenes of *The Magnificent Seven*. I had sat through the movie fourteen times and knew it almost by heart.

Mina insisted that we rehearse the reopening of the cinema every day. She wanted it to go perfectly. Levon had fine-tuned the projector, dusted and oiled it, cleaned the lenses. He could now run it blindfolded. During our practice sessions, Philomene was assigned the role of a customer, along with Rosie and Sandy. They stepped outside, then up to the booth, where Charlotte pretended to sell them tickets. Mina had us on such a strict budget that we used strips of paper for tickets. I tore the strips in half, slipping one piece through the slot, returning the other to the customers with a smile. Mina worked the popcorn machine. We had popcorn every night for dessert. I gave a bag of it to Levon; upstairs he put it in his satchel. Once Philomene, Sandy, Rosie, and I were seated, Levon would start the movie. Philomene got quickly bored, the girls fidgety, and they would go back upstairs. I watched as long as I cared to. When I left, Levon would rewind the film.

Each morning Charlotte, Mina, and I had painted walls, scrubbed floors, and nailed down carpets, while Levon and his family kept to the projection room, which Philomene had transformed into a home. She had hung white curtains over two windows. Four fold-up cots were stacked against the wall. Blankets, sheets, and pillows were neatly arranged in a cupboard below the table with the film-rewinding equipment on it. A stew pot, silverware, and frying pan were in a crate next to the linens. The percolator that Mina had purchased was on a table next to Levon's chair. Philomene would be cooking, using the hotplate, but by early afternoon she would have opened a window and ushered out the smells with an electric fan.

Afternoons Mina and I did paperwork and took naps in the back row, while Charlotte sat in the front row with her tutor, a college student named Bethany. Bethany was tall and slim and held her stack of books atop a clipboard. She would kick at the door to announce her arrival. We could tell she had a special fondness for Charlotte because each time they saw each other Bethany would beam and her eyes would crinkle up at their edges. Bethany was prompt; we would hear her kick at one-fifteen, and at three forty-five she expected to be paid for the lessons. Mina placed her check in an envelope between napkin holders on the refreshment counter.

Watching their animated faces, the pats on the head and quick smiles of encouragement Bethany gave Charlotte as they studied, I felt distant from our lessons at Paduola Lake and had little inspiration to attend regular school. However, my secret ambition to try electronics school had been strengthened by Levon's example. Just look, I laughed to myself, Levon went to electronics school and he found a great job even before he finished! I saved dimes and quarters for a shortwave in one of a matching pair of porcelain turtle banks Mina had bought, and studied every pawnshop window, and tried out new radios in electronics-store showrooms. I had frequented one on College Street so often the proprietor finally said, "Hands off the merchandise, kiddo. Unless you're going to buy. Got it?" I had forgotten the frequencies of my favorite overseas stations. I had little interest, however, in Charlotte's transistor radio; it was not capable of bringing in news, concerts, or soccer games from great distances. Nor did I even care about *Lights Out, Great Men of Vision,* or *Great Books.* I had simply lost interest in Toronto radio once I arrived there from Quill.

Around the time Bethany would arrive, Levon and his family usually disappeared down the fire escape. Once, Mina asked, "Levon, where do you go in the afternoons?"

"It's like this," he said. "We got a whole city, out there. There's machines. Cigarette—them machines. Telephones. Coffee machines. Jukeboxes. All got slots, eh? We check 'em. Hundreds. Come back, sometimes with ten dollars, dimes, quarters. Then, there's stadiums. Just walk in, or—climb a fence. Get under seats. Pretty good day, slots and stadiums—maybe twelve, maybe more dollars. Then we go to the bingo. Sometimes, that. Bingo games at the Salvation Army. Lots of Indians there. Play that bingo. Sometimes, win money that way." Then he walked up the stairs, and Mina stood nodding to herself.

Though they were otherwise lackadaisical about what they called "clock time," Levon and his family always returned punctually at four-fifteen, when Mina took us through our paces. Later, Mina, Charlotte, and I would lock the front door and either go shopping or go straight home. Levon's family would eat supper, and then he would set out for the parks, ravines, railroad tracks. The next morning when I entered the theater I would catch the smell of raccoon, opossum stew, or duck grease. I would go upstairs and chat with Philomene and Levon as best I could in Cree, the way I had with Hettie while she cooked. Both Levon and Philomene spoke Cree fairly well. Rosie and Sandy heard it most often in lullabies and occasional bedtime stories Philomene knew from her own childhood, or in reprimands, or when Philomene and Levon wanted to keep a secret from them.

On the night before the reopening, Mina said to Charlotte and me, "I hope all this amounts to something. The cinema, my darlings, is no halfhearted endeavor. This *has* to work. Otherwise we'll have to go to Vancouver. Of course we could live with my parents. To think you've never met them! But that would be admitting defeat. My defeat, and I'd have included you both in it. You see, even now my thoughts are racing, aren't they? This is not good. It happens too often of late. Do you know how I stop the racing? By saying to myself, Mina, you cannot count on luck. You cannot hope for refuge on the Ark. You cannot count on much at all. Except for Noah and Charlotte, and keeping up our loan payments, and oh, I hope the dome doesn't peel tomorrow night. Amen."

Early the next evening, a delivery truck stopped out front and a man hauled in a crate of soda bottles with a bill taped to the top. I got our handcart from the downstairs closet while Mina signed for the crate.

"Where you want this?" asked the man.

"Oh, I'll get it," Mina insisted.

"Part of the job," he said, tilting the crate onto the cart. "So, where to, ma'am?"

Tightly wound from worrying about the reopening, Mina took the exchange to imply that she was incapable of simply wheeling the crate herself. As the delivery man and I stepped back, she yanked the top off the crate bare-handed with a loud grunt, nearly falling over backward, and took up four bottles in her arms, carrying them behind the counter. There she wiped each bottle clean with a dish towel, placed two in the small refrigerator, two on the floor.

Now both the delivery man and I followed suit, until the crate sat empty on the car near the front door. "You want the crate, or what?" the man said.

"Take it," Mina replied.

"Okay if *I* put it on the truck?" he said.

"Noah can do it," she said, looking at me.

"I give up," the man said.

Mina went back to finish arranging the bottles.

When I came from the truck, I said, "You look worried the world's going to end. Let's go upstairs, Mother. Philomene and the girls are all dressed up. Even Levon! You should see. Let's go up and look."

In fact we were, all of us, dressed for the occasion. I had on the same clothes I had worn to the dance in Quill, including the herringbone jacket, though I now had a pair of good-fitting dress shoes I had bought at a thrift store on Temperance Street. Mina wore a formal dark blue dress with white buttons and a white corsage pinned to a wide lapel. She had on dark red lipstick and a little rouge, and she walked with self-conscious deliberation, fussing over this and that, moving the napkin holders an inch or two, dusting poster frames, sitting down on a couch in stiff repose, all the while picking bits of lint from the armrests, trying to be every inch the proper hostess. Charlotte wore a blue skirt with her favorite white cotton sweater, and she had a smaller, pale green corsage pinned to her hair.

Mina had ordered a giant cutout of all of *The Magnificent Seven* on their horses, which she prominently displayed on the left side of the lobby. At some point, maybe in a booth in the train station, Levon had had his picture taken and then enlarged, which he pasted over Yul Brynner's face on the cutout. Neither Mina nor Charlotte had noticed, and I couldn't look at it for fear of bursting into laughter and giving it away.

Upstairs Charlotte helped Sandy on with her socks and shoes. Rosie sat in a chair swinging her legs. Sandy had crayons out and drew faces on paper plates on the floor. The girls each had on a new sweater and old jeans. They both wore magenta stocking with leather soles and alligator faces on top, button eyes and yarn grins. Philomene, too, had gussied up. She wore new jeans and a red T-shirt, and her hair hung in two braids, each with a ribbon tied in a loose bow halfway down. Levon, who stood barefoot near the percolator, had on old jeans and a black T-shirt, but they had been freshly washed, and he had bought a new belt whose steer-head buckle reminded me of Job's.

"Hello," Philomene said, quickly looking away. She could be so painfully shy. Even that brief greeting caused her embarrassment. Her remedy was to to fuss at the girls and rearrange things—flowers in a vase, coffee cups, toothbrushes—to do anything more useful than talking.

"You all look lovely," Mina said, a little calmed. "Will you sit downstairs and watch the movie?"

Though Mina had so carefully orchestrated rehearsals, she obviously had not noticed that Philomene and the girls could not bear to sit through more than five minutes of the movie.

They would limit their participation in the evening's event to getting dressed up. "Oh—no," Philomene said, head bowed down.

It had rained lightly that afternoon, and by evening there was a damp chill in the air, so some of the earliest customers arrived wearing raincoats and carrying umbrellas. One of the first to arrive was Mariya, from the newspaper office. When she displayed her complimentary ticket, Charlotte turned to me and grinned, knowing that neither she nor Mina had given such a ticket away. "Noah's right by the door," Charlotte said, purposely loud enough for me to hear.

Once inside, Mariya looked directly at me. She had her hair in bangs in front and long curls in back, in a French style, much different from when I had seen her at the newspaper. I smiled and gave a little wave, which she smugly rejected as she disappeared into the ladies' room.

Customers entered the lobby and stood around sipping complimentary punch or drifted over to the refreshment stand. Others went in right away to find seats. During a brief lull at the counter, Mina walked over to me and said, "How are you doing?"

"No one else is really dressed up," I said.

"That's good," Mina replied. "This is a neighborhood theater. People should dress as comfortably as they wish."

But at that very moment two little boys and their parents walked in dressed as if they had come directly from church, each boy tugging at his bowtie. Soon groups of students arrived in jeans and sweat shirts, sandals or loafers. "Good evening," I said, tearing their tickets. "Enjoy the show."

I wore a name tag with the word "Manager" underneath. From my post I could see Charlotte turn every so often to survey the crowd. It was clear that we would not have a full house, but by seven-fifty the center rows were full, the side rows were filling, and there were still people in line at the refreshment counter, and some people waiting at the door, glancing anxiously at their watches.

Mariya appeared. She had changed her hair back to a style closer to what I had remembered. She walked directly over to me. "It appeared you didn't recognize me, Mr. Krainik," she said. "I thought I'd help out."

"Didn't you see me wave?" I said.

"I most certainly did not," she said. She wore a pearl necklace in a deep loop in her red blouse, and gray denims and loafers, and I caught the light scent of her perfume. She was even prettier than I recalled. Something of that surprise must have registered on my face because she said, "I have a life other than at the newspaper, you know."

I tore her ticket, absentmindedly putting both halves in the slot. Intently observing this, she said, "If I need to come out into the lobby, I'll have to ask for you personally, I suppose. So don't forget my face, all right?"

She knew I was watching as she started down the aisle; she stopped and sat in the back row and did not so much as glance back at me.

The only time I left my station was when Mina had called me over to back her up at the refreshment stand. The line there had grown long, and she wanted to avoid seeming flustered in front of the customers at all costs. So for five minutes or so she worked the cash register while I reached in for candy, filled popcorn boxes, and worked the spigots.

Returning to the door, I saw that things were progressing smoothly, except that a little girl was positioned in front of the cutout, staring at it, saying nothing. Tearing tickets, smiling, offering my cheerful greeting, I still managed to keep an eye on her. She had on a green raincoat, black galoshes, and a transparent plastic hat, under which I could see curly black hair.

She was peering at Levon's face on the cutout and must have been disturbed by it because she began to shriek, stomping her feet and running in place, until her parents hurried over. Each clasped one of her hands, glanced at the cutout, then stopped and gave it a hard look. The father crouched down for a moment to solace the girl, then scowled at me and I turned away. When I next looked they were leaving. They didn't even stop to ask for their money back. They just walked out the door, the little girl still sobbing, and were gone.

At eight o'clock there were a dozen people still in the lobby. I glanced over at Mina, who checked her watch, then nodded at me. I knew what she meant. I took a small bell from my jacket pocket and tapped it a few times with a mallet. This felt a little ridiculous, but Mina had insisted on this particular piece of decorum to signal that the movie was about to begin. In the lobby was a short woman with light red hair and a black hat with two pheasant feathers sticking out from it. "Charming," she said, touching the bell. She smiled at me and hurried to her seat. But the last person in line, an elderly man with wispy white hair, a neatly folded raincoat over his arm, handed me his ticket and remarked, "Didn't think I was to be called like a sheep!" He walked slowly down the aisle, and I closed the door firmly behind him.

While Levon ran coming attractions, Charlotte remained in the booth. When it was clear that no more customers would arrive, she bound up the bills in separate denominations with rubber bands and emptied the change into a small, zippered pouch. After switching off the booth light, she carried the money to the office, where she closed it into a small floor safe and spun the combination dial. Flashlight in hand, she walked into the lobby, then stepped into the theater. Mina sat on a stool behind the refreshment counter, counting up the money she had taken in, then putting it in her purse. She started a new batch of popcorn, in case anyone should want some during the show. She looked relieved yet weary, and when she noticed me watching she waved me impatiently into my office.

In the office I sat with my feet propped up on the desk. Mina and I had caught up on paperwork and organized files and catalogs so well that there was little for me to do. I had the catalog description of *The Magnificent Seven* taped to the phone. I could vaguely hear the sound track through the wall behind my back: the movie had been on only a short while—the lead outlaw was harassing the peasants. Hearing a bullet shot, I knew he had just gunned down a man who dared protest the pillaging of his village. A stain of blood, I knew, spread across his shirt. His wife would cry out and bend over him, then press her face to her hands.

From all the work and last-minute excitement, I was exhausted and slept a while, head down next to the radio on the desk. When I woke I heard through the wall, "Where you from?"

"Tombstone."

I looked at the clock: 9:05. Then there was a knock at the door. "Come in," I said.

There stood Charlotte, all jitters. She crumpled up a candy bar wrapper, smoothed it out on the desk, crumpled it again, all the while talking jibberish.

"What's wrong with you?" I said. "Calm down, what's happened?"

Charlotte hugged herself, closed her eyes, sighed deeply, then opened her eyes. "Uncle Anthony's in the theater," she said.

"Can't be, no way."

"Wrong."

"Are you *sure*? Don't fool around, I mean it."

"As sure as anything," she said, collapsing into the swivel chair in front of the desk. "He didn't buy a ticket from me. He just walked in. He had on a big coat I'd never seen before, and a hat down over his face so I could hardly recognize him. Kept his head bent down, too, but I *know* it was him. I couldn't say anything. I froze up. I didn't *dare!* I didn't dare, Noah, I just didn't dare."

"Where is he now?"

"Center front, I'm pretty sure. I walked down the aisle a ways, and I think that's where he's sitting. It's crowded right there, too."

"Did Mother see him, do you think?"

"No, I don't think so. I looked. You were behind the counter helping out. And she was real busy."

"Now, listen. Listen to me a minute, Charlotte. Don't tell her. Whatever you do, don't tell her. I know you tell her everything, but this might be too much. So don't okay?"

"I won't."

"Promise me."

"I promise, I promise."

"No, cross your heart and hope to die promise."

Charlotte placed her hand over her heart and looked solemn. "Cross my heart, Noah," she said.

"Okay—now, just go back out there. When the movie's done, just . . . I don't know what. Mother probably won't be in the lobby. Most likely she'll be upstairs lying down on the cot in the storeroom."

"What if she isn't?"

"She will be, I just know it. She said as much. Otherwise, I'll have to try and distract her some way. Lie that somebody's on the phone or something—No—that's no good. I don't know what yet. You just go back out there. If you want, when the movie's over come back in the office here and wait."

"Can't I stay here now, Noah, *please?*"

Seeing how upset Charlotte was, I said, "Sure you can. I'm going upstairs to talk with Levon."

"You going to say anything to Uncle Anthony?"

"I'm going upstairs."

I walked into the lobby, shutting the door behind me. Mina was sponging the countertop. "Everything all right, darling?" she said.

"Just fine. Charlotte's minding the office a few minutes. I'm going up to check on Levon." I said, sounding as managerlike as I could. "Movie'll be over in half an hour. You look pretty tired, Mother."

"As soon as I'm finished here, I'll go up and lie down. You come get me when customers start to leave, all right? I've got a little suprise."

"I'll get you as soon as the credits come on," I said.

I walked slowly up the stairs, trying not to let on that anything troubled me. In the back of the projection room, Philomene sat on her cot between Sandy and Rosie, who were each tucked under their own cot blankets. The room was dark, except for the illumination of the projector's motor light and a nightlight in a baseboard socket in a corner. Through the viewing window I saw the tunnel of dusty light from the projector swallowed in midair blackness a short way out. Philomene stroked her daughter's hair, humming a Cree lullaby. Levon sat on the stool next to the projector, focusing intently on the screen.

Quietly I closed the door behind me. "Levon," I whispered.

Levon shifted toward me on the stool. "These guys, they are kicking *ass*," he said, referring to the hired gunslingers. "Why, are you up here?"

"Got a little problem," I said.

"What's that?"

I stepped over to the viewing window, craning to look down at the audience. But it was all a dark blur. I tried to focus on the front center rows, but it was useless.

"Don't block—the light," Levon warned. "What's going on, eh?"

"Just checking on somebody."

"Somebody, who?" he whispered more loudly than I had.

"My father, that's who."

"Who you was telling me, 'bout last week? Who cut out on you, up north? Him? Can't be. Otherwise—you would tear ass down over the seats, like a fuckin' pirate. Was *my* old man, I'd be doing that. My girls, Philomene, too—them, too!"

"I didn't tell you much about it all, Levon. It's pretty complicated."

"Complicated—*shit*," Levon said out loud. Philomene hushed him, then continued with her lullaby. "Complicated, fuck that, eh? I can take care of this little *problem* you got, direct. I walk down the stairs. Down the aisle. Tell me where he's sitting. What's he look like. I walk down, the aisle—nice and slow. Lean over very quiet, like with the ducks, eh? Say: *'What the fuck are you doing here?!'* Perfect English, eh?"

"That'd screw up the movie. Mother would kill me."

"Got to make a choice here, Noah. What you told me—he was jacking your family around, how long? *Years.* You said *years.* That's what you told me. Years. So, I am only saying, what *you* said. So—what's a fuckin' *movie* worth—compared to having, a flashlight, in his face like a convict, eh?"

"That's past—the cinema, here, is what we've got from now on, Levon."

"Can see you aren't—interested, in my help. You want to stay here, looking at the top of his head, eh? Me—me, I'd turn them fuckin' lights on. While them customers, they'd be enjoying the dome, you'd be facing down, *him*."

I looked at Levon in disbelief, worried he was going to take charge of the situation and do exactly what he advised me to do.

"What, then, are you gonna do, Noah?" he said, turning away on the stool.

"Leave it alone. See what happens, that's what."

"That's one plan," Levon said. "But—there's other ones."

"Thanks for the advice, Levon."

He relaxed his shoulders but did not look at me again. "No problem," he said.

"See you later," I said, wanting any kind of encouragement, knowing there would be none. Levon walked over and sat next to Philomene, then began to explain things in Cree. I went out the door, down the stairs, and found Charlotte still in the swivel chair. I sat down and switched off the desk lamp.

In a few moments we heard the inside door opening and closing with a squeak. In the near darkness we both stepped to the office door, each so intent on what we had heard that we bumped into one another. Charlotte wedged herself just under my arm as I opened the door a crack, and we both peered out.

Anthony was in the lobby, right out in the open. Pressed against her, I felt Charlotte inhale sharply in recognition, but she had placed her hand over her mouth, so she remained silent. Anthony revolved slowly as a toy soldier winding down, fixing his sight first on the refreshment stand, then the ticket booth, then the cutout. Mina's story of their meeting in this very lobby decades before raced through my mind, as I imagined it might be doing in Anthony's as well. Now he faced the theater door, as though deciding whether or not to return to his seat. I could see him best at this angle. He looked much the same as when I had seen him up north, just as gaunt, in the same greatcoat, his hair slicked back from his forehead.

"He knows we're watching him," Charlotte said in a whisper, which in the dark seemed to come from no source and be no louder than my heartbeat.

"If he does," I whispered back, "he's got a choice to come in or not."

In a moment Anthony turned, opened the theater door. "He's going back in," Charlotte said.

But then Anthony reappeared, having retrieved the French horn case. "You didn't tell me had had it with him," I whispered to Charlotte. Anthony put on his hat, pulled up his collar, and, without so much as looking to either side, walked out the front door.

I felt Charlotte tremble. "Uncle Anthony," she murmured, "what are you *doing?*"

A few people came out into the lobby, and I said, "It's over."

We heard applause. "People clapping at a movie," Charlotte remarked, forcing a small laugh. "That's funny, don't you think, Noah?"

"I can't say what's usual or not," I said, "I have to wake Mother up."

I stepped out and half smiling jostled my way between customers toward the stairs. Suddenly I was face to face with Mariya again.

"So," she said, "now you know where I work and I know where you work. That's a start, don't you think? I didn't like the movie too much." She raised her eyebrows slightly and shrugged, then walked out to the street.

Soon Mina, Charlotte, and I stood in the empty lobby. Mina walked to the refrigerator and took out a bottle of champagne. "Surprise!" she shouted. "Now let me warn you, this stuff can put you a mile away from yourself very quickly, and it's hard to get back—if you want to, that is. So drink a little at a time!"

She popped the cork, which ricocheted off the cutout. "We deserve this, don't you think?" she said, holding up the overflowing bottle. "It all went well, wouldn't you agree, Noah?"

"Yes, I would."

We all got paper cups, and Mina poured us champagne. Heeding Mina's words, Charlotte and I sipped ours cautiously, while Mina drank her entire cup in three gulps and immediately poured herself seconds. "To The Northern Lights!" she toasted.

Levon appeared on the steps. "*Everyone* gone, eh?" he said, looking at me.

"All except us drunks," Mina said, her voice slurring. "Want some bubbly, Levon?" She held forth the bottle.

"Got coffee," he said, turning back up the stairs.

Mina switched off the lobby and marquee lights, leaving on only a floor lamp near a couch, placed there to try and give the lobby the comfort of a living room. Charlotte and I continued to sip our champagne, while Mina, with great relish, drank a third and fourth cup. She now carried an edgy, even aggressive, tone in her voice. "I think we made a profit," she said. "I'm sure that when we finally calculate it, that will be true. *Nothing* went wrong—hallelujah!" She put her hand to her mouth, then slid it out rapidly as if playing a trombone. "Whoopee!" she cried.

Charlotte looked uncomfortable, even alarmed, but Mina's enthusiasm was such that we tried to go along. We tapped our cups together with each toast Mina offered. "Here's to the profit," she said, finishing another cup of champagne. Closing her eyes, she swayed forward, then snapped back as if suddenly awakened. "Here's to the nothing wrong! Here's to poor old Gus. . . . Here's to . . ." She tilted backward, righted herself. Turning to the cutout, she said, "Here's to *The Magnificent Seven!*"

Barely maintaining her bearing along the brief route to the cutout, she stopped, made a sweeping bow, and asked it to dance. "May I have the pleasure?" she said, giggling. She did not even notice the photograph of Levon. She hugged the cutout, lifted it, and said, "You bad old meanies certainly can dance!" Then she looked at us and frowned. "Oh, ooohh, you party poopers!" she said. "You stick-in-the-muds. Standing in the dark not dancing." Then she gave a sidelong grin, pointed to one of the horses, put a finger to her own mouth, and said, "Ssshhh," as if about to reveal a secret. Still holding the cutout, she hopped up and down once, then literally galloped a few steps and collapsed on the couch. The cutout fell away face-down on the floor.

"Go upstairs and get some coffee from Levon," Charlotte said. "That used to help Uncle Anthony, remember?"

I ran upstairs and knocked on the projection room door. Levon opened it, holding a lantern. "I need some coffee, Levon," I said, almost pleading, out of breath. "Strong—okay?"

"Coffee?" Levon said. "You?" But he went to the percolator and returned with a cup. "Here," he said. "Wouldn't start, drinking this shit, late night."

"It's for Mina," was all I said.

Head propped up a little but still curled on the couch, Mina sipped the hot coffee. "Lovely, lovely party," she said. "Just lovely. Ask me back, will you?"

"Yes, we will," I said. Charlotte sat on the opposite couch, watching.

Slowly Mina drank the entire cup. Finally, sobered a little, she sat up stiffly.

"Auntie," Charlotte said, "we can get the bus almost right out front, you know. Let's go home, okay? I'll clean up the aisles and seats in the morning."

We were the only passengers on the brightly lit bus and sat in the back seat. Mina sang "Across the Alley from the Alamo" loudly, all the way to Olive Street.

Once in the apartment Charlotte and I went quickly to our rooms. Mina, now inventing unrhymed verses, ran bath water, but after a while I realized that she had forgotten the bath. So I turned the spigot off and found her asleep on the couch, still wearing her corsage.

Yet later, as I lay on my bed, I heard Mina knock on Charlotte's door. Once she had gone into Charlotte's room, I walked into the hallway and listened at her door. "Charlotte," Mina said, "darling, I'm all right now. Just a bad headache, I'm afraid. Did I frighten you?"

"A little, Auntie. You were funny, though."

"Well, I was trying to keep a secret and I was having great

difficulty doing that. I'm going to tell you what it is, but you must promise not to tell Noah. Can you promise that?"

"I think so."

"Please try, for Noah's sake. Because if he knew, I think it would upset him. Deeply upset him. You see, tonight, at the cinema . . . how do I say this? Your uncle Anthony was there. There's no mistaking it. It's not my imagination playing tricks. I saw him. He didn't look at me, but I saw him come in. Noah had stepped from the door to help me, and he was busy with something or other. Soda, I think. I looked up and saw Anthony go into the aisle. He was so much thinner, but still, it *was* him. My Lord, I thought, *why?* Why? Not only Toronto, but here in The Northern Lights? Because of your letters, I imagine. When I went upstairs to lie down, I thought that what I had asked Noah at supper the day he arrived might be true. That Noah read Samuel Bay your letters, and perhaps Anthony learned about The Northern Lights. . . . What does it matter now? I've feared this would happen. I've thought about it every day."

Though at first it seemed Mina was solacing Charlotte, Charlotte's response had the calmer tone. "Auntie," she said, "I know you had to tell *someone*. Now I'll tell you a secret of my own. *I* saw Uncle Anthony, too."

"Oh, dear," Mina said, her voice caught up short.

"It's okay—nothing happened. Funny, he didn't even buy a ticket. Yep, I saw him go right in without saying one single word."

"He must've snuck out the emergency exit," Mina said.

"What else did you think about upstairs?" Charlotte said.

"That—" Mina hesitated. "That by appearing, Anthony has let us know that he knows where we are. He wants us to see him thin, in old clothes . . . perhaps feel sorry for him. To feel like we've locked him out. Then again, he may have wanted to shock us. To give us a shaky start with the cinema."

"Could be all those things," Charlotte said.

"Or reasons we'll never understand. But an important thing

for now is that what I've told you and what you've told me should stay between us. And that you won't breathe a word of it to Noah."

"I promise."

"Sweet dreams, then. I'm ashamed of how I behaved tonight, but try and understand. Good night, darling."

I could not sleep, so I kept the clock radio with its luminescent dials on and listened to it for hours, trying to track down a station from beyond Toronto, and failing. I imagined Anthony, having fled the theater lobby as he had the cabin, wandering the city. Where did he live? In one of the dingy apartments Levon and I had walked past? In a shabby room above a market shop, where one day he saw the dancing silhouettes in Mina's advertisement?

When the sun came up, I got dressed and quietly made my way down the hall and out the door. On Olive Street I was met by a cold, damp wind. As I walked briskly on, life felt woefully dreamlike one moment, desperately real the next. Perhaps Pelly, having been sent away by his real parents to live with Sam and Hettie, had known the same confusion. Perhaps it was like learning to ride a unicycle, keeping perfectly balanced despite fierce crosswinds. Walking down Palmerston Avenue, I drew strength from thoughts of that kinship.

At first I thought I'd stop where I could watch the small planes arrive and depart from the City of Toronto Airport, on the island in Toronto Harbor, and let the planes remind me of Wilfred Gaboriault, Willie Savoie, and other mail pilots. But when I reached where Palmerston turned into Tecumseh Street, I turned toward Union Station and the skating rink. I hurried my pace until, out of breath, I was flush up against the railing. A single skater glided through the icy light and in his first turn past nodded and said hello.

He was a slight man with an aquiline nose and whimsical mouth, and his thinning dark hair, tinged with gray at the sideburns, was parted on the left. He wore a trim, brown tweed suit and trousers, a plaid scarf, and old-fashioned black skates —Sam had a pair like them—that buckled up high, secured by ankle straps. He was hardly skating, more leaning his body and allowing what weight he possessed to propel him.

When it became apparent that I was intent on watching, he began—almost from politeness, it seemed—a gradual conversation, asking another question each time he passed. "Lovely morning, wouldn't you say? Fond of skating, or do you prefer to watch?" But by the time I could reply, he would be out of hearing range.

Finally I caught on and spoke first as he approached. "I skated my whole life," I said. "Since I was five."

Silently he drifted past.

"On your way to work?" he asked his next time around.

"Out for a walk, is all," I shouted after him.

After another turn round the rink he stopped at the railing, "I see," he said.

I could not imagine why his voice should be so familiar, as I had spoken to so few people in Toronto—basically Levon and his family, Charlotte, Mina. Yet it was strikingly familiar, that was certain. "Talk more," I said. "Your voice . . ."

"I'd enjoy a conversation, but I don't quite understand . . ."

Then I knew.

"Please," I said. "The radio . . . at night."

He looked both curious and startled.

"Charles Dickens."

"Why, yes. That would've been several years ago."

"Fabian Bennet."

"Good Lord, correct again. But then of course I've read aloud for . . . let's see, some twenty years. There was another time. Yes. I was in a grocery, talking with my wife. About soups, something altogether silly like that, you see. When all of a sudden a woman said, 'Haven't I heard you on the radio?' Decidedly more uncertain than you, I might add. Still, quite extraordinary, don't you think? Once, now twice in twenty years."

"I heard you in Quill."

"Beg your pardon?"

"Quill. Up north—a village."

"How nice, Mr . . . ?"

"Noah Krainik."

"Yes, well then, Mr. Krainik, how fortuitous to meet like this."

"I heard you up until April, then I moved here, to Toronto."

"Well, you can tune in *Great Books* here as well, you know."

"For me, it's not . . ."

"Not . . . ?"

". . . The same. The *books* are, but the listening wouldn't be, is what I meant."

"I see . . . it's a personal matter."

"I had this idea, Mr. Bennet."

"Fabian, please."

"Fabian, this idea. That if—and I know it might seem—if you'd *consider,* just once, before or after your broadcast, to say something. A *hello.* There's a person. Lives in Quill, that is. Name of Hettie. Quill is small. On the map, but very small. And there's this radio Hettie and I listened to. She even wondered what you looked like."

"Imagine that," he said. "But I'm afraid, Mr. Krainik . . ."

He went on, but I could no longer hear him; I was lost in the vision of Hettie, in her kitchen, astounded at hearing her name over the shortwave.

He calmly pushed off in a long stride, his hands clasped behind his back. His movements were simple, but as he rounded the far end of the rink my thoughts took another turn, and I saw a figure fly into an expert zigzag, halt, perform a counterclockwise spin. I heard my lone applause echo against the domed, star-filled sky above Quill.

236

About the Author

Howard Norman is the author of two books of translation from North Canadian Algonquin languages: *The Wishing Bone Cycle: Narrative Poems from the Swampy Cree Indians,* which was awarded the Harold Morton Landon Prize by the Academy of American Poets, and *Where the Chill Came From: Windigo Tales and Journeys.* He received a Whiting Writer's Award for his first novel, *The Northern Lights.* Mr. Norman lives in Massachusetts and Vermont and travels extensively in the Northwest Territories. He is at work on a new novel.